E

Jane Eyre's Daughter

WITHDRAWN

Elizabeth Newark

SOURCEBOOKS CASABLANCA™
AN IMPRINT OF SOURCEBOOKS, INC.®
NAPERVILLE, ILLINOIS

Published by Sourcebooks Casablanca, an imprint of Sourcebooks, Inc.
P.O. Box 4410, Naperville, Illinois 60567–4410
(630) 961-3900
Fax: (630) 961-2168
www.sourcebooks.com

Originally published in 1997 as *Consequence*, ISBN 0965914704.

Library of Congress Cataloging-in-Publication Data

Newark, Elizabeth.
    Jane Eyre's daughter / Elizabeth Newark.
        p. cm.
    A sequel to: Jane Eyre.
    ISBN-13: 978-1-4022-1237-6
    ISBN-10: 1-4022-1237-2
    1. Eyre, Jane (Fictitious character)—Fiction. 2. Mothers and daughters—Fiction. 3. Young women—Fiction. 4. Great Britain—History—19th century—Fiction. 5. Yorkshire (England)—Fiction. I. Brontë, Charlotte, 1816–1855. Jane Eyre. II. Title.
    PS3564.E86J36 2008
    813'.54—dc22
                                                  2008010201

Printed and bound in the United States of America.
BG 10 9 8 7 6 5 4 3 2

Dedication

This book is
dedicated
with great appreciation
and much affection
to my English teacher,
Dorothy Wallis.

Contents

PROLOGUE

My Mother

"She looks sensible, but not at all handsome."

◄§ JANE EYRE §►

*T*HE OAK PULPIT RISES high above the congregation.

The wood gleams dark and mellow from centuries of polishing by docile female hands. Brass and silverware shine in the midmorning sunlight, which streams through the stained glass windows. Standing there, exulting in his captive audience, the Rector, the Right Reverend Ambrose Pimlico-Smythe, unaware that his beaky nose and fishy mouth are splashed with green and blue and his immaculate white lawn and lace clerical robes are overlaid by purple and cyclamen reflections, so that he appears to inhabit a veritable coat of many colours, grips the rail and glares down at his congregation.

"God's will be done," he thunders. "Let woman bring forth her child in pain. Only thus can Eve's guilt be purged—Eve, who defied our Lord, ate the forbidden apple, corrupted Adam, and let evil into the world! Her deed can never be forgotten! Her sin contaminates all females. Each must suffer in her turn."

He pauses and coughs portentously. "There are women among you so lost to true Christian feeling, so little aware of the gaping mouth of Hell, who would use this new Devil's brew, chloroform, to mitigate the pains of childbirth. But God is not mocked! Again we hear the hissing of the snake and see his darting tongue. The flames of Hell leap high! Listen, and you will hear the screams of those cast down into that fiery furnace. Better far to scream at the pangs of childbirth than for all eternity! Pain is woman's reward from God, a sign of his true love, a sign that after due penance even she, vile though we know her to be, may be admitted to his sight. Only by meek submission, by womanly acceptance of this pain, may you redeem yourselves from your earthly sins and avoid eternal damnation. Do not deceive yourselves. Any among you who seek to escape this earthly fate are the Devil's disciples."

He runs a pale tongue over his lips. I hear my mother draw in a deep breath.

She smoothes her gloves over her hands and picks up her reticule.

"Let a woman travail and labour and bring forth her child in torment!" rants Mr. Pimlico-Smythe. "God's will be done! Yea, again I say …"

At this point, my mother takes my hand and rises from our pew. "Come, Oliver," she says to my brother in clear, conversational tones. "Come, Janet, my dear. Don't dawdle." Turning her back with quiet deliberation on the clergyman, who stops in midsentence, gazing down at her openmouthed, she leads us from the church, looking straight ahead, ignoring the stares and whispers of the congregation.

Once seated in our carriage, she shakes herself and brushes her mantle, as if throwing off some noxious dust. She looks earnestly from Oliver to me.

"Mr. Pimlico-Smythe is a very foolish man," she says. "Remember, my dears, no ceremony bestows wisdom upon a man born with neither intelligence nor understanding; ordination of a fool provides us merely with yet another ordained fool."

It is a scene I never forgot.

❖ ❖ ❖

My name is Janet Rochester, and the story I have to tell is my own. But it must start inevitably with my mother, for no history of myself can be understood, can be in any way complete, without an understanding of that remarkable woman. I can see her now as she was that day, seven years ago: small, erect, back straight as a guardsman, every hair in place, her head held high, her expression calm. My mother, Jane Eyre Rochester.

I was twelve at the time we swept out of the Hay church, but back we must go, even farther, long before my birth.

My mother first met my father, Edward Fairfax Rochester of Thornfield Hall, when she was engaged as governess to his ward. My mother and Mr. Rochester fell in love and, after the death of the first Mrs. Rochester (who, I must tell you, was mad and kept confined in an attic room, out of sight) in the fire that destroyed Thornfield Hall, eventually married. *Their* love was a deep and wondrous thing, but hers, I always thought, did not extend so lavishly to me. There was a constraint between us. I could never run to her with a scraped knee or cut finger as of a right. I approached diffidently. She always attended to me promptly and carefully, but she seldom lifted me onto her knee for a final kiss or hug, as is so usual with a loved child. It was a source of regret to me that, through some inadequacy of my own, as I thought, I did not have her full love. Yet I was not affected as strongly as I might have been. My father was the centre of my world, as he was of hers, and this seemed quite natural to me. She loved my elder brother, Oliver; he was, after all, physically very like my father. I, if you will forgive a somewhat *outré* description for a female, was the odd man out.

How did I feel about her? I loved her, and I was ready enough to show it, but I felt she preferred a calm control to strong demonstrations of emotion. I did my best to please her, paying strict attention to her likes and dislikes and trying to emulate her high standards, thinking if I could not have her spontaneous love, I might at least have her approval. But overall, I was proud of her in a somewhat wistful way. I was always quite sure she could face anything, anyone, especially in defence of her principles—or her beloved husband. She had what is called moral fibre.

My father, quite simply, I adored.

After their marriage, dear Reader, my parents made their home at Ferndean Manor, my father's hunting lodge (Thornfield Hall, home of the Rochesters for many generations, had been burnt to the ground). My mother, with the practical good sense and energy that is such an integral part of her, promptly oversaw the clearing of the long neglected woods around Ferndean Manor, where young saplings battled with each other for existence, intertwined in a deadly embrace among the fallen trees. They blotted out the sun and, in consequence, moss grew on struggling trunks and sickly branches, and nettles and fungus grew in the glades. My mother made sure the woods were cleared some two hundred yards back from the house, and conduits were dug for drainage of the water that seeped down from the hills, ending in a large ornamental pond. The trees were thinned, and dead wood hauled and stacked for winter fires. Then my mother tackled the house. Ferndean Manor was dank and dark. The ivy that covered the walls and smothered half the windows was ripped away, the dull red bricks were repointed, dark green paint was applied to the window frames and doors, and from the grim and Gothic ruin of a house—smelling strongly of mildew, home to mice and bats, and declared ghost-ridden by the local inhabitants—emerged a tidy, well-proportioned manor. The sun danced once more through freshly polished windows. Fires burnt clearly in the grates. The smell of mice and mould was replaced by the scent of lavender polish.

Ferndean, built as it was in a small glen, was never the most salubrious site for a dwelling, but once the glen was cleared and drained, its lawns tended and flower beds established, it became a cheerful likable spot enough. It was there that my father first developed the interest in landscape gardening, which was to be one of his principal occupations over the years. And it was there, two years after their marriage, that my brother Oliver was born. Little Oliver grew strong and healthy playing in the Ferndean gardens. (I never lived there, but I visited the tenants with my father many times.) A year later, a second son was born, a difficult birth. Sadly, this child was stillborn. My mother was devastated. She was ill for some time.

As soon as she was well enough to travel, my father transported his family, complete with nursemaid, lady's maid, and manservant, to the south of France and thence to Italy and Greece, even Egypt, returning to Ferndean after some twelve months of brilliant sun and *wine-dark sea* had done their work and restored my mother's health and spirits. Her energy flooded back and then it was she who persuaded her husband to rebuild Thornfield. He was reluctant, although it was the ancestral home of his family; he had no great respect for his forebears, since the greed and selfishness of his father had done him harm. For him the ruins left by the fire were still haunted by his first wife's mad screams and rages. But my mother loved Thornfield. To her its very shades were hallowed by the fact that within its walls she came to know her beloved mate. She reminded him of his happy childhood there and of the burgeoning of his young manhood. There was little he could deny her; plans were drawn up and work commenced.

It took two years. A handsome house emerged. *New* Thornfield, as the country folk who lived around Hay called it, was not as large nor as imposing as the old; there were no battlements, but windows were larger, rooms were airier; even the servants' quarters were more generously built. There were no stifling internal attic rooms in the new Thornfield, no guarding of grim secrets. It became at last a very pleasant seat, surrounded by great old trees that had outlived the fire that destroyed the old building. A small part of the ruin was left intact at my father's design (there was a fashion for such ruins, which were thought picturesque, romantic). Between the crumbled walls, the space was turfed and planted and became a favourite playground for Oliver and later myself.

I was born at new Thornfield Hall three months after the move from Ferndean. My father was delighted to have a daughter, but my mother was disconcerted. She had taken it for granted she should bear another boy, to be called Edward for his father. I was christened after her, Jane Eyre Rochester, but I was always known as Janet.

It was unfortunate that within three weeks of my birth my five-year-old brother tumbled from a tree and broke his leg. It was a clean break and quickly set, but he was a restless patient, disliking confinement. He cried for his mother, and she went to him, leaving me with my wet nurse. I believe my patient father held me more than my mother as, long before, my mother's Uncle Reed had carried *her* at Gateshead Lodge, where she lived as a girl. Molly, my wet nurse, was kind and cheerful. She was one of Bessie Levin's daughters, Bessie who had been my orphaned mother's only friend at Gateshead after her uncle's death. Molly was married to our lodge-keeper, Joshua Parrott. Mrs. Parrott stayed with me to be my nurse, and I was fond of her. It was she who came in the night if I cried. Her daughter, Annie, my fellow nursling, the same age as myself, was my favourite companion. Later, Mrs. Parrott became housekeeper at Thornfield. In my early years, my mother seemed less a parent than a visitor to the nursery, kind but brisk, observing my development and testing my skills as a tutor would. Oliver was with her always.

How is it that I am cognizant of all this ancient history, some of which might well be hidden from a daughter? My mother kept a journal, and from this, after her marriage, she wrote an account of her life up to that point, beginning at Gateshead (where she was mistreated by her Aunt Reed and her cousin John) and continuing through her years at the

ELIZABETH NEWARK

miserable school of Lowood and her arrival at Thornfield Hall as governess to my father's ward, Adele Varens. I was always precocious and, as compensation for my somewhat lonely life, a prodigious reader. When, at the age of twelve, I found the manuscript in an antique desk, seldom used, in my father's library, I spirited it away and hid it in one of my own private hiding places. I read it eagerly, puzzling sometimes over her small, spidery handwriting, engrossed. It explained for me many things about my mother I had not understood. In particular, I understood her love of Thornfield, for (in the heartfelt words she poured out to my father and faithfully inscribed in her journal later) after her cramped, controlled, unhappy childhood, there, at Thornfield:

… I have lived in it a full and delightful life—momentarily at least. I have not been trampled on. I have not been petrified. I have not been buried with inferior minds and excluded from every glimpse of communion with what is bright and energetic and high. I have talked, face-to-face, with what I reverence, with what I delight in—with an original, a vigorous, an expanded mind. I have known you, Mr. Rochester …

The passion of her words, the depth of feeling, went to my heart. It was a declaration of love, and her love for the house was entwined with her love of the man, my father. He was maimed in the fire that destroyed the old Thornfield, losing a hand and an eye. She could not repair his body, though she had restored his mind to courage and happiness, to the pleasure of living. But she could rebuild the house. What a woman she was, my mother.

My father saw me reading the manuscript but did not stop me. My mother, to the best of my belief, did not know I was acquainted with her past. She did not take much interest in my activities, though she liked to see me occupied. Luckily, she saw reading as a fitting occupation for a young girl. She came to be my model. Thinking of her at eighteen, setting sail as a governess on the dangerous sea of life—alone, without protection, braced to face whatever gales and wild storms might come her way, with no compass save her religion—filled me with awe and a strong wish to emulate her courage and integrity. She had longed for liberty, she wrote, for change, stimulus. But if that were denied her, she was prepared to accept a "new servitude."

That old story reminds me: I must not forget to tell you what became of Adele Varens, my father's ward, who was, of course, the reason my parents met. She was sent to school after my parents' marriage but came home each summer and then, when she was eighteen, joined our household for good, living contentedly as part of the family. But I was only one-year-old when she married, at twenty-two, a Frenchman—somewhat to my mother's dismay. My mother was never able to believe that good moral sense and true judgment were to be found in the French. Adele went to live in Paris but came back on rare occasions to visit us, beautifully dressed in fashions subtly different from any I saw in Yorkshire. My mother clicked her tongue at extravagance and vanity, but on at least two occasions, I saw her try on her visitor's bonnet. Adele remained a stranger to me; I did not come to know her well.

It was perhaps a pity—and always a source of regret to me—that my resemblance was to my mother, not my father. I believed this influenced her feelings for me. Oliver was at first sight a true Rochester: his eyes large, brilliant, and black, his hair also black, swarthy of skin, robust, intense, looking much as my father looked before the fire (Vulcan was my mother's fond name for her husband). However, as I grew up I came to realize he was but a mild copy of my father. His temperament was diluted. He was not quite as tall, not as broad in the shoulder or deep in the chest. His brow was not as high, as developed in the organs of intelligence. He had not the depth of feeling my father had, and his eyes did not flash with my father's passion for life. Oliver was a follower, where my father was a leader, and he followed my father. But my mother, less clear-sighted here than she was with me, accorded Oliver such adoration as she had left over from her husband.

In contrast, I was quite tall for my age (taller already at twelve than my mother), with light brown hair and, my father said, hazel eyes. But the looking glass contradicted him. My eyes, dear Reader, are green, the colour of seawater rippling over seaweed in the deep rock pools on the Devon coast. I was sturdier in build than my mother, whose infancy and childhood had not been conducive to health. My complexion was fair and touched with colour after exercise, whereas her skin had an even, ivory pallor; my hair waved however long and hard I tried, at her direction, to brush it smooth, and my green eyes were shadowed by lashes of a darker brown than my hair. I took as my model my mother's neat self, not a hair out of place, all plain and smooth and controlled, but I could not emulate her. My father's more robust blood vied with hers in my veins; I longed for action and exercise, for adventure. I did not dislike my appearance; I felt I was well enough: plain but not repulsive; not beautiful, but not ugly, either.

My father would have me painted, as a child. I believe he hoped my mother would paint a miniature of me, as she had of Oliver; she was skilful enough. But this did not suit her, and instead he engaged an artist to make a study of me at the age of twelve, which he hung in the library on the opposite wall to a full-size portrait of my mother. I do not remember ever seeing her gaze at my picture. Oliver's miniature hung in her sitting room on the first floor, and a portrait painted on his twenty-first birthday hung in the drawing room, in full view of the sofa where she often sat.

Do I sound resentful? Sometimes I was; sometimes I longed for her to throw her arms around me in impulsive affection. I wished I could run to her in times of pain or trouble and bury my face in her bosom. Instead, I ran to my father. But my mother was a remarkable person—strong, outspoken. I felt she made her own rules. So I loved her in a somewhat detached way, keeping my distance, but my admiration was wholehearted. She believed in self-control, in keeping one's emotions under guard—her one exception being in relationship to my father.

I did love my brother. Oliver was a good friend to me and had his own troubles in my mother's expectations. He confided in me that he was afraid he was not my father's equal in intelligence or strength; my mother never for a moment admitted that. He was put on earth, she seemed to assume, to repeat my father's virtues, so that the model continued; he was not allowed to be himself. And in his heart, he knew he fell short of this demand. He was always fearful of disappointing her. I was not jealous (though, as I have said, I was sometimes wistful) when she reserved her strongest feelings for the males in her life. That was her way.

Her feelings for my father were strongly depicted in her journal. I was but twelve when I first read her story, and I was puzzled and even dismayed at the strength of her passion when she wrote about how it was revealed to her (on her supposed wedding day!) that he was already married, and she decided to leave him. I turned the pages hastily, believing I should not linger over such private thoughts. But later, when I was fifteen, I reread these paragraphs, and my own heart swelled within my developing bosom, and my cheeks flushed with echoed emotion. For I, too, thought my father perfection. I thought I knew how it would feel to be forced to leave him.

I knew I had his strong affection—as his daughter but also, it must be admitted, because I resembled my mother (oh, irony of fate). All through my somewhat lonely early childhood, onlooker that I was of the tie between my mother and my brother, my father was my affectionate friend, demonstrative and loving. He guided my studies, read poetry and Shakespeare with me. (I loved *As You Like It* and *Much Ado About Nothing*, the wit and sparkle of the play between lovers; he the splendour and conflict of the histories. I can hear his voice now, that rich, deep voice, reciting speeches from *Henry V.*) As the years passed and I grew towards womanhood, I hoped he would come to see me less as a child and more as a companion, as a young woman, but sometimes, it seemed it was that very growth that kept him from me. When I was thirteen, Oliver left for Cambridge. He spent Christmas with new friends, and it was a full year before he returned. When I heard his voice in the hall, I ran to him, and he held me off and looked me over, and he too treated me differently.

"You are quite the little woman," he said. "Janet, you are growing handsome!"

I laughed. I thought he teased me. But then I saw my father look at me and then at my mother, and away again. Her head came up sharply.

"Nonsense, Oliver," she said. "You will fill the child's head with vanity. Internal beauty—of mind and spirit—must be Janet's aim."

I stared long and hard at myself in the looking glass that night, but I could not see that I had changed so much or were so much improved. Or why it made a difference if I were.

But after that, my father's casual caresses, kisses, and physical greetings in the morning and the evening grew less frequent. My mother, too, as I moved towards womanhood, treated me with more formality, her normal tranquil regard tempered with some new emotion. She had always been opposed to finery. Her own dress was plain and subdued in colour, and she encouraged me to follow suit. My clothes were of good fabrics, but simply cut and without ornamentation. We met few people socially. I had no way of knowing how I appeared to outsiders. I grew up shy and reserved, full of dreams and longings for what I feared was unobtainable.

They were so different, my parents—he tall, she short; he of rich and worldly background, she with few worldly goods (until she inherited money from her uncle, when she was nineteen) and of Puritanical tastes; he of little faith, she deeply religious. His robust and sardonic sense of humour was always present; she had none of that (though she had some wit and a taste for quirks and oddities). He and he alone could make her laugh aloud. Yet they were identical in their love. For it was always clear to me that my mother loved my father, and he loved her, and their love was a very physical love. No one talked to me of the love between a man and a woman; it was not a subject for discussion. Marriage was approved by the Church. It was the authorized union of man and woman for procreation. That was all it was necessary to know. But when an Eshton daughter married and we attended the service, I listened to Mr. Pimlico-Smythe as he intoned the marriage vows. "*With my body, I thee worship,*" came the nasal clerical voice, devoid of all expression. But I felt a jolt, a sudden strong beat in my heart; the blood rose hot to my cheeks. This, it was clear to me, defined the attachment of my father and my mother. This was married love.

It was therefore through watching my parents that I learned the nature of adult love. To love someone devotedly meant to want them close by, ever near; to exchange a hundred small caresses every day; to allow fingers to touch, arms to brush, words to be spoken in low, deep tones meant for one ear, one listener alone among many. As I grew older, I sometimes watched them retire, arms entwined, to their bedroom and I dreamt about them as I lay restless through warm summer nights in my own narrow cot, while the scent of honeysuckle stole through my window, intoxicating, disturbing. What was it like, I wondered, to share my father's bed, to be held by those strong, muscular arms close to him throughout the night, so safe, so cherished? My cheeks would flush, my limbs grow moist with perspiration at the thought. I would stretch out on the cool sheets and roll and flex my body like a cat. These things I could not talk about; they were forbidden, wrong. I disciplined myself. My thoughts must be suppressed. I tried to clear them from my mind. But as I grew older and became, as my brother said, "a little woman", I knew I must seek in life someone who in mind and body would meld with me as a glove fits a hand. This could be the only true marriage.

I had little hope, however, that it would be my fate to find such a partner. Although we did not mingle with many other families, I was aware from conversations overheard that most marriages in our society, most male and female partnerships, were not as theirs. Men and women in the County married for social advantage: great estates were united; men whose lands were hard-pressed married wealth;

women of rank with little in the way of a dowry sought husbands with means. And if marriage for love were so rare—if, indeed, most men and women were so ordinary (as I found them)—how was I, so muted in colouring, so undistinguished in appearance, to attract so rare a mate, surely sought by others more beautiful than I?

How could I win the equal of my father?

I came to believe, as I grew older, that my mother saw me as a rival and perhaps had always seen me so from my birth—a second, small Jane Eyre who might bewitch my father (as *she* had bewitched him, changeling that she was) and steal him from her.

My father. His whole appearance was of strength, akin to the Yorkshire moors; to the hills, where the underlying bones of the earth thrust through its skin in the form of flint; to our wild and rugged countryside, where the wind wailed over the rooftops and distorted the trunks of the trees and, in winter, sent its icy blasts through heavy clothing to the skin. I loved the moors. There kestrels and peregrine falcons hovered, seeking their prey. Once I saw a golden eagle and thought immediately of *him* as it rose into the air on urgent beats of its powerful wings. But although he seemed built for endurance, for battle against the elements, my father had a great need to love and be loved. The years he had been tied to his first wife, whose ravings and violence made a mockery of everything marriage should stand for, had been bitter indeed. The affection my father showed to his great dog, Pilot—half Dane, half Mastiff, with his lion's head and mane and black coat blotched with white—and Pilot's utter devotion to *him* gave a glimpse of my father's inner depths. Pilot died when I was young, but his son took his place and then *his* son, each dog looking much the same and named the same: Pilot.

I learned to walk clutching Pilot's back. He stood up, I stood up. He walked, I staggered along beside him. When I was three, I tried to ride Pilot and from this moved to my first pony. My father encouraged me, protecting me when Oliver laughed and teased the pony and tried to make it gallop. My father was himself an intrepid rider. And riding became important to me both because I saw that it pleased him and also because it gave me freedom. However restrained and subdued my daily life within the house, on horseback I was free, physically and mentally. I was in charge of myself and of the powerful beast beneath me. I soon became a good rider. I regretted only that I might not ride astride. My father was proud of me, my mother (I felt) ambivalent; she did not ride herself. Although in theory she believed in education and independence for women, valued her own emancipation, and felt strongly that it was wrong to deny a woman a full life, her religious beliefs, combined with her deep love for my father, led her to believe that submission was a womanly virtue—*not* indiscriminate submission (early she had rejected the domination of Mr. Brocklehurst, director of Lowood School, and later that of her cousin, the masterful, righteous St. John Rivers), but submission with love to a strong, honourable male: on the one hand, God the Father; on the other, Fairfax Rochester. I believed she shared her adoration between her God and her husband. *Mrs. Rochester* was for her the sweetest name.

I confess my mother puzzled me. I think she admired my riding ability but felt I was somehow flouting heavenly authority (and hers) when I rode away, often alone, exploring the countryside. And when I returned, flushed and excited, my hair blown from its neat bands into tangled curls on my forehead and long strands on my shoulders, she looked severe.

Her reaction may also have been coloured by the fact that my father once expressed interest in a young woman from one of the local County families. The Hon. Blanche Ingram was a notable horsewoman and was first seen by my mother riding with my father. (Again, I learned of this through her journal.) Miss Ingram's arrogance and assumption of social superiority were symbolized by her position high in the saddle of a horse, from which she looked down her nose on my mother. Miss Ingram was long gone from the neighbourhood. She had married a worn-out man of fashion, considerably older than herself, and lived now in London; her brother, Lord Ingram, had inherited Ingram Park and had, I believe, two or three children. We did not meet. We were not part of their social world, though this, I believe, was my father's choice rather than theirs. My father's family was an old one, long established in Yorkshire, and he was very wealthy; birth and money cover a multitude of sins. But my mother did not forget the past. In her time as a governess, she had been snubbed by these very people. And to her, riding may still have been associated with arrogance. My mother would not have stopped me riding altogether, but left to herself, I think, she would have curbed my rides, turned them into ladylike excursions on a leading rein, escorted by a groom. But in this my father ruled, and I rode free.

I was free, too, of her stern unquestioning religious beliefs, for my father—whose history had taught him no love of the clergy and Society's conventions, who had no taste for unquestioning obedience, and who was, in fact, too proud to brook any unearned authority and too intelligent not to examine traditional beliefs—taught *me* to question from an early age. He had turned to God, he told me, when he thought he had lost my mother and in desperation blamed the misdeeds in his past. He had prayed desperately for forgiveness and for her restoration. And his prayers had been granted. That he acknowledged with the deepest gratitude. But religions, the rules and regulations that controlled the ways in which man was allowed to worship, those he firmly believed came from man, and he did not accept their authority. He read the works of the new thinkers and theologists of our time and discussed them with me. From the writings of Professor Thomas Huxley he culled the term "agnostic" to cover his own beliefs; that is, that while God existed, religions were the invention of man. This did not suit my mother, though; as I have shown you, she was quite ready to criticize the clergy. But she always believed my father a law unto himself.

After the Rector's denunciation of chloroform and my mother's pointed withdrawal, we went seldom to the church in Hay. In fact, we did not live a very sociable life. Sometimes my mother's cousins, the former Diana Rivers, with her husband, Captain Fitzjames of the Royal Navy, and Mary

Wharton, with her clergyman husband, all of whom lived on the Devon coast, came to stay with us or we went to them, but not more often than once a year. (Devon was my only exposure to the sea, which my father loved.) We knew their children as well as we knew any, but not well.

Our neighbours fought shy of us. The events leading to the fire, and the discovery that the lunatic known to be living at Thornfield Hall was in reality Mrs. Rochester, made a great stir. The fact that my mother had been living in the house as governess to little Adele and that my father had attempted to marry her bigamously was a scandal that lost nothing in the telling. The stories ripened with the years, and my parents, self-sufficient as they were, made no attempts to conciliate or reconcile. Mr. and Mrs. Eshton were welcome acquaintances until they moved to Scotland. Sir George and Lady Lynn exchanged social calls. Colonel Dent remained my father's good friend, and we paid occasional visits to his estate of Highcrest Manor to take tea with quiet Mrs. Dent, and even more rarely they visited us. But Nigel Dent, their only son, was five years older than Oliver (he was destined for the Indian Army). There was no child at Highcrest for me to play with.

My father's interests were broad. At home, his interest continued to be landscape gardening. His impaired eyesight was no handicap here, nor his lack of a hand. With my mother's help, he read widely on this subject. Our park was beautiful. And when, at the age of five or six, I tagged at his heels, stole a trowel, and begged to be allowed to dig and plant, he encouraged me, had the local blacksmith make me a set of tools to size, allotted certain beds to be known as mine, gave me seeds and cuttings, and taught me, as I grew, the art of propagation. Gardening became one of my great joys. Whatever my small worries, my self-doubts, a morning spent with my bulbs or weeding in my flower beds, kneeling on my own special mat, my hands deep in the rich soil (for I must confess I often forgot my gloves, despite Molly's scoldings), always served to smooth the wrinkles from my mind and to leave me serene.

My father also kept abreast of politics, with the reformation of Parliament and talk of a universal vote, with industrialization and unrest among working men, and with the spreading of the railways. Queen Victoria had been in seclusion since the death of Prince Albert in 1861, and this caused considerable discontent among the populace, with some eccentrics talking republicanism. My father discussed all this with my mother, and I listened when he spoke. There were also important events overseas that interested him, such as the consequences of the Civil War in America in 1865 and the abolition of slavery there (made law in England long before, in 1833); the war in the Crimea and exploration in Africa; plant-hunting in China. The unrest of the field hands in the West Indies deeply interested him, connected as he was with Jamaica through his first wife and the wealth she had brought to their marriage. He had lived there several years. He told us stories of his own travels in those early years when he had fled as far as he could from Thornfield. He read with great interest Mr. Charles Darwin's book, *On the Origin of Species*, and discussed it with us eagerly; my mother felt it came close to blasphemy. My father also kept pace with much contemporary prose and poetry; he was always adding to our library. As I have said, my mother read to him several hours each day. He rode and walked, with Pilot at his side. Sometimes he went to London on business, and he always returned full of the happenings of the day. But he brought no friends home with him. My mother communicated regularly by letter with her Rivers cousins but saw them once a year at the most.

So, all in all, we were an isolated family, but I was happy enough, bolstered by my father's support and my deep love for him. Left to myself, I played with Annie Parrott or created imaginary playmates, imaginary adventures. I was fond of my fellow nursling, but she was a practical soul. She would play house with me in the ruins, sweeping clean a patch between the roots of a tree and collecting stones and twigs and berries for furniture and food, or ride a fallen tree, pretending it was a horse. But she looked at me askance when I added unseen play-mates. I learned to keep such fantasies to myself, lulling myself to sleep at night with imagined adventures in which my father was hero. Oliver did not go to school—my mother taught both him and me our early lessons—but later tutors came to us both. I found in myself a talent for piano playing, which both my parents encouraged. It gave me much pleasure to play for my father. At eighteen, Oliver went away to college. And by then, Annie was already helping her mother with housework; such schooling as she had received she gained through me, and at twelve she was considered old enough to work (when I was sixteen, she became my personal maid).

Alone, I read and studied, practiced my music, and wandered the estate. I sketched and drew from nature, not portraits like my mother, but tiny detailed drawings of ferns and fungi; the "sticky buds" unfurling on the horse chestnut trees and later conkers, as we called horse chestnuts, richly polished, emerging from their prickly cases; catkins dangling from witch hazel bushes; toadstools emerging from a crevice in a rotting tree; seedpods on poppies; and flowers and leaves on hawthorn twigs. I had a little of my mother's skill.

And so I grew to sixteen, idolizing my father, striving to live up to my mother's high standards, with no great expectations of my future life. For what could happen to tall, plain, silent me? I had little hope of a rewarding marriage. My father, the unobtainable, was there before my eyes. Where was I to find his equal? And what else was there in life for a young woman? I resigned myself to ending my life as a recluse.

Only at times would I daydream of a life shared with someone I could not define, of a life of exploration and adventure, of travel to far-off lands with a companion who would share with me his experience yet leave me to make my own discoveries, someone who treasured me for my own uniqueness and relied on me for help and comfort even as he offered help to me. It was a happy dream. I would return to myself with a sigh and a feeling of incompleteness and longing.

Oliver came home once or twice a year. He returned home for good after the completion of his college terms. It was the following April, shortly after my sixteenth birthday, that change did indeed come to the Rochesters of Thornfield Hall, and my story truly begins.

CHAPTER ONE

I Am Sent to School

This was an uncomfortable crisis ...

⊰ VILLETTE ⊱

"Miss Janet? Miss Janet!"

My maid's calm country voice called me early one morning as I dawdled in the orchard before breakfast. It was a fine April day, the air fresh and cool after a night of rain. There were crocuses, patches of yellow and purple, visible in the grass and daffodils in bloom under the apple trees, and somewhere a robin sang, proclaiming his territory. As I left the orchard, a kestrel flew up, lofting high in the rain-fresh sky: windhovers, the Yorkshire people call them, a name I have always loved. I watched it float overhead, poised, wings still, eyeing the ground for prey.

"Miss Janet?" The call was louder.

I picked a daffodil. I held it between thumb and finger and inhaled its fragrance with enjoyment. Its clean, astringent scent filled my senses. Only then did I turn towards the house.

"Yes, Annie. I am here."

My mother wanted me, she said. I was to join the rest of the family in the library. Quickly she straightened my collar and smoothed my hair, braided and looped at the back of my head.

There could be no dawdling if my mother had expressed a wish. I made my way to the library, where my father sat at his desk and my mother stood behind him with one hand on his shoulder. Oliver lounged in a leather armchair. They had been talking eagerly, but now they stopped and looked towards me.

"Come in, Janet," said my father as I lingered on the threshold. It was sometimes difficult for me to intrude on their close-knit group. He sat me down in a chair opposite his desk. His glance at me was sober and assessing.

"We have something to tell you, Janet, of an important nature. We are making a change in our lives." Cool fingers seemed to play about the nape of my neck. I shivered, shrugged my shoulder blades, and held my tongue.

"Your mother and I are leaving shortly for Jamaica," he said. "Within a month. And we will be gone perhaps two years. Oliver will accompany us. It is a scheme that has been long in the planning." He looked at me kindly. "You are too young, we feel, for such a trying journey. You will stay safely in England and go to school. So, Janet, what do you say?"

I felt as if I had been struck a blow. But I stiffened my spine and returned his gaze. "It is a long way off, sir," I said. And again, "It is a long way."

He winced. My father had travelled considerably during the difficult years of his first marriage to Bertha Mason. He believed he travelled in an attempt to leave behind his unhappiness and despair with his marriage. In fact, I believe he would always have had a wandering bent. He was interested in other ways, other lands. Apart from their yearlong European tour, my mother had not travelled, though when she was young she had yearned for "far horizons." She took up the tale. They had decided, she said, that now, while they were both in good health, was a suitable time to make a journey they had long considered. (This was an oblique reference to my father's age; he was twenty years older than my mother.) It was, they explained, their intention to investigate the affairs of the Masons, the family of my father's long-dead first wife, to see how needy they might be after years of upheaval and revolution in the West Indies and, if they felt it advisable, to make recompense for the money that had come to my father on his marriage to Bertha Mason. (That was my mother's influence, I thought. My father's conscience was well developed, but I doubt if he would, left to himself, have felt guilt over Bertha Mason's dowry. That a husband assumed a wife's property was a fact of life. It would be my mother who felt that every last reminder of that disastrous marriage should be excised.)

I had read in my mother's journal the story behind that ill-fated marriage. My grandfather had arranged for his younger son to marry Bertha Mason, a Creole, living in Jamaica and the daughter of a wealthy sugar planter, although he knew that both her mother and grandmother were of unsound mind, the mother now confined in a lunatic asylum. Through this marriage, my grandfather planned to make his son's fortune without having to divide his own property and thereby lessen what he could leave to his eldest son, Rowland. Bertha Mason's fatal mental inheritance had been disguised before the marriage, her coarse behaviour glossed over. She was handsome, that was enough. (In the Islands, she was widely known to be unchaste and intemperate, indulging in strong drink—the fiery local rum—smuggled in by her servants and given to extreme bursts of temper and even violence to those serving her; local gentlemen of marriageable inclination knew better than to seek her hand despite her wealth.) To Mr. Rochester senior, her dowry was all that mattered. As it turned out, this venal marriage was unnecessary. My uncle Rowland was unmarried, and when after some years he was thrown from his horse and broke his neck and then, shortly after, my grandfather died, my father inherited Thornfield and all his father's property. He had grown steadily more prosperous over the years.

My mother took over the explanation once more. "As your father says, *you*, Janet, are to go to school in London. Your father believes you have lived too long in seclusion here with us. The establishment is a finishing school for young ladies, run by my friend Miss Temple, and there you will not only continue to study art and music and to follow a course of reading but also learn to dance and to comport yourself with ease in the social world." The corners of her mouth turned down a little. "I do not imply I wish you to indulge in the more vapid ways of Society, to become vain and self-centred, concerned only with appearance, dress, gossip, and petty snobberies. Your whole upbringing must protect you from such false indulgence. We have tried to instil in you such standards and true moral principles as will preserve you from frivolity. But to be at ease in society is an asset."

My father broke in on her discourse. "Mrs. Rochester, you will fill our sweet Janet with dismay. This is no banishment. I feel sure you will lead a pleasant life. We have investigated this school thoroughly. You are green yet, my dear.

Grass green—as I once was. Our life here is quiet. You are unaccustomed to society. It will do you good to live for a while in London, with other young ladies. There will be trips to museums, galleries, concert halls. The school is in Kensington, not far from the Royal Albert Hall, of which we have recently read."

"It is run, as I said, by Miss Temple—my old friend and school mistress." Once again, my mother took up the tale. "Her husband, the Reverend John Nasmyth, is dead. She needs to amplify her income, and she has returned to her old calling and to the use of her maiden name."

Miss Temple, as quite a young woman, had been the superintendent of Lowood, a charitable institution, the school to which my mother's relatives had consigned her. That school had been bad, conducted with meanness and religious strictures at the orders of the Reverend Mr. Brocklehurst (severity and semi-starvation in God's name), but Miss Temple had been an exception to the rule of harsh discipline, false economy, and petty spite. My mother had loved her, and it was Miss Temple's marriage that had impelled my mother to advertise for a position as governess and to remove herself from the school to work for my father, taking care of Adele. "She and her sister-in-law, Miss Ada Nasmyth, own quite a large house in Kensington, sufficient to provide bed and board to twelve young ladies from sixteen to eighteen years old. In two weeks' time, you will join them."

Two weeks? I shrank, and I know my face paled.

"We have been planning this trip for some time, my dear," said my father. "We expect, as I say, to be away for two years. You will be an accomplished young lady of eighteen by the time we return." He smiled at me, and my mother coughed sharply. "Everything has been thought of. Thornfield is to be let. Mr. Briggs will be in charge of my estate and property. Miss Temple will join with him in temporary guardianship of you until you are eighteen. We expect to be home by that time, but all contingencies must be covered."

He stood up and took a quick turn about the room, pausing by the window to look out at the prospect, which was fair indeed: thin, bright April sunshine making diamonds of the raindrops on the lawn, trees coming into leaf, daffodils and crocuses adding colour to the scene. Fat clouds overhead promised more rain. When he turned around, his face was sober, and his eyes met mine with gravity and solemn intent.

"If, for any reason, we are delayed—or worse—through some misadventure on land or sea, Mr. Briggs has our instructions for your future life. You will leave Miss Temple's school at eighteen and live with a joint guardian until you are twenty-one. Mr. Briggs will continue to be your primary guardian; he has my full confidence and direction. This second guardian is not unknown to you; it is Colonel Dent. You would live with him at Highcrest Manor. You will have an allowance from the estate and will be consulted in all minor things, but you must stay with your guardian. At twenty-one you may return to Thornfield, if you wish, with a suitable companion. Indeed, you are to choose a companion before you go to Colonel Dent, since he, as you know, is a widower." My father hesitated. "Colonel Dent has been a soldier all his life, accustomed to army discipline, an authoritarian. He is a stiff-backed man, conventional, rigorous in his attention to the social strictures of our time. You will not find him as tolerant, as willing to discuss new ways and new ideas, as perhaps I have been. But he is a *good* man, Janet. You may trust him to do what is right and give you the careful protection a young woman—a *wealthy* young woman— needs. Our property is left in trust, and the full income will be available to you when you are twenty-five. We should not wish you to marry before your twenty-first birthday, although an engagement would be countenanced, if it were considered by your guardians to be appropriate."

The ideas so smoothly laid out before me, this close organization of my future life, distressed me. The thought of losing my parents and my only brother, of living with a little-known guardian, of precautions being taken to preclude my marriage to a fortune hunter (for that, I clearly saw, was what they had in mind) was overpowering.

"Oh, stop!" I cried, jumping to my feet. "I cannot listen!" I placed my hands over my ears and stared at my father in anguish.

"Janet!" said my mother sharply.

"Janet," said my father in his deep voice, looking at me with patience and love.

"I am going to ride," I said. "I must have time to take this in. It is too much, too much!" And I ran from the room.

I waited impatiently while my groom saddled my mare, Nimbus, a recent birthday present from my father. Not until I was in the saddle did I let myself think. I was appalled by the prospect in store for me. Tears stung my eyes as I galloped down one of the rides, Pilot at my heels.

I rode for over an hour. My mother had schooled her daughter to control her outward emotions. Never had it been so hard to achieve such self-discipline, but I managed at last; I grew resigned. When I returned, calm but very hungry (for I had missed my breakfast), I found my family at luncheon. I was by that time able to apologize for my wilful behaviour and to seek more information about my life in London.

First and most importantly, I asked whether I should be able to continue with my riding in London and what would become of my new mare. My father assured me that lessons were given at a riding school in Hyde Park and that the students were able to ride in Rotten Row. My mare would be brought to London by a groom and stabled in the park for my sole use.

Their plans continued to unfold. Pilot, my father's beloved dog, was to live with Colonel Dent.

My father, looking grave, then went over again the provisions that had been made for possible contingencies. If, at the end of two years, when I was eighteen, no letter had been received by Mr. Briggs or myself within six months, the second arrangement would come into force. My father would leave a sealed letter with Mr. Briggs giving instructions for my care. A generous allowance would be made for me from the estate. I should inherit nothing at that age, and, if I were to form an attachment and wish to marry, an engagement might be entered into, but no marriage would be concluded until I was twenty-one, and then only with the consent of Mr. Briggs and Colonel Dent.

At twenty-one, if my parents were still missing, or if news had come of their and my brother's demise, a different set of instructions would come into place. If, on the other hand, Oliver returned to England alone, a third set of instructions had been left with Mr. Briggs to cover this contingency.

Matters of such grave portent could not but distress me. I felt stunned by the barrage of instructions, by feelings of foreboding. Both my parents kissed me and reassured me. They had no doubts of their safe return. Such journeys were quite common these days. It was practical, however, to be prepared for anything the future might hold, and they did not want to leave me, a young girl, at the mercy of a harsh and greedy world. We had no close relations. But I had known Mr. Briggs all my life; he was an old friend. I could place my trust in him to deal with me as my father had ordained.

I went to bed in a state of considerable dismay. I could not sleep. My quiet and pleasant life had turned head over heels, and nothing in the future was certain. Deep within me grew a thought I hardly dared admit—that I was being left behind (punished) by my mother for my father's fond affection. The bitter thought occurred to me that, although the reasons for travel given to me were true, a secondary motive of my mother's was to remove my father from me now that I was becoming a young woman. My figure, though slim, was now well formed, my complexion good, and my hair glossy. I was moving towards the marriageable years. Did my mother indeed see me as a rival? I cried that night and several more, but I rose each morning, splashed my face with cold water, and greeted my family with a calm and cheerful demeanour. My mother's keen eyes noted such evidence of distress as was left, but she smiled and nodded with approval at my resolution.

The days passed all too soon, and we left for London together, an adventure in itself, since we travelled by railway from Millcote. My father had travelled by train to London on many occasions; it was by far the quickest mode of travel; but all was new to my mother and me. I was deeply excited. First and foremost, I was amazed at the rapidity with which we travelled—more than thirty miles an hour. The train itself was a dragon, spitting live sparks and specks of soot. When we passed through one of the many tunnels, my mother opined we had glimpsed hell: the funnels spewed forth concentrated gusts of fiery smoke into the blackness. We could not breathe. My father made haste to close the windows. We came provided with luncheon baskets, shawls, and small pillows and were able to purchase hot tea at the various stations along the line. Our more intimate needs were handled by hasty dashes into the waiting rooms by the platforms. We left early in the morning, and we reached London by the end of the day, grimy and gritty (we wore special gloves for travelling that we discarded on our arrival) and very tired with the exertion and stress of such an unusual journey. Our very bones felt rattled and out of kilter. We drove at once to the Hyde Park Hotel.

Two days later, somewhat restored by sleep (though the noise of the London streets, even in such an elegant part of town, was considerable to our country-bred ears) and having ventured to inspect some of the grand London emporiums and made such purchases as were necessary, I was escorted to my future home. Miss Temple's Seminary made its home in a Georgian house in a London square, Rutland Gate. It was a tall, narrow house, four stories high, painted white, and with an iron railing in front, guarding the area, as it was called. Narrow steps led down to the area from an ornamental gate in the railing. An area was in fact a brief flagged courtyard from which doors led to the kitchen in the basement, to the servants' quarters, and also to the laundry and coal cellar. A handsome portico sheltered the front door, which was painted a glossy indigo and was flanked by four Grecian pillars. The stairs were of white marble. Similar houses formed three sides of the square, differentiated mainly by the colour of the front door; the fourth side looked onto the Knightsbridge Road and Hyde Park. In the centre of the square was a pleasant garden, with flowers and bushes and many fine trees, surrounded by ornamental iron railings and a gate, which was kept locked. Only residents of the square had a key to the gate. Tucked away behind the stately houses, down a cobbled slope, was the mews, with stables for the carriage horses and accommodation overhead for the coachmen and their families.

Miss Temple was waiting for us with her sister-in-law, Miss Nasmyth, two steps behind. Miss Temple was quiet, gently spoken. Her forehead was high, her look intelligent, her smile warm. Her dark hair was streaked with grey, and fine wrinkles netted her complexion. Miss Nasmyth, some ten years younger, seemed reserved, withdrawn; she was very thin, and her lips were pinched together. She did not smile and seldom spoke. We inspected the rooms together. The schoolrooms (lecture rooms, Miss Temple called them) were on the ground floor. One was equipped as a studio, with easels and statuary, and several young ladies were at work there. They looked at me with some curiosity but were called briskly to attention by an attendant instructor. I could hear music close at hand. At least two pianos were being played: on one a series of dramatic trills and scales were produced; the other was used more tentatively to play a slight and shaky melody. The dining hall was also on the ground floor, and below were the kitchen premises, which we did not inspect but which intruded themselves with a smell of baking. The library (used also by Miss Temple as her office) and the sitting room for pupils were up one flight of stairs.

The bedrooms were up a second flight. Two young ladies passed us on the stairs, their heads bent demurely; I noticed the quick, surreptitious glances as I passed. Each bedroom contained two narrow beds with white counterpanes, a wardrobe, two chest of drawers, and a washstand with two jugs and basins in what I noted was pretty china, scattered with blue flowers. The curtains were made of a flowered cretonne in which blue predominated.

My mother had told me that two young ladies shared each bedroom. This, in particular, had perturbed me; I had never shared a bedroom, and the thought of sharing with a *stranger* was particularly dismaying. I was reserved by nature and modest by training. My mother, knowing my feelings— which, indeed, she had instilled in me—brought up this subject on my behalf, and I found that, to begin with, at any rate, I need not share. There were only ten other girls in residence; I should make eleven. Until a twelfth arrived, I should sleep alone. I sighed with relief.

We returned to the study, and now the dreaded time was at hand. I embraced my mother. As I moved back from the embrace, my mother patted my cheek and said, "Dear Janet, I know you are as good as you are clever. May God watch over you." She left a small, tissue-wrapped package in my hand as she removed her own.

"A keepsake, my dear," she said.

I turned to my father, who hugged me closely. "My dear," he said. "My very dearest daughter." And then, under his breath, "'Stiffen the sinews,' my brave spirit."

My brother kissed my cheek. I stood stiffly in that close, book-lined room and heard them descend the stairs. I would not cry. There was a murmur of voices in the hall, the click of the latch, and then the sound of the closing door. Miss Temple turned to me with a smile and put out her hand, but I walked past her to the long window, heavily draped in a plum velour and curtained with lace. I pushed the lace aside. My family walked away from me to the waiting hansom cab.

I watched first my mother and then my brother enter the cab. My father stood alone on the pavement, his broad back towards me. He spoke briefly to the cabdriver, then turned, slowly and deliberately, towards the house. I withdrew behind the curtain. For a scant moment he gazed up at the window. I saw him blink, and his mouth contract. Then he turned abruptly away and mounted the cab steps, the cabbie slapped the horse's back with the reins, and the cab moved away and trundled up the street out of sight.

I was reminded of a sentence of my mother's, which I read long ago in her journal: *"He made me love him without looking at me."*

Then and only then did I examine my mother's parting gift. Inside the fragile wrapping was a small velvet jeweller's box. Inside the box was a ring, nestled in satin. It was familiar to me, as was all her jewellery. A Rochester family heirloom, it was a fine emerald surrounded by diamond chips set in a golden circle. I was strangely pleased. *Her* gifts tended to be sensible: books, expensive enough; clothing; a set of silver-backed brushes on my last birthday. Since the ring came from the Rochester inheritance, it might be said to come from them both, yet I knew my father had given the jewellery that had come to the Rochesters from the female line (indeed, from his grandmother, *not* herself a Rochester) freely to his bride.

It was the most valuable thing I had ever owned. I slid it on my finger for a moment, admiring the blue flame curled deep within the shimmering green, and then I placed it back

in its box and gave it into Miss Temple's keeping to deposit in her small safe.

I allowed Miss Temple to take my hand. She guided me back to my bedroom, where Miss Nasmyth was supervising the delivery of my luggage. Then they left me to settle in. I took off my cloak and bonnet, smoothed my hair, and rinsed my hands in the basin. There was a chair by the bed and, for a few moments, I sat looking down at my hands. I felt appallingly alone. Then I shook myself and stood erect. I would not disappoint my father's expectations of me. I looked around my bedroom with a better heart than I had expected. The blue-flowered china and the matching curtains were gay and pretty. I unlocked my trunk and hunted for a few precious objects. The room was comfortably furnished and, when I had unpacked my particular treasures—my favourite books, framed sketches, and ornaments from home—it seemed a pleasant enough refuge.

There was a sudden disturbance. A musical gong sounded once, twice. Almost at once, feet mounted the stairs, voices called, dresses rustled. I heard Miss Nasmyth calling out a reprimand to some wild soul who dared to run along the passage. The bedrooms on either side of mine were invaded. I heard chatter, subdued laughter, nothing to dismay me. Then the gong sounded a second time, five steady beats. Miss Nasmyth came to my door and led me down to luncheon, and I met my companions.

CHAPTER TWO

Rutland Gate

I like the spirit of this great London which I feel around me.

◊ VILLETTE ◊

I DID NOT SEE my family again before they left. My mother thought it best that there be only one farewell. Two days later, they took a steam packet downriver to meet the *Albatross*, the ship that would take them to the West Indies. I was left alone for the first time in my life.

My days passed pleasantly enough. After the first week, I slept well. The city noises ceased to disturb me, and if I woke in the small hours, wrenched from sleep by an aching loneliness, a feeling of desertion, I soon slumbered once more.

I was not used to the company of young women. At first I remained an onlooker, responding to direct communication but without making any advances on my part. Most of the girls were agreeable enough, two or three silly or in some way ill-natured. I left them alone. Two in particular I came to call my friends: Paulina Fanshawe and Davina Trevelyn, always known as Daisy. Both these young ladies had parents living in London, and their mothers on occasion gave tea parties for the pupils of the school, half at one time, at which we learned to make polite conversation while handling our cups and saucers. Various undemanding guests were asked to meet us. Once or twice an impromptu tea dance was got up as good practice for the young ladies, and so it was I came for the first time to dance with a man. We were at the Fanshawes.

Paulina's aunt, Miss Fanshawe, who resided with the family and acted as companion to Mrs. Fanshawe, played the piano. I sat near the tea table, behind which Mrs. Fanshawe was ensconced with the silver tea service in front of her. I was wearing a new silk dress of a dark violet, and I looked down with pleasure at my skirt, smoothing it with my gloved fingers and admiring the sheen. There were four young men present: Paulina's brothers, Frederick and Aubrey, and two of their friends, Evelyn Trent and Geoffrey Allerton-Smyth. There were six of us young ladies and a scattering of other people: a married couple or so and two of their daughters. I thought it unlikely I should be asked to dance, nor did I wish it, though I had come to enjoy the dancing lessons we had twice a week at the Seminary. I was light on my feet, and the steady exercise I had riding my horse in Hyde Park gave me balance and physical control. I found that I held my own quite well with the other girls. But I had no great opinion of my charms. I continued to find myself "well enough," as I had of old. And I had come to realize that the most attractive girls were those who acted as if they *believed* themselves attractive, those who smiled and fluttered and talked with ease, if not necessarily with sense. I watched them, studied them, but I could not join them. I counted myself an onlooker. I was startled, therefore, when a voice at my side said, gently, "Miss Rochester, may I have the pleasure of this dance?"

I looked up to find Frederick Fanshawe at my side. He was Paulina's elder brother, a slight young man with warm brown eyes and a long and silken moustache, aged about twenty-three, I understood; he was acting as a political secretary to a friend of the Fanshawe family, a member of Parliament. I had spoken to him once or twice, asking him questions about parliamentary debates in which I had been versed by my father. I remember plainly his surprise; politics were not a subject for debutantes, but he answered me sensibly and offered observations on the topics of the day on other occasions.

I now gave him a quiet assent and stood. He took my hand and led me into the set that was forming in the angle of the L-shaped drawing room that was to be used for dancing. I found it strange in the extreme to stand thus, with a man holding my hand, but almost at once the music started. The dance was one I knew well; we advanced and retreated, *chasséd* and curtsied, and then in turn led the way between the dancers in the set. All at once I found myself smiling. Frederick Fanshawe smiled back, and we danced our way down the set and around again. He took my hand and released it, as required, and I forgot to find it strange. I held my head high and gathered my skirt in my left hand. The silk whispered pleasantly about my limbs. When the dance ended, I was quite sorry.

Frederick Fanshawe asked me again, and then one of the other young men, Evelyn Trent, partnered me. I missed no steps, made no mistakes. I said very little, but my partners seemed to enjoy our dances. Paulina and I returned to school arm in arm in great content.

"My brother likes you," she told me, making a prim mouth but laughing at me with her eyes.

"Oh, Paulina," said I. "He is a grown man, out in the wide world. He is being kind to your young friend."

"Perhaps you are right," she conceded. "But I think he enjoyed being kind to my young friend." And she laughed at me until I felt myself blush, and I fell silent.

I had only the slightest interest in Frederick Fanshawe as a man. He was pleasant enough, but there was no strength in his physiognomy, no vigour in his port. But as a partner I appreciated him; my enjoyment of dancing was confirmed. I looked forward to our lessons and, on those not infrequent occasions when a dance was got up, I did not shrink back or play the wallflower.

I have mentioned my riding. This my father had arranged with Miss Temple. My beloved mare, Nimbus, had been brought to London, and I rode her regularly twice a week, Mondays and Wednesdays, very early in the morning, accompanied by a groom. Hyde Park was almost deserted—the air was fresh, birds sang, and I rejoiced. On Saturdays, I joined with other pupils in a demure group ride on Rotten Row, pleasant enough, but my weekday rides were my great pleasure. One could not gallop in the park as I did in the Yorkshire countryside, but a brisk trot was permitted. The groom was a lively young Cockney named Albert Higgins, and we dealt well together. Riding with me was a release for him from hard labour at the stables, and he enjoyed it as much as I did.

A year passed, too slowly but not unpleasantly. I did indeed feel, as my father had said, less "green" in the ways of society. During that time, I was the happy recipient of several letters from my family. My father wrote from the ship, describing their life, with its circumscribed routine, its comforts and discomforts, and the adaptations that had to be made. *"Your mother bears up well,"* he wrote, *"though rough seas upset her health."* She did not like this mentioned, he added. He wrote also of the grandeur of the sea in a storm (he, needless to say, was never seasick), the fiery splendour of the sunsets, the startling clarity of a full moon in a cloudless night sky over an ink-blue sea, and the unexpected pleasures, such as the sight of dolphins swimming at the prow, an albatross flying overhead with its colossal wingspan (did I remember "The Ancient Mariner," which we had read together?), a whale spouting, and then the first flying fishes, a sign they were entering the tropics. Oliver wrote of climbing the rigging and learning to dance a sailor's hornpipe. He spoke briefly of the sailors, packed together in the hold, sleeping in hammocks, and the casual brutality of their daily lives. My mother wrote, typically, of the lack of privacy, of the difficulties one faced in daily tasks, such as the washing of one's clothes: a sailor had been appointed to do this chore, but she was unwilling to entrust him with her own more intimate garments. She made sure they were hung to dry inside a pillow case and not exposed to the vulgar gaze. She spoke of the endless days stretching out one after the other so that time ceased to have meaning. She said, proudly, that none of them had been seasick, and I smiled to myself. Then she spoke of my father. *"It delights my heart,"* she wrote, *"to see your father so bronzed and vital, glowing indeed with health, thanks to the salt breezes and tropic sun. His hair, still so thick and crisp,*

blows in the wanton winds. He seems one with the wild tempes-
tuous sea, the storm-whipped waves, the glory of the tropic night."
Tears stung my eyes; I saw him so clearly. I shut them briefly
before continuing to read. It seemed there were two other
women on board, a Mrs. Akenhead, a naval captain's wife
going out to join her husband at the West Indies Station, and
her daughter, Miranda, pleasant women with whom my
mother had made friends. She was keeping a journal, she said.
When they docked at Madeira, she spoke of the joy of exercise, of land that stayed still beneath one's feet, of the scent of
orange blossom. They had joined forces with the Akenheads
and had hired a carriage to drive around the island. Then
there was a gap until letters came dealing with life in Jamaica,
an island rent by troubles between plantation owners and
their black workers. The Masons were dead, they had discovered, their plantation long owned by others. My parents were
making arrangements to bestow a goodly sum of money on
the local school for the children of plantation workers.

At the end of my first year at the Seminary, there were
changes in the pupils. Three of the elder girls left, to be
presented at Court and formally introduced to Society by
their Mamas. Four more young ladies arrived, and I was faced
with the fact that I must now share my bedroom, which had
for so long been my sanctuary, for I was still solitary. Paulina
and Daisy were my good friends. I talked with them at mealtimes and in our recreation periods, I walked with them, and
I visited their homes, but I continued to find that I needed
time alone if I were to retain my peace of mind. When the

closeness of other bodies, the pressure of socializing, the shrill buzz of female chattering were too much for me, I retired with a book to my room. I had established that it was my custom, and Miss Temple gave her permission for me to withdraw in this way on occasion. Miss Nasmyth, I believe (she was never a good friend to me), would have denied me; she thought me proud and above my company.

Now this indulgence must end. Moreover, one of the new pupils was from my neighbourhood and was known to me, though by name only. The Hon. Isabella Ingram was the daughter of Lord Ingram, and the niece of that Blanche Ingram who had been in a sense my mother's rival for my father's hand, as my mother related in her journal. Ingram Park was some ten miles north of Hay. This was not a family with which the Rochesters had visited—there was little goodwill between them—but they were very much part of County society. Isabella was a few months my junior. She was to attend the school just until she was eighteen, when she would be presented at Court. She had black hair, worn in a multitude of ringlets, black eyes, and a fine complexion with a high colour. Her nose was arched, as were her eyebrows. Her mouth was fashionably small but thin-lipped and supercilious. On her introductory visit to the school, she immediately made her presence felt with her constant high-pitched chattering and piercing laugh.

Isabella looked, and was, arrogant and disdainful. It was she, I was told, with whom I must share my bedroom, and I at once rebelled. Apart from my need for time by myself,

I had quietly conformed to the school's routine, making few demands. Now I spoke up, but first I approached Paulina, whose bedroom companion was one of those leaving the school. With her agreement, I proposed to Miss Temple that I share with Paulina. There was nothing here to object to, girls who became friends often expressed a wish to share and, although it was desired that such reorganization as took place each year should be achieved with a minimum of upheaval, it was in no way an unusual request. Miss Nasmyth, however, did object. She claimed that once again I was particularizing myself in an effort to make myself out as superior.

"You seem to find it difficult, Miss Rochester, to conform to the ways of the community. Perhaps you feel yourself to be privileged?"

"In what way, Miss Nasmyth?" I responded. "Miss Browne and Miss Entwhistle have also requested to share. How do you find me different?"

"In your manner, Miss Rochester. Aloof. Cold. Miss Browne and Miss Entwhistle are sweet, womanly girls. It is a pleasure to accede to their request."

I looked at her in what I could not but feel was an aloof, cold manner. "I hope you enjoyed the chocolates they gave you," I said.

Her mouth closed tightly. Miss Nasmyth's taste for sweet-meats was well known and catered to by girls with special requests. I had never so indulged her. I knew also that she liked to caress those girls she made her particular favourites.

There were odd rumours in the school about Miss Nasmyth, rumours I only half understood but could not like. Miss Temple joined the conversation.

"I see no reason why Miss Rochester and dear Paulina should not share a room if they both wish it, Ada. Isabella Ingram can share with Maude de Vere perfectly well."

And so it was settled. But it soon became plain that Ada Nasmyth had informed Isabella Ingram of my request and had relished her response. Isabella Ingram, within the first week of her residence, spread a garbled version of my father's first marriage and my mother's career as a governess before her marriage throughout the school, and Miss Nasmyth, meeting me as we gathered in the drawing room before dinner, as was our custom, curled her upper lip and said in a voice loud enough to be heard by all: "I now understand your reluctance to share a room with dear Miss Ingram, Miss Rochester. Your position in life is hardly that of her equal. You could not have felt comfortable."

My father's voice spoke in my ear, *"Imitate the action of the tiger ..."*

"Nor do I feel comfortable with you, Miss Nasmyth," I replied clearly. "It is a question of manners. But that, I fear, you do not understand."

Someone tittered nervously. Miss Nasmyth glared, and I knew that in the future her dislike of me would harden. I thought too little of her to let it worry me. But Paulina, after-wards, shook her head at me. "Miss Nasmyth controls the school in so many small ways," she said. "Miss Temple takes a larger view, but she is not well; she is growing old. Miss Nasmyth will do her best to make you uncomfortable."

Oh, to be gone, I thought. When should I hear again from my parents? When would they be home? In our first year of separation, several letters had reached me, my parents taking turns to write. At the end of the year, they had written stating that their affairs in Spanish Town were in order and they were beginning to think of their journey home. Then had come a startling letter. Their plans had changed. They had decided, having travelled halfway around the world, to complete the circle. They were going to cross Panama by land and take a ship from the Americas across the Pacific on a voyage that should take them, eventually, to Singapore. From Singapore, they would sail for home.

It was the adventure of a lifetime, my mother wrote. "This is something I have always wanted to do," wrote my father.

Since then, all I had received was a letter from Oliver, telling of their preparations for the land journey by mule: "Mother is outwardly calm, inwardly a little apprehensive, but we will take great care of her." Months had gone by since then without mail. Where were my mother and father? In nine months I should be eighteen. I longed for Thornfield, my true home.

It was about this time that I dreamt (a dream that would recur) about my father. Time and again I saw him, with that unmistakable, familiar back view, walking ahead of me along what seemed to be a tropical beach. There were palm trees and large crabs, which alarmed me. I called, but he did not turn. Try as I would, I could not overtake him. I awoke from this dream with my eyes full of tears.

Isabella Ingram joined our riding parties. Her habit was dashing, her style showy. She objected to "the slug of a mare" she was offered by the stables and, having inspected my Nimbus, at first requested that she be allowed to take turns with me on the mare. When refused, she went as far as to attempt to bribe Albert to let her take the mare out behind my back. Albert promptly informed me. When it was made clear to her that Nimbus was my personal property and not for anyone else's use, she vowed to transfer a horse of her own to London. Some three weeks later, the horse arrived, a showy, lively young gelding sent by her brother at her request.

When Albert brought out the gelding, a chestnut whose name was Beau, the horse objected strongly to the London scene, the noise, the uneasy bunch of riders, the carriages coming and going into the stable yard, the passersby, the women with their parasols, the men gesticulating with their walking sticks. Miss Nasmyth, who did not ride but escorted us to the park and waited for us at the stables, began to remonstrate with Isabella, advising that she allow Albert to ride Beau at first until he had run the fidgets out of his feet. I was waiting to one side of the group, Nimbus, with her perfect manners, standing calmly by the railing. Isabella looked at me with scorn. "I have no need of a tame and biddable horse," she scoffed. "Bring him to the mounting block!" Albert, holding Beau, made some quick comment, but Isabella, mounting quickly, struck at his controlling hand with her riding whip and jerked at the reins.

Beau reared. A chorus of squeals went up from the waiting young ladies. He took a couple of quick, dancing steps on his hind legs, his eyes rolling, dropped to the ground, reared again, then leapt away, twisting and cavorting, before breaking into a gallop down the row. Someone screamed. Isabella was doing her best to control him, but the second time he reared, he displaced her in her saddle. Half around his neck, she clung to him; then, as he plunged to right and left, she rolled off his back and struck the ground. Beau kicked his hind legs and disappeared down Rotten Row.

I went after him. It was not a planned reaction. As Beau leapt away, I dug my heels into Nimbus's sides, and she sprang forward. Beau, his reins flapping on his neck, raced ahead, and I thundered after him. I had often longed to let the mare try her paces; now the chance had come. Behind me, I heard the grooms shout, and hoofs began to thud. But Nimbus was off like the wind. Down Rotten Row we plunged, with people shouting and waving on either side of the railings. I found time to hope no one would run onto the ride in front of us, as trees, railings, and people blurred together with our speed. We must have galloped half a mile before the horse ahead slowed. There were other riders on the track. They hastened out of the way of the pounding hoofs, but they served as a deterrent to Beau. I came up behind him, keeping to one side so as not to egg him on. Horses are natural competitors. We were steadily overtaking him when a dog ran onto the track, barking and leaping up at the runaway. Beau swerved away from the dog, saw the railing, and jumped. In a moment he was off again, running now between pedestrians and playing children. Nannies screamed and plucked their charges out of his way. I saw my chance and jumped in my turn from farther up the track, riding now at a tangent to meet him as he plunged across the turf. He was right ahead of me … he was just in front … I had him.

I caught his flapping reins and pulled. He tossed his head but slowed, and Nimbus came up level with him. The gallop became a trot and then a walk. Then we stood, the horses head-to-head, and I began to catch my breath. Hoofs behind me made me turn. Albert appeared, jogging along on one of the jobbing horses, his face red and sweating.

"Gawd 'elp us, miss," he said. "Ow, miss, I thought you wuz a gonna."

"Not I, Albert," I said, and I laughed. I felt thoroughly alive for the first time in an age.

"My dear young lady," said a voice nearby. "That was a remarkable ride." I looked around and found a small crowd collecting. Close at hand a tall gentleman in grey reached a hand for Beau's reins. He was accompanied by a lady nearly as tall as he, with smooth ash-blond hair visible beneath a grey hat with a curving brim trimmed with a sweeping peacock's feather. It was their likeness that first struck me, then their remarkable good looks. They were both so tall and fair, with wide-set grey eyes and straight thin noses, arched eyebrows and mouths perhaps a little thin-lipped but beautifully curved. The man held Beau in a strong grip and passed a soothing hand over the horse's sweating neck and shoulder. He smiled up at me, and his eyes gleamed. I looked back at him with as much self-possession as I could.

"I'll take 'im, Miss," said Albert jealously. A second groom, Jack, now approached, riding with caution over the grass, which was strictly forbidden by custom. I knew we should return to the row and the stables as quickly as possible so the grooms would not be blamed.

"I thank you, sir, for your assistance," I said formally to the tall man in grey. He handed the reins to Albert and raised his grey top hat to me. At his side, the lady smiled and nodded. The man still quizzed me with his eyes. "I hope we meet again, my fair centaur," he said. "I'll not forget you."

I flushed. Albert moved off, leading Beau, and I wheeled Nimbus to follow him. "Good-bye," said the lady. "Go in safety." The man raised his grey gloved hand in a farewell salute. The lady pulled at his arm. "Really, Hugo," I heard her say. "This is London, not Vienna."

We rode slowly back to the stables, first Nimbus, then Albert leading Beau, and Jack bringing up the rear. Isabella was seated with Miss Nasmyth in a hansom cab. She looked pale and shaken but enough herself to scowl at me as I drew up alongside them.

"Really, Miss Rochester," scolded Miss Nasmyth. "That was surely unnecessary. Such hoydenish manners, galloping in that way! The grooms were quite capable of recovering the horse."

"It was your mare that startled him in the first place," said Isabella sullenly. "Very true," agreed Miss Nasmyth.

"I suggest you learn to ride before you mount a half-broken yearling in the park," I said coldly to Isabella, ignoring Miss Nasmyth. My upbringing had taught me reserve; it had not taught me to be meek. "You might have caused an accident to someone other than yourself. And do not blame others for your own mistakes."

I wheeled Nimbus and rejoined the group, but they were beginning to dismount. Seemingly no one had a taste for the morning's amble around the Row.

Miss Nasmyth complained of my behaviour formally to Miss Temple and did her best to have me disciplined for outrageous conduct and gross impertinence by foregoing my rides. I told Miss Temple firmly that I did not appreciate the dishonesty of either Miss Ingram or Miss Nasmyth. Miss Temple spoke to me in private about controlling my outspokenness and of my need to live in harmony with the community. I heard her out in silence. I was quite fond of her, but I knew her grasp of the running of the school was slipping. I hoped to be gone before it became time for her to hand over control to Miss Nasmyth. From that time on, during my remaining months in the school, Miss Nasmyth spoke to me only when she was compelled to do so. Mostly she would instruct one of the maids to pass on a message she could not avoid giving me. It affected me very little, except that I wished more keenly to be gone.

Sometimes at night, however, I would relive that wild ride after Beau in the park. There had been joy in the speed, my oneness with Nimbus. And I saw again that pair of Vikings, the lady and gentleman dressed in grey, with their blond hair and grey eyes. And I saw his smile and the deeply masculine provocation of his look.

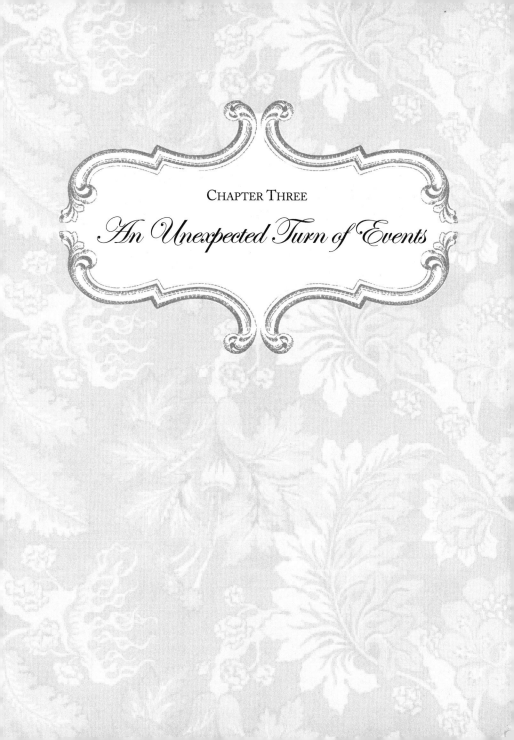

CHAPTER THREE

An Unexpected Turn of Events

It was a tall, fashionable-looking man . . .

‣ JANE EYRE ‣

$\mathcal{P}$AULINA AND I SHARED our bedroom in comfort. She was modest and reserved. We dressed and undressed (discreetly hidden by our nightgowns), washed at the washstand behind a screen, and made our toilets with a regard to the privacy of the other. I was infinitely relieved. We were both quiet sleepers. I suffered quite often from insomnia, for I still missed my father and was beginning to feel anxiety over his return. He had been always the centre of my life, and nothing was changed by his physical absence. My dreams became more frequent, more full of anxiety. Once awake, I would lie in bed in the small hours, tears still stinging my eyes as I thought of him. Then, as I lay awake, I would listen to Paulina's quiet breathing, and I found it soothing and as nonintrusive as the patter of rain on the windowpane.

Our rides continued. The young gelding was returned to Yorkshire and was replaced by a well-schooled mare, chosen this time by Lord Ingram, not the Hon. Adolphus, Isabella's brother. She did not join me on my weekday rides.

But I am leaping ahead. One notable event took place a few days after my headlong ride through the park. I was practicing my music in one of the ground floor studios early one afternoon when one of the maids came to fetch me. I was wanted, she said, in Miss Temple's room. Did she know for what reason? There were some strangers come, she said.

Miss Temple often rested at this time, when the school was quiet; it was beginning to be acknowledged that she was not in the best of health. If the weather were good enough, small parties of girls would visit picture galleries, the South Kensington museum, the gardens of the Horticultural Society, or even the International Exhibition in the afternoon. If all else failed, we walked in Hyde Park or Kensington Gardens. Today there had been heavy rain in the morning, though this had abated. But the day was still overcast, and the wind was chill. Winter would soon be upon us. I had taken advantage of a cancelled outing to spend some extra time on a Mozart sonata that was giving me trouble. Now I followed Mary up the stairs and wondered at the break with routine. Perhaps someone had brought a letter? Some news of my parents? I began to be excited.

Mary tapped at the study door and opened it for me. I passed within and found myself in the presence of two visitors whom I at once recognized: the elegant strangers I had seen in the park as I brought the horse Beau under control. They were distinctive indeed; I could not fail to know them. The lady smiled and inclined her head. The gentleman bowed more fully. I looked at Miss Temple in some surprise.

"Janet, my dear," said that lady. "I have to introduce to you Sir Hugo Calendar and his sister, Mrs. Deveraux. I am informed that they saw your recovery of the runaway horse in the park last week and were sufficiently struck by that happening to enquire at the stables as to the circumstances. On learning your name and your residence within this Seminary, they came to me, anxious that they should be made known to you. They are acquainted with your father and, indeed, are living at Thornfield Hall. Sir Hugo is the tenant of Thornfield Hall."

My eyes widened. I was considerably amazed. Such a coincidence seemed to me remarkable. I took the slender, grey-gloved hand Mrs. Deveraux held out to me and then made my curtsey to Sir Hugo.

"I am pleased indeed to know you, sir," I said to him. "And I should welcome any news you can give me of my home. It is some eighteen months since I was there. I miss it sorely."

"The Hall is in excellent shape," he returned. "We are much enjoying our sojourn there. My sister Alicia"—he bowed in her direction—"has been keeping house for me since her arrival from India. I am in London now on business, but I hope to continue to lease the Hall for some time to come. On which score, I wonder if you have any knowledge of your father's proposed return?"

"I regret that I do not. It is some time since a letter reached me. It is a source of considerable anxiety."

"The mail from a place so distant must have a hundred chances of going astray," Sir Hugo said gently. "Perhaps your parents will outrun their correspondence. Will you yourself be returning to Yorkshire in the near future?"

"I shall be leaving this Seminary in the coming spring," I said. "And I hope then to take up residence again in Yorkshire."

"Sir Hugo has been telling me how impressed he was with your riding skill and ability with horses," put in Miss Temple. "He has also told me that he was quite fully informed at the Stable of the circumstances of the runaway and that no one there considered you in any way to be to blame. It was Miss Ingram's impatience and inability to hold so strong a horse that was at fault." She smiled at me and patted my arm. I noticed the slight tremor of her hand.

I smiled back at her but did not in my heart appreciate the knowledge that an outsider's evidence was necessary to assure her that I had spoken the truth. Sir Hugo and his sister left a short time afterwards, Alicia Deveraux taking the trouble of telling me how much they should enjoy welcoming me to Thornfield. I murmured my appreciation but hoped with all my heart that my return to Thornfield would be with my parents once more in residence. I saw no prospect of enjoyment in the experience of being a guest in my own house.

But Sir Hugo and his sister made a considerable impression on me. Sir Hugo in particular seemed to meet my eyes with more than common courtesy in his gaze. His well-cut lips twitched into a smile whenever he spoke to me, and his look lingered on my face and his hand on mine as we made our good-byes. There seemed a consciousness in all his attention to me, which I found disturbing. Alicia Deveraux was not as forthcoming; she seemed polite enough but had considerable reserve. I wondered about their relationship. She was a widow, it seemed, and had lived abroad. Perhaps her husband had been an officer in the Indian Army? She was not wearing black. Her costume that day was a dark peacock blue, the jacket flaring at the waist into a *basque* over the full skirt and trimmed with a high collar of astrakhan and cuffs to match. Her suede gloves were the same grey as the collar, and she wore grey boots of such elegance I could only guess they were made in Paris. Her small, close-fitting hat, of peacock blue to match her costume, was set at a slight angle on her head and was decorated, once again, with a sweeping peacock feather. Her waist was tightly laced, and her skirt brushed the doorway as she entered. With her ash-blonde hair glimpsed smooth as satin beneath her hat and her calm, self-possessed air, she was a figure of considerable style. I could not help but hazard a guess that all her clothes were Parisian. And this interest on my part was a source of some wonder to me. Was I becoming vain and superficial, some-what less my mother's daughter?

It was true that I was beginning, coaxed on by Paulina and Daisy, to be aware of fashion and to enjoy the purchase of suitably flattering costumes. Money was not a problem— Mr. Briggs advanced whatever I needed—and the afternoon parties and concerts we attended, the tea dances, encouraged me to experiment with colours and textures. I did not now confine myself to the sober shades of my mother's recom-mendation, although I looked my best, I felt, in the deeper shades of blue and green, wine red or violet. Not for me were the pastel pinks and blues of the prospective debutantes, and never white, in which I looked insipid. I had grown quite tall; my training in dancing and deportment ensured that I stood erect and walked with grace. (We practiced each week walking and dancing with heavy books balanced on our heads, and I no longer had the slight stoop that had once marred my posture. I was not one of the girls directed to use the backboard.) My health was excellent. Paulina told me that her mother was impressed by my air of self-possession and that her brother admired me. I was beginning to realize that, though of course I was still plain, like my mother, my appearance was acceptable, even stylish. Oh, I was not extravagant. My early training went too deep for that. My parents would not find me frivolous on their return. But I paid attention to such of the fashionable world as I glimpsed in my quiet life and made sure my dresses were becomingly cut and properly fitted.

In talking thus of clothes and fashion, I am avoiding a subject that indeed I find disturbing to remember. It was the night after the visit by Sir Hugo Calendar and his sister. The rain returned, and the wind grew wild. By suppertime we were all conscious of the wailing of that wind in the chimneys and the rattling of windows. Looking out at the garden in the middle of the Square, I saw leaves whirled into the air like the astral bodies one heard of at séances now fashionable in London society. These fragile, ghostly shapes seemed to dance with abandon before they disintegrated, becoming fragmented and scattering before the elements. The rain lashed the outside of the house. A leak was discovered in one of the attics where the maids slept, and there was much running to and fro with pails and dishcloths. We began to retire at an earlier hour than usual, seeking the warmth and reassurance of our beds. As I reached the landing, a great crash resounded outside. Paulina and I rushed to the window and saw that a branch torn from a giant elm tree in the garden had fallen across the railings surrounding the basement area. It still vibrated with the force of its descent. The pavement was littered with leaves and twigs and smaller branches, torn from the trees in the Square. I looked up at the sky. All was pitchy dark, with the glass globes of the public lighting showing pale and spectral. The gas flames, lit by the lamplighter at dusk, flickered inside the globes. Many were extinguished.

I could not sleep. The wind still howled outside, reminding me of the fierce winter storms of Yorkshire. I thought of the moors, dusky purple with heather, colourless and drenched with rain under heavy grey clouds or white with snow and swept by blizzards. I longed to see my home again. The visit of Sir Hugo and his sister had revived old memories. The loss of my family was as keen as on the day they departed. I braced myself; I was not inclined to give way to my emotions. *Soon,* I said to myself, *soon now they would return.* I should see my father's strong, craggy face, his eyes, one blind and useless, the other fiercely black—*like an eagle,* I thought, *as I had so often, like some great bird of prey,* though I knew well how that eye could glow with tenderness, beam at me with love and approval. I would feel his great arms close tightly about my shoulders, the warmth of his being radiating through my person.

He was such a vital presence in my memory that it is not surprising I dreamt that night of Thornfield. But not, at first, of him. When I finally slept, I dreamt of the moors, swept bare by the cruel wind, cold and empty save for wolves running before the wind, hunting a great stag. Then the dream changed to Thornfield, and I walked the corridors, noting each familiar piece of furniture, each painting. Somewhere the wind still howled—or was it the wolves? But it seemed to me I could smell the old familiar mixture of the lavender polish the maids always used and my father's tobacco. Surely cigar smoke still curled in the air? I entered the study, looking eagerly about, sure I should find him. But it was Sir Hugo I saw, standing behind my father's desk. I stood before him, silent. "I am the Master of Thornfield now," he said. "No!" I cried. "This is my father's house. He will return." Sir Hugo advanced towards me and suddenly I was frightened. His hands reached out, and I shrank back, but then, at the last moment, I realized that it *was* my father, that it was he I was shrinking from. The room had gone, and I was staring out to sea. Waves crashed against a great sailing ship. I cried out, "Father!" He was there, struggling in the turbulent water. I made haste to stretch down my hand but could not reach him. As I watched, helpless, I realized it was Oliver, not my father. The figure vanished slowly, and I awoke, my heart thudding, tears streaming from my eyes. The rain still lashed the windowpane; the wind wailed outside with the voices of a thousand ghosts.

Across the room Paulina stirred and half sat up. "Janet?" she said, still half asleep. "Go back to sleep, Paulina," I said. "I was dreaming." She sank back beneath her bedclothes, asleep again at once, but I lay awake for hours. Never had I had so vivid a dream. What did it mean? Where was my father? Was he in need of help?

The next day, as we dressed for breakfast, I told Paulina what I had dreamed. "Do you believe in dreams?" I asked her.

"Not as prophecy," she replied. "Perhaps as something one wants—longs for? Dreads? You want so badly to have news of your family, yet you are afraid of what you may hear. You are building pictures for yourself. But they are not necessarily true pictures." I am not demonstrative, but I hugged her as we moved towards the door.

Then two letters arrived at once, though they had been written some months apart. They had been very much delayed. The first was from Oliver, telling something of the land journey, partly by mule and partly, as it turned out, by coach, and then of their embarkation on an American clipper; the second, from my mother, describing the exotic sights and peoples from Singapore. I was at once relieved and yet made more anxious. Where were my parents now?

The winter dragged slowly on. No other letters came from my parents, either to me or Mr. Briggs. He too was beginning to feel concern. He visited me at the Seminary about once a month and did his best to reassure me for, he said, letters went often astray and ships were held up, but travellers returned safely in the end. He was indeed a comfort to me. I knew that my father had trusted him thoroughly and that he took a personal interest in my well-being. His manner was quiet and businesslike, his turn of speech dry and unemotional but not without a touch of humour. He was a man of below medium height, with dark hair now turning grey and receding in front, and with shrewd, hazel eyes. His face was as wrinkled as a nut, as if he had shrunk a little with age and his skin was a size too big.

He came soon after the storm. When he was very much in earnest, he would lean forward and tuck his chin in, and his spectacles would slip down his nose. They did so now as I told him my dream, and he assured me it was the storm, the disturbance of wind and rain, that had so aroused my imagination. He did his best to dispel any morbid fancies I might encourage in the nights when I could not sleep. I now regarded him much as I would a favourite uncle.

And after that, indeed, though I occasionally dreamt of my home, occasionally saw my father walking ahead of me, such dreams were mild and pleasant. No dire phantoms came again to haunt me.

During that long winter, I came to know Miss Temple better. She was compelled to spend long hours resting, though she still kept a hand on the reins. Miss Nasmyth grew more arrogant; it seemed obvious to me that, once Miss Temple retired, the school would lose in reputation if Miss Nasmyth did not choose to be more receptive. But sometimes in the late afternoon, in the quiet time between practice or lectures and dinner, Miss Temple would send for me. She had, it seemed, a great affection for my mother, and she liked to reminisce about those bleak, grim days at Lowood. She told me more than once about my mother's arrival: the small, pale girl named Jane, very upright, with her mouth firmly closed. How tired and lost she had seemed after her long journey and how determined not to show it. And there was little at the school to make her welcome. But over the years, she and Miss Temple had become close friends.

"What I always admired about your mother, my dear," said Miss Temple, "was her courage and her strength of will. She was not well grown, she was none too sturdy; her strength came from inside her. She was so young but already so true to herself. She saw clearly through hypocrisy, however bolstered by authority. If she felt something was right, she would not be changed from her course. She had true delicacy of principle. She was not at all usual; her artistic talents were considerable, and some of the subjects of her drawings were upsetting, almost morbid, not what one expected of a young girl. Her early years were not happy, and her imagination had a dark side to it. A most interesting child and a remarkable young woman. I was very fond of her; she was like a younger sister to me. I was so very glad when her fortune changed, and she married your father."

I found I liked to hear my mother recalled in this way. My own loneliness seemed more bearable in comparison with hers. My parents were now far away, but they had brought me up with care and regard. And I now had good friends. My mother had been so alone. No wonder she always urged the importance of standing on one's own feet. It was interesting, moreover, to compare Miss Temple's account of life at Lowood with the anecdotes I had read in my mother's journal long before.

❖ ❖ ❖

At last it was spring. Almond blossoms coloured the trees in the Square, and daffodils opened eager trumpets to the thin sunlight. I picked one and held it to my nose. The clean, distinct, somewhat herbal fragrance—what one might almost call an intelligent fragrance compared with the blatant, mindless sweetness of, say, violets or the romantic dreamy scent of the rose—carried me back to the spring two years before and the day on which my mother announced her plans for travel. Where were they now? What honey-sweet tropical blooms made dizzy the air they breathed? I carried my daffodil to my bedchamber. The scent clung to my fingers.

My eighteenth birthday arrived. Mrs. Fanshawe, Paulina's mother, gave a party for me. I wore a new dress of shot silk, blue-grey with a hint of red, that gleamed in the lamplight; a cagelike crinoline supported its bell skirt. (I had practiced in my bedroom, with Paulina, sitting and moving in that odd garment, of which my mother would not have approved.) Frederick Fanshawe, waltzing sedately, opined that my dress was the colour of my eyes. Perhaps the blue was reflected there; perhaps his eyes deceived him. He was a conventional young man; he would look for blue eyes in a young girl. I quite liked him, but I found him dull. I had no wish to encourage his attentions.

Pleasant though the party was, all I could think of was that my time in London—in exile—was nearly over. I was eighteen. Under the instructions my father had left with Mr. Briggs, I was now to go to Highcrest Manor, the home of Colonel Dent. I should leave at the end of April. There were dresses to order, and shoes, of London's fashionable cut; in particular, I needed a new riding habit and boots. (London,

Paulina told me, was the only place to buy a riding dress. French women came from Paris for this particular item.) There were books and music to buy while I was still in a great metropolis—and more trunks to hold all these additional items. There were friends to whom I must say good-bye.

❖ ❖ ❖

But first I must engage a companion. This duty had been laid on me in my father's instructions, because Colonel Dent was a widower; Mrs. Dent had died some five years previously, and there was no older woman resident in his house other than his housekeeper, Mrs. Brotherhood. For convention's sake, and for my own comfort, it was considered I should engage a suitable young woman aged about twenty-five, older than myself by some years but not too old to be a pleasant companion. I did not at first know how to go about this task, but Miss Temple placed an advertisement in *The Times*, and, when two or three applicants had written, it was arranged that I should meet them one by one in Miss Temple's study. A day was appointed.

Three women came at the appointed time; two I knew at once I could not live with. The third, a Miss Alleyn, Laura Alleyn, appealed to me on sight. She was twenty-seven, quietly but not unbecomingly dressed. Her hair was the colour of dark honey, her skin fair with pleasantly rosy cheeks, which seemed to indicate an appreciation of the outdoors. She was two or three inches shorter than I, but held herself very straight and looked at me with a directness of gaze that was reassuring. She had a pleasant smile and a quiet voice, with a slight Scottish accent—an elongation of her e's and a curling of her r's—which was refreshing. She had grown up in Carlisle, she told us, had accompanied her parents to London, and the previous year had had the misfortune to lose them both to influenza. Since then, she had been living with an aunt and uncle by marriage. There was something in the way she spoke of her present circumstances and of her uncle in particular that conveyed to me a certain distaste, but she gave no details. Her reticence did not displease me. Her means were small, and she was looking for a post where a good education, some knowledge of music and art, and active habits would serve her. I withdrew with Miss Temple to confer and, since our impressions coincided, returned to the study some ten minutes later to engage her. Her smile when I told her she was thought suitable was a heartfelt one. Holding out her hand to me, she said, simply, "I am so glad, Miss Rochester. I think we shall deal well together." I assured her that it was my thought also. Details of salary and employment were soon arranged, and when she left the house, it was with the intention of returning in a week's time, with her luggage, ready to accompany me to Yorkshire by the railroad. We were to travel from Kings Cross Station, an amazing edifice of yellow brick, said to be built on the site of the old smallpox hospital.

It was a busy week. First in order, I arranged for Nimbus to be taken back to Yorkshire by Albert Higgins, the young man from the Hyde Park Stables, whom I had come to know and trust over the past two years. He would remain in my employ as my personal groom at Colonel Dent's house.

"Fank you, Miss. Oh, fank you," said Albert. He had a wide mouth, and his grin stretched across his face. "I'll not le' you down, Miss. You'll see."

He came, I believe, from a large and poor family, struggling to survive in the London slums. His father drove a cab, but his horse was getting old. I knew it was Albert's ambition to buy a new horse for his father. Albert worked hard at the Stables, mucking out twenty stalls and grooming and feeding the horses with little help. I worried about removing him from London, but he told me his younger brother was to take his job and with it the filial responsibility to his parents. I met young Ernie on my last ride before Nimbus departed. He was somewhat shorter but was otherwise a recognizable member of the Higgins clan, freckled and wide-mouthed, a cheerful soul, missing a front tooth. He whistled tunefully through the gap.

The last of my clothes was delivered. My trunks were packed. I spent a pleasant afternoon with Mrs. Fanshawe and declined my first proposal. Frederick Fanshawe asked for my hand in a diffident, low-keyed manner (of one perhaps with little expectation of an acceptance) that made it easy for me to decline. I was not attracted to him, but I did not dislike him, and I found he had left me with some fortification of self: I no longer thought it impossible that anyone should seek my hand in marriage; a man had declared his love for me. However, my father was still my guiding star, and I saw little chance of finding a man who matched him in my evaluation.

I remained deeply grateful to kind Mrs. Fanshawe for the trouble she had taken with the girls from Miss Temple's school and for her special friendship to me. It is always encouraging to know that one is liked. Under her gentle direction, I had learned to be less gauche, less reticent. I learned to handle my cup and saucer of eggshell china, my silver teaspoon, my napkin, and a plate of fragile cucumber sandwiches and crumbling sponge cake or of brittle meringue with melting cream—it was a juggler's art, but I learned. There were occasional blunders, not necessarily mine; tea was spilt, jam dropped on the carpet, butter marred the front of a dress. We girls learnt to minimize our distress, to conceal our blushes of mortification—all this and make small talk, think of something to say within the rules of polite conversation, yet not only speak of the weather! There were so many subjects forbidden to young women. Yes, I felt I owed Mrs. Fanshawe a debt. And from my heart I envied Paulina her mother, so warm in her feelings for her daughter, so kind, so encouraging. Paulina had a sunny nature; her feelings were open, her judgments (to my young mind) on the whole true. Whatever came her way in life, she knew she would always have her mother's love and trust.

Paulina was to be introduced to Society that year with the intention, though unstated, of finding a husband. She was already attracted to Evelyn Trent, one of the young men who came to the house with Frederick. And there, perhaps, I did doubt her judgment. Her feelings changed her. My modest, reserved friend, intelligent and clear-sighted, sighed and blushed and clasped her hands. I asked her what she knew of him. Little, it seemed. His attraction lay in his well-cut features, his smiling eyes. He was polite, attentive at tea parties. She never saw him under stress or at a disadvantage. Was this enough, I thought, for her to commit her life to a stranger? Young women seemed so vulnerable to me. We knew so little of the world. How could we judge except by instinct? And yet the traditional idea of marriage to a man chosen solely by one's parents was unappealing. *They* would be impressed with respectability; attention would be paid to appearances, possessions, and position. Did they ask into a suitor's temper, mild or hasty? Was he kind? Did they look for humour and imagination, both of which I felt desirable in a lifetime companion?

Paulina lived for Mr. Trent's smiles. Some days she persuaded herself he returned her affection; some days she feared he did not. She was not at all sure that her parents would favour such a marriage for her. He was a friend of Frederick's, but he was not rich. His grandfather was a bishop, his father a parson in a small town in Kent. Poor Paulina.

My relations with Isabella Ingram had been distant since the episode with Beau. We had arranged our inevitable close contact so that we spoke and interacted as little as possible. On the last evening, when Miss Temple said a few words of regret at our parting and gave me a splendid cashmere shawl as a keepsake and Paulina and Daisy filled my arms with flowers, chocolates and comfits, embroidered handkerchiefs, and combs of tortoiseshell, Isabella dropped me a slight curtsey and made one small comment: "I shall return to York-shire myself in six months' time, Miss Rochester. It is likely we shall meet again. Perhaps we may ride in the same hunt or dance at the same hunt ball." Her smile was empty, a mere curve of the lips.

"I shall look forward to it," I returned, with as little honesty as she, and turned to more pleasant company.

The next day, with Miss Alleyn at my side, I rode in a hansom cab to the grandeur of Kings Cross railway station, and we travelled by train to Millcote.

CHAPTER FOUR

Highcrest Manor

I looked up and surveyed the front of the mansion. It was three stories high . . . a gentleman's manor house, not a nobleman's seat.

❦ JANE EYRE ❧

*J*HAD FORGOTTEN HOW long it had been since I visited Highcrest Manor. I was still a child—ten or eleven—shy, unused to strangers, and I had stayed close to my parents, although Oliver had gone down to the stables with Nigel Dent, then a subaltern about to leave for India. Mrs. Dent, a sweet, quiet-voiced lady left delicate by the rigors of life in India, was then still alive. I remember her lying long hours upon a chaise longue, Kashmiri shawls draped over her feet and around her shoulders. I now eyed the grim outlines of the house, which was large, sprawling, built to the taste of previous generations, and gloomy—not unlike, I imagine, the old Thornfield Hall. It was a forbidding pile of grey stone: bleak, unfriendly, with battlements around the roof giving it a medieval touch, three stories high, with two wings angled out to east and west. A stand of tall old trees—oaks, maples, and chestnuts—stood behind it and housed a rookery. The tenants rose cawing to circle over us, wings black and ragged against the declining sun. It made an ominous picture.

While the butler, whose name was Ramsbotham (a traditional Yorkshire name that brought a smile to my lips), directed two footmen to carry our luggage into the house, I entered with some trepidation, expecting heavy oak furniture from a previous century, even rushes on the floor, suits of armour, and a minimum of comfort, but I was very pleasantly surprised. The light was dim, but I could make out a deep, oblong hall that was indeed panelled in dark oak, but the wood glowed with generations of polishing. A great staircase rose to the left, built of matching oak, and curved up to a gallery over our heads. The floor was flagged with stone but was richly carpeted with a Turkish design of deep reds, black, and gold, as was the staircase. Although it was June, a fire burned in the stone fireplace in the hall and gave needed warmth and light, even a possibly deceptive appearance of cheerfulness, to the chill entrance. An animal, sprawled before the fire, stirred as we entered and rose. He stood tall and square on four long legs, his head low, his ears back, and his hackles raised; I heard a growl gather in his throat. "Pilot?" I said. I saw a quiver run over his chest and legs, and in two great bounds he had reached me to stand on his hind legs, as tall as I, to lick my face with his tongue. It was two years since I said good-bye to Pilot, my father's great dog. "Oh, Pilot," I said, and I hugged his great body. I had the odd and comical thought that here was my family back, my home. I turned to Laura and made a formal introduction of the dog. She laughed and offered him her hand, and he accepted her.

I continued to examine my surroundings. The walls were thick, and I imagined the temperature inside the house would change little with the seasons. "A man's home is his castle," I thought to myself as Colonel Dent came to welcome us. I could well imagine him in armour or carrying a sword.

He was a tall man, thin almost to gauntness, with a strong hooked nose and bushy eyebrows, still dark, in a narrow, bony face. His thick head of hair was white. My chief memory of Colonel Dent, in fact, was of his hair. His hair turned white quite young, but what had once made a pleasant contrast to his dark eyes and ruddy complexion now, a decade later, with the coming of old age and the loss of his once high colour, added to the severity of his appearance. He wore riding clothes of old-fashioned cut and beautiful boots of black leather. He was a few years older than my father, which placed him somewhere in the late sixties, but he looked still older, like illustrations I had seen of Father Time. I had heard that the death of his wife five years before and later, the sudden deaths of his son, Nigel, and his young daughter-in-law in a cholera epidemic in Bombay, had greatly changed him. I now believed it.

A woman stood with composure in the background as Colonel Dent made us welcome. I introduced him to Laura Alleyn, and he, in his turn, beckoned the woman forward. "My housekeeper, Mrs. Brotherhood," he said. "You must look to Mrs. Brotherhood for all you need for your comfort. She will be happy to do everything in her power to assist you."

Mrs. Brotherhood was short and full-bodied, and her hair was black streaked with grey. She had a rosy, countrywoman's complexion, but her dark eyes, it seemed to me, were watchful, and her mouth was firmly compressed. However, she spoke to us pleasantly enough and shortly led us upstairs. Her black satin dress rustled as she walked, hinting at taffeta petticoats beneath. Her keys jingled at her waist. Our way took us down stone walled passages. There was carpet beneath our feet, centred on the stone flags, and tapestry hangings on the walls, but the air struck chill and drafty. Our rooms were in the West Wing. The East Wing, she told us, was never used and was, indeed, kept locked. There was some evidence of dry rot in the floor beams, and it was not considered safe. Laura and I had adjoining rooms, large and well furnished. I was pleasantly surprised to find the floors carpeted and the windows curtained with flowered chintz. The Colonel had married an heiress, I remembered. He had had property; she had brought money. Whatever the background, it was a pleasant place. Laura and I smiled with pleasure. Beyond our bedrooms, at the end of the passage, was our sitting room, with windows on two sides overlooking the park. Looking out, I noticed that the grounds of the Manor were well set out with lawns and hedges, trees and shrubs, but I noticed no flower gardens. There was little colour to be seen at that most flourishing month of the year.

The furniture in our sitting room was of recent design and beautifully kept, the carpet and curtains nearing the luxurious. I saw with pleasure that a grand piano stood in one corner of the room. And there were empty shelves and brackets prepared, it seemed, to receive our books and ornaments.

We dined with the Colonel in a large and gloomy dining room. The walls were papered with a deep red Chinese paper decorated with figures only dimly to be seen. The pictures on those bloodred walls were of that somewhat macabre school that considers dead animals appropriate for the titillation of diners. Deer and hares, pheasants and quail, their dead eyes glazed, blood on occasion beading their noses or beaks, were tumbled on tables or hung from hooks on walls, together with strings of onions, bunches of herbs, quantities of fruit bringing some variety of colour—lemons and rosy apples and bunches of purple grapes—and flagons of wine painted to glow in the light of the lamps. The room was carpeted with a Scottish tartan design of the kind made popular by the Queen at Balmoral. The food was good but somewhat heavy after our purely feminine fare at school. Mulligatawny soup was removed with a round of beef, served with a large Yorkshire pudding and rich brown gravy. The dessert was a plum pudding. I was tired yet somewhat feverish with travel and change. I ate little but was grateful for my glass of red wine. Laura made gentle conversation with the Colonel. He looked at her, I thought, with approval for her low voice and smooth hair. When he looked at me, his eyes narrowed. He seemed in some way puzzled by me. I could not think why this should be.

When dessert was placed on the table, he cleared his throat as if he had an announcement to make. We waited, but for a moment he said nothing. Then, hurriedly, he said, "We are a small company for such a room as this. I remember when we were a goodly number … but those days are gone. However, there is one resident of Highcrest Manor who is at present away from us on business. My secretary, Roderick Landless, will join us within a week or so. He is nearer in age to you than I and is, though somewhat reserved, in general, a good conversationalist. I think you will get on well together. I look forward to his return."

This announcement reminded me of someone else I looked for. "Colonel Dent," I said. "Mrs. Brotherhood introduced us to the maid you have engaged for us, Milly Allnut."

"Ah, yes," he said. "She is the daughter of my gamekeeper, Joseph Allnut. A worthy family and a good girl."

"I had hoped," I continued, "to find my own maid, Annie Parrott, here at the Manor. I understood from Mr. Briggs that he had been in touch with her mother, the housekeeper at Thornfield, and that Annie was willing to come."

"I am sure you will find Milly an obliging, hardworking young woman," the Colonel said gruffly.

"Indeed, yes. But if there is no particular reason Annie should not come to me, I should very much like to have her here. It was arranged that she should do so. Is there some problem?"

"No, no," said the Colonel. "Speak to Mrs. Brotherhood. It is she who manages such things."

I did not think he looked pleased, but I saw no reason my old playmate and maid should not join me at the Manor and, I thought, though I should speak to Mrs. Brotherhood as he suggested, if I had no word from Annie, I would ride over to Thornfield at an early opportunity. In London it had seemed to me that I should not wish to visit Thornfield while it was in the hands of strangers, but now that I was once more in Yorkshire, my feelings had changed, and I longed to see my old home once more. I had also to admit that I was curious to meet Sir Hugo Calendar and his sister again.

Laura and I soon adjourned to our own quarters, leaving the Colonel to his port and cigar. Pilot rose when we did and accompanied us. The Colonel called to him as he walked with us to the door. The great dog stopped and looked back at the solitary figure still seated at the dining table, then he followed us through the door. Old loyalties proved stronger than new.

Our trunks had been brought upstairs and were unstrapped. Our valises were already unpacked. We had much pleasure in unpacking and arranging our books and personal belongings. Our sitting room, the chintz curtains rosy in the lamp light, began to belong to us. Pilot lay before our fire.

"Laura," I said, looking at her across the room. "Do you think you can be happy here?" I had already come to like and trust her; I hoped she liked me.

"Oh, yes, Janet. My uncle's house is receding. I feel calmer and more comfortable than I have felt since my parents died. We will make a good life for ourselves here, I am sure."

"I should not wish to pry, Laura, but was there something about your uncle's house that you particularly did not like?"

Laura pursed her lips. She stared at her hands. Then she raised her head to look at me. "My uncle was most kind in offering me his protection, but I must confess there was much about him that I could not like. The sisters had not met for many years, and my mother was quite astonished at the change in her young sister since her marriage. I barely remembered her. My aunt had been, it seemed, a lively active young woman, very musical and with a fine singing voice. Now she seemed sad and depressed. She had three young children with whom she spent much time during the day. They were quite charming, and I enjoyed helping her play with them, teach them. But by late afternoon, when my uncle was expected home, they were left strictly to their nurse. He did not like her to spend time with them when he was there, and he saw them himself solely to question their conduct, small though they were, and to correct their faults. My aunt had long ago given up her music. She seldom spoke unless my uncle asked her a direct question. When I came to live with them, I soon decided she was afraid of him. He was a cold man, authoritarian, very masterful in his dealings with the servants—and it was he who made all household decisions. No one ever questioned his pronouncements.

"That did not make for a happy house. But soon, to my dismay, his attitude to me changed considerably. He seemed to wish to charm me, bought me small gifts, asked me to sit with him and read to him in the evenings. Where once he had insisted on his wife's presence, he now sent her to the nursery to attend to the children while he stayed with me. He even suggested that he tutor me in certain literary readings he thought would improve my mind. He would say that I looked pale—and he would take my wrist to count my pulse or lay his hand across my forehead. I did not like his touch. I began to try to avoid him, but then, one day, he began to scold my aunt in my presence, accusing her of trying to turn me against him. He reduced her to tears, and I could not conceal my indignation. I withdrew from the readings. Then there came a time when, late at night, he would come to my bedchamber and knock at the door, a gentle persistent knock, knock, knock … He would call my name. I never answered, just covered my head with my blankets and tried to sleep. Fortunately, there was a key to my door. I kept it locked at night and carried the key with me in the daytime. It was just about then that I saw your advertisement. I came to see you with such desperation in my heart, hoping you would find me suitable as your companion. My uncle was angry at my decision, but I am twenty-seven; he has no authority over me. It was just a matter of resolution. He was not my guardian. He tried to impress on me that women are not fit to stand alone, that every woman should be guided by an older man, that I needed his protection, but I was adamant in my decision. I was sorry to abandon my aunt, and I loved the children, but I was oh so glad to leave his house behind me."

I looked at her. Her face was gentle in outline, delicate in colouring, but her mouth was firmly set, her eyes at that moment clear and determined. Her back was very straight, and her shoulders squared. Her situation seemed to me appalling, and I admired her very much for her courage in breaking away. I sought for a change in subject.

"I wonder about this young man, Mr. Landless. I hope he will be an agreeable addition to our party." There had been something in the Colonel's manner as he spoke of his secretary that intrigued me. I was not particularly given to romantic fantasies, but I wondered at that moment, as I watched Laura, with her smooth hair and sweet face, arranging her books by subject on the shelves, if he might be someone she could love. It was a sad necessity for young women that they should find a husband if they were to have any kind of life, and for someone like Laura—no longer a girl, educated and refined but lacking any dowry—it would not be easy. As for me, with the ideal picture of my father ever before me, I doubted I should ever marry.

The very first morning, I found my way to the stables. Albert Higgins was there with my mare, both of them in fine fettle. The ride had been without problem, he reported. "Right innerestin', Miss," he said with a reminiscent twinkle in his eye. "Learned a lot, I did." He seemed content with his quarters and was getting on well enough with the head groom, though, he reported, he had some difficulty in understanding him. "An odd way of talkin' they 'as 'ere," he said. "Furrin like. But I copes." I was surprised to find several horses in residence, both carriage horses (a matched pair) and good mounts for riding. One would be the Colonel's, perhaps two if he still hunted, but four? Albert was helping to exercise them, he said with obvious relish. I had him saddle Nimbus right away, and I rode off, with Pilot at my heels, uphill to the moors. A wonderful feeling of freedom settled over me. The confinements of school, of London life, were gone. This was no tame ride in a park; I was in my own stamping ground once more. The moors stretched around me, broken only by outcrops of flinty rock. The heather was not yet in bloom, but grouse scuttered away from under the horse's hoofs, curlews wailed as they took to their wings, and overhead a skylark sang joyously, as free as I. I stopped on a rise and stretched my arms to the heavens. It was a day part cloudy, part bright, but as I held up my face, the sun broke free and caressed my brow. To be here, to be back where I belonged, was "very heaven."

After that, I visited the stables every day. I saw Milly Allnut on more than one occasion sitting on a mounting block or dodging around a stable door and guessed Albert was the attraction. He was a personable young man with his ready, wide-mouthed grin; his face was freckled, his brown hair curled, and his nose was snub. He probably seemed exotic to the local girls, with his Cockney accent and his city experience.

Our life began to take shape. I dreamt less in Yorkshire. I enjoyed waking up and realizing I was no longer at school in London, but back in my own northern county, with the breeze, cool and invigorating, coming off the moors and in at my window. It was sweet, but the bitter came quickly as my mind admitted the nagging worry about my missing father—oh, and mother and brother. There was, however, nothing I could do but wait.

Our mornings were quiet. Laura and I walked the grounds with Pilot, finding no formal gardens but many beautiful trees. Much of the land near the house was surrounded by walls of the local flint stone, with locked wooden doors. We wondered why this was necessary but respected the Colonel's privacy; there would be time enough when we knew him better to question him. Afternoons I often spent in riding. If I did not venture out, our time was spent at needlework or music or reading in our sitting room. My piano playing was far superior to Laura's, but she had a pretty singing voice, and I had pleasure in accompanying her in songs of her choosing. Laura liked needlework better than

I, in particular, tapestry work. She was engaged in a cover for a footstool.

As she sewed, I would often read aloud to her. I soon discovered the Colonel's library, a handsome room with dark oak panelling and a splendid tiger skin flung across the dark red Turkish carpet. This was quite different from his study, a small crowded room where he spent a good part of his time. The study walls were decorated with guns and spears, daggers in embroidered sheaths and belts of beaten silver, not books, and there were many strange Indian carvings set on small inlaid tables, including some that looked like idols. An elephant's ivory tusk, capped with chased silver, swung from a silken cord above the fireplace. However warm the day, a fire always burned there. What the Colonel did with his time, I did not know. I had the impression he brooded, staring at the portraits of earlier Dents in their dress uniforms and snow-white topees or at the many amateur paintings of ruined temples and bazaars, women in saris, and dark-skinned men in turbans, perhaps painted by Mrs. Dent. But whether he saw them or withdrew into the past, I could not tell.

Colonel Dent seldom came into the library, although a writing table set with an inkwell and a blotting pad, on which some books were neatly piled, and a mahogany rolltop escritoire and matching bookcase indicated someone worked there, presumably the absent secretary, Mr. Landless. The escritoire was locked. (I must admit I indulged my curiosity, perhaps rudely, and received a merited check by this fact.) I browsed along the shelves and found that, as well as bound sets of the classics, looking stiff and as if seldom opened, there were works of travel and exploration, books on archaeology, palaeontology, ornithology, and the like, as well as many books on India. There were sets of novels—Scott, Trollope, Fielding, several by Dickens, collections of the essays of Addison and Steele, some poetry, and bound copies of *The Ladies Magazine*, belonging presumably to Mrs. Dent, as had the fat, dusty volumes of novels by Mrs. Gaskell and George Eliot. Here were riches. Three shabby volumes, obviously much handled, revealed a charming book, *Pride and Prejudice*, written by "A Lady." Laura and I read alternate chapters to each other and found considerable quiet amusement therein. In one corner, however, not far from the writing table, there was quite a different selection on gardens and horticulture filling several shelves. Beginning in the late eighteenth century, the books added up to a comprehensive history of landscape gardening and of the propagation and cultivation of the hundreds of new plants and bushes that had been brought to England by our intrepid explorers in Asia and the New World. Some I recognized from my father's library; as I have mentioned, landscape gardening was one of his enthusiasms. He could indulge this interest in the grounds of Thornfield unhindered by his poor sight. He had made sure I understood this was indeed the century of gardening. All these books were well-worn, marked with slips of paper, and with pencilled notations in the margins. But as I have said, there was little to be seen in the park of modern design. The

Colonel's grounds were of an earlier style, when nature was in command, and the ideal was to hide all traces of man's interference. Gardening did not seem to be one of the Colonel's interests. Whose were these books, then? And if this was a practical interest, where were the gardens being worked on? These strongly individual shelves seemed private. I did not like to disturb them. But the novels and books on travel and exploration I devoured with pleasure.

Laura was not an experienced rider and was a little nervous, but she enjoyed the exercise, and we found a gentle mare in the Colonel's stables to suit her. She took to the sport with enthusiasm and soon began to improve. However, in the afternoons, I rode by myself on Nimbus, exploring the neighbourhood. Pilot came with me, but I took no groom. I did not forget my plan to ride to Thornfield, and so it was, when a week had passed and I had had no news of Annie from Mrs. Brotherhood, whose manner was repressive, I decided to pay a visit to Sir Hugo and his sister.

The day was bright with a scattering of clouds. There was a brisk wind. Albert feared it promised rain, but I felt the fine weather would hold long enough for my purpose. Thornfield was just seven miles away across country. "It will not take me more than an hour!" I said to Albert. Pilot barked at my heels, but I thought it best to leave him and called to Albert to hold his collar. I did not know what dogs now lived at Thornfield. Pilot would feel possessive, and a dog fight would not make for a pleasant introduction. Nimbus was eager for exercise, and we set off from the estate at a brisk trot. As we left the driveway for the road across the moors, a kestrel rose from the branch of a spruce overhanging our path. I saw its rounded head, its fierce curved beak, and glimpsed briefly its keen, wild eye. It flew out of sight over the park.

We made our way along the lanes winding across the moors, sometimes little more than tracks and sometimes running deep between stone walls expertly crafted, one flint fitted in above another without mortar, stacked so carefully that the walls could stand the fiercest blast of winter wind. Down the centre of the lanes ran worn white stones, a guide on a moonless night. It was three miles to Hay. I skirted the little town, which I had not yet visited; I had no wish to draw attention to myself and face questions about my family. Then I trotted on between hedgerows of hawthorn and hazel. The scent of the hawthorn blossom was piercingly sweet. It had made my mother sneeze uncontrollably, I remembered. Molly Parrott had been superstitious about it. She called it *may*, as the local people did. She claimed it was unlucky to pick it, and she would not have the flowers in the house. A heron passed overhead as we joined the lane, which ran downhill all the way from Hay. I heard the sound of its heavy wings, beating, beating as it flew, its feet trailing behind. As a child, I thought them magical birds. I learned to recognize those throbbing wing-beats, even when the bird was not in sight. Fields of half-grown corn and oats extended on either side, far and wide. The clouds were gathering fast, and I began to admit some fear of rain.

At the first sight of my beloved home, I reined Nimbus in. A jumble of emotions set my heart beating fast, and my cheeks felt flushed. Almost I turned back. Could I bear to see strangers there, in possession of my father's house? But I had come a long way, and I was anxious to enquire for Annie. I pushed myself to continue. We entered the driveway and trotted towards the house and, as we did so, the rain began to fall.

CHAPTER FIVE

Return to Thornfield

From behind one pillar I could peep around quietly at the full front of the mansion.

◄ JANE EYRE ►

I STOPPED IN FRONT of the main entrance and dismounted. It seemed odd—disturbing—to me to pull, as if I were a visitor, the great iron handle that rang the bell in the hall. But it was raining quite hard, and I was glad to gain shelter. As the door swung open, a groom came from the stables. His was a familiar face. "Micah," I said, and he grinned at me and touched his forelock before he led Nimbus away, giving her a welcoming pat on the neck as he did so. She whickered and bent her head to touch his shoulder.

When I turned back, Barley, our long time butler, stood at the open door. Warmth and light spilled out onto the marble steps from the house behind.

"Miss Janet!" he said, in tones of some amazement.

"I am glad to see you, Barley," I said. "I have come to see Sir Hugo. Will you please tell him I am here?"

I stood in the hall, looking around me at the familiar sights: the rich, red Turkish carpet on the squares of black and white marble, the great curving staircase of polished oak leading up to the gallery, the oil paintings of country scenes (two were by John Constable) on the panelled walls. Everything was immaculate. My home was being well taken care of. As I stood there, I felt as if I had stepped back in time. Even the smell was familiar: the wood smoke from the fire in the hearth and the lavender-scented polish that was of Molly Parrott's own making. I remembered my dream and felt for a moment dizzy, as if I were out of step with time. I bit my lip. My eyes smarted—but it was the smoke, the smoke. I would not show weakness before Sir Hugo Calendar by greeting him with tear-filled eyes.

But it was not Sir Hugo who entered the hall with Barley close behind. Mrs. Deveraux, cold, upright, elegant in an afternoon gown of primrose silk ornamented with black velvet bands, appeared before me. Her hair, swept high on her head in elaborate braids and curls, echoed the colour primrose. She seemed to take in every detail at once—my wind-whipped hair beneath my hat, my flushed face, the rain-drop sliding down my nose, the sheen of moisture on my habit and gloves. I felt like an awkward schoolgirl again. But I was as tall as she and my parents' daughter still, with my father's pride and my mother's blunt and candid tongue (she who was overawed by no one).

"How do you do, Mrs. Deveraux," I said and held out my hand. "I hope you will forgive my unexpected appearance. I have come for some news of my maid, Annie Parrott, whom I was expecting to find at Highcrest Manor on my arrival."

"Miss Rochester." She bowed her head in greeting and touched my damp glove briefly. Belatedly, I stripped off my gloves. Her eyes were still on my habit and hat. "You are intrepid indeed to ride so far on a day such as this. It is my brother's custom to refer to you as the Amazon—how right he is!" She gave a small, chill laugh. There was no humour in it. "Please come into the drawing room and warm yourself. Barley, bring some Madeira."

I took off my hat and handed it with my gloves to the maid who had now appeared. I smoothed my hair as best I could; wisps were curling around my forehead and cheeks. My waves turned to curls in damp weather.

Once seated, I returned at once to my reason for such an unconventional visit. It was obvious that Mrs. Deveraux considered it a considerable breach of etiquette. Her face showed a scornful amusement at such uncouth behaviour. But I was not prepared to be snubbed in my own home, and I repeated my statement.

"I realize you must find my sudden arrival somewhat startling, but I am anxious, as I said, Mrs. Deveraux, for news of my maid. Is there some reason why she has not joined me at Highcrest Manor? Is she perhaps indisposed?"

She looked at me in silence for a moment. "It was my understanding from Colonel Dent that he had satisfied your requirement with a young woman of his own household. Is this not so?"

"Colonel Dent has indeed offered me the use of a young woman who is the daughter of his gamekeeper. But, as I am sure you were informed by Mr. Briggs, it was always my wish to have my former maid join me once I returned to Yorkshire. It is still my wish. Is this a difficulty?"

"Annie is an excellent seamstress. I have found her most useful in the upkeep of my own wardrobe and as an assistant to my own maid, Marie-Jeanne, who is, of course, French."

There was a settled complacence in her manner that indicated she was unused to any dispute of her own requirements. She was a lady of fashion, strong willed, and quite sure of her own superiority. She must have seen me as little more than a gauche schoolgirl, windblown and weather marked, unused to the ways of society. Her manner made clear that she expected nothing from me but compliance. My back stiffened. My eyes met hers.

"I am sorry to cause you any inconvenience, Mrs. Deveraux, but this arrangement is of long-standing. I must insist that it is honoured. I wish Annie to join me at Highcrest Manor as soon as possible."

"And if I say it is *not* possible?"

I was puzzled in the extreme at what could be her motive for denying me Annie's assistance. Barley entered the drawing room at that moment, accompanied by a maid bearing a tray with a crystal decanter of Madeira and a plate of macaroons. He set them down on a nearby table. I spoke to him directly.

"Barley, will you please ask Annie Parrott to come to the drawing room?"

"Miss Rochester!" said Mrs. Deveraux. "I think you are forgetting our circumstances. It is I who give the orders in this house. It is you who are the visitor." She turned to Barley. "You will disregard Miss Rochester's request."

I nodded to Barley, who left the room. I knew he would do as I wished.

It was perhaps a useful diversion that we were at that moment joined by Sir Hugo. He looked from one to the other of us, Mrs. Deveraux flushed with annoyance, I flushed with determination. He smiled broadly. He was not a man to be overawed by conventionalities, I thought. In fact, it seemed he might extract a certain sardonic enjoyment from such a situation as he found.

"Miss Rochester, I was delighted when I was told you had paid us a visit, and I am sorry that I was not able to join you sooner. But I know my sister has made you welcome, if that is not an impertinence in your own home. I am only anxious to know how we may serve you?"

"Miss Rochester has ridden here *alone* from Highcrest Manor and is demanding her maid," said Mrs. Deveraux. "I find the situation quite extraordinary."

"But from our first meeting I have always known that Miss Rochester was extraordinary. And an equestrian of the first rate. I often think of your intrepid ride in Hyde Park." His voice was mellow and calm, but the look he gave his sister was quite at odds with his words. "Is there some reason why Miss Rochester's maid is unavailable?"

"I find her of considerable use," said his sister. "And I was assured by Colonel Dent that a satisfactory substitute had been found at Highcrest Manor. He distinctly informed me that there was no need for Annie Parrott to leave Thornfield."

"I regret there has been any confusion," I said. "But in this matter it is my decision that must take precedence. Colonel Dent was not authorized to change my directions."

"Not authorized! Miss Rochester, you talk in a manner hardly suited to your age and position."

"My age is irrelevant," I responded. "My position is that of deputy to my father and owner in default of Thornfield Hall. His servants are very much my responsibility. This arrangement was made at the time of the lease, and there has been no change in the terms of that lease."

"Surely there is no need for any such legal-sounding complications!" exclaimed Sir Hugo. "My dear Alicia, there can be no great problem caused by the removal of one country-trained maid among so many. We were aware of Miss Rochester's stipulation in regard to her maid, and we will, of course, make sure it is fulfilled. Come, Miss Rochester, let me offer you some Madeira."

His smile was full of charm, his voice determined. Abruptly, Mrs. Deveraux altered her stance. She gave a little laugh, looking straight into his eyes. She put one white and slender hand on his sleeve. "Oh, if you put it like that, Hugo, of course it is of no great matter. Miss Rochester, I am sorry to have discomfited you in any way." She smiled at me with her mouth; her eyes were winter cold. She was once again the calm, elegant woman of our first meeting, yet only a few moments before she had been passionate and wilful, displaying a strong antagonism to me—as a woman might behave to a rival. (But this was ridiculous. Who could regard me in such a light?) She definitely viewed me as an intruder.

And then Barley returned to the room with Annie at his heels. She looked just as I remembered her: rosy-cheeked, merry-eyed, a little plumper perhaps, but trim in her mauve-striped cotton uniform, with lace embellishing her cap and apron.

I smiled at her but did not speak. Sir Hugo spoke to her directly. "Annie, Miss Rochester has come to remind us of her need for you now that she has returned to Yorkshire. With your consent, my dear," and he bowed to his sister, "you will leave for Highcrest Manor in the morning."

"There are one or two tasks Annie must complete before she leaves," broke in Mrs. Deveraux. "Perhaps Wednesday morning will suit?" She looked at me. It was a matter of power, I thought. She must show mastery.

"Certainly," I said. "When you have finished anything you are at present engaged in, Annie, pack your box and come to Highcrest. I shall look forward to welcoming you there on *Wednesday*." I let my voice emphasize the day; I could imagine Mrs. Deveraux continually finding some other incomplete task to delay Annie, and I was not prepared to accept this.

Annie smiled at me with her eyes; her mouth stayed prim. "Yes, Miss Janet. Certainly, Mam." She dropped me a curtsey and then curtsied to Mrs. Deveraux, a slightly briefer bob, and left the room.

"And now," said Sir Hugo. "You must tell me about your ride here. Is your groom in the stables?"

"I came alone," I said, and felt warmth rise in my cheeks once more; my behaviour seemed more remiss seen through his eyes than it had through his sister's. He raised his eyebrows but continued to talk, asking me questions about my reaction to my return to Yorkshire and to Highcrest Manor. "You will, of course, take dinner with us this evening?" He glanced at the window. Raindrops streamed down the windowpanes, but the day had lightened and I could see, above the trees, that the clouds were breaking up.

An exploratory ray of sunshine suddenly turned the summer leaves a brighter green.

All I wanted was to leave as soon as possible, but he would take no denial. When the dressing gong sounded, Mrs. Deveraux led me upstairs. She was occupying my old bedroom, I found, with a resentment I quickly hid. She installed me in a guest room, and her French maid, dark-haired and sharp-faced, was directed to find me a suitable gown. "I should wish to loan you something in white," she said. "But I fear I have nothing so naïve."

I was attired in lilac silk when I made my way back to the drawing room, my hair expertly rewound. Marie-Jeanne had at first offered me a dress of pale aqua, which I found most attractive; but Mrs. Deveraux waved it away and pointed to the lilac, not a favourite colour of mine. Marie-Jeanne, as I would have expected, was a practiced hairdresser and obviously a lady's maid *par excellence*. I wondered again what possible use Mrs. Deveraux had for Annie with such an experienced maid at her service. Marie-Jeanne having come to me only when her mistress's toilet was completed, Mrs. Deveraux had already returned to the drawing room when I myself was ready. I came quietly down the stairs and approached the partly open door. Through the door I could see the great mirror above the mantelpiece, with its heavy frame finished in gold leaf, gleaming in the candlelight. In the mirror were reflected two persons: Sir Hugo, in elegant evening dress, and Mrs. Deveraux, arrayed in a rich wine-red satin with rubies at her throat and ears. They were standing close together, face-to-face. Her white-gloved hands, her wrists encased with twin gold and ruby bracelets, were holding his lapels, and she was gazing up into his eyes. She stood on tiptoe to brush his cheek with her lips. I could not see her expression, but his face was directly in my view. His cheeks were flushed, his clear eyes aglow, and his lips were parted. There was excitement in his aspect but also some irritation. As I watched, he tried to step away, but she held him. And then *he* kissed *her*—she plainly offered him her lips, but he inclined his neck and kissed, in his turn, her cheek. I backed away from the door to the foot of the staircase. The intimacy of the scene shocked me. I found myself breathing quickly and blushing yet again. Then Barley came through the green baize door from the servants' hall, carrying a tray and a decanter. I let him pass ahead of me, then followed him into the drawing room.

For the first time, I was glad to be wearing lilac. It was not my colour; it stole warmth from my hair and complexion and made me look pale. In these circumstances, I knew it would reduce the effect of my blush, and I was relieved. I did not understand what I had seen, but I knew it should have been preferable that I had *not* seen it.

Once seated at the dining room table, I raised my eyes to Mrs. Deveraux's face. Her face had little expression, but I could not believe her happy. For the first time, I found fault with her own dress. Her fair hair, which had echoed her primrose afternoon dress to perfection, was too light for the dark red of her evening gown. The colour—or her mood—

aged her. I had thought her ten years older than myself, in her late twenties perhaps, but now I wondered. In that dress, in the light from the candelabra, she might have been ten years older again.

The meal was substantial, rich with sauces, well cooked and well served. It seemed likely Sir Hugo had imported his own cook; I did not think that this was Mrs. Barley's cooking. Sir Hugo led the conversation, asking me about my family and, in particular, my father's background. It seemed to me he was anxious to learn my father's worth. This was not something I wished to discuss, and I changed the subject as soon as I could, talking of India, where I knew Mrs. Deveraux had resided, and Colonel Dent's travel books. I gave silent thanks to Mrs. Fanshawe and Mrs. Trevelyn, the mothers of my friends, for their careful exposure of their daughters' friends to society and to the making of polite conversation. Mrs. Deveraux said little; she kept her eyes on her plate. When she raised them, she looked at Sir Hugo.

When dinner was over and we had once again withdrawn, I brought up the subject of my departure. It was not yet dark, though the sky was partially overcast; I knew the ride back to the Manor would take me over an hour; I needed to start on my way.

Sir Hugo had objections. He suggested I stay the night at the Hall and send a groom to the Manor with a note explaining my absence. I anticipated that Colonel Dent would already be displeased at my unexplained absence, and I had no wish to stay at Thornfield. I was not comfortable in the company of these two sophisticates. Mrs. Deveraux stayed silent during Sir Hugo's invitation. I knew she wished me gone. It seemed likely I should once more encounter rain, but I would not give in. I insisted I must leave, and I changed once more into my habit (now dried and brushed by Marie-Jeanne). My horse was brought from the stables, and by eight o'clock I was once more in the saddle and on my way, accompanied, at Sir Hugo's insistence, by Rufus, one of my father's grooms, a gruff man in his fifties, whom I knew well. Mrs. Deveraux had given a *moue* of disapproval at my suggestion I ride alone.

The road was sticky underfoot. I set off at a steady pace, disregarding the drips that descended from the trees as we passed underneath, glad of the white stones defining the path. There were glimpses of a pale summer moon, not yet full, peering out from behind the dark nimbus clouds that straggled across the sky. Moths and small flying insects were everywhere. A bat flickered ahead of me and was swiftly gone. The air was full of the scent of wet earth and grass and flowering hedgerows. A hedgehog scrabbled across my path. An owl hooted once, twice. I saw its ghostly shape flying beyond the hedge. All at once I was happy. I was tired both mentally and physically from exercise and from what had felt like a long-running sword fight with two skilled opponents. But I had gained my point. Annie would join me in two days. And if she did not, I was quite prepared to follow up my visit to Thornfield with another. But I was sure she would. Whatever Mrs. Deveraux's feelings and motives, Sir Hugo would

ensure she did as he wished. I wondered about the relationship between them. She seemed at once to defer to him, yet
to make demands of him. (A thought crossed my mind out of
nowhere. Was she indeed his sister? Could a closer, less
conventional relationship be theirs? But I had not yet enough
exposure to the world willingly to explore such thoughts)
But I soon ceased to think of them. Nimbus trotted on
through the fields, skirting the moor, sure-footed in the
meagre moonlight. Rufus, on a sturdy cob, stayed close
behind me.

Once past Hay, it began to rain again—a gentle,
persistent rain, not unpleasant. It was a warm night, and a
mist was rising from the ground as we reached the narrow
lanes with their dense hedgerows below Highcrest and
wound our way uphill. I was glad to be so near to home (as I
must now consider Highcrest), and I touched Nimbus with
my whip. She sprang forward as we rounded a corner in the
lane leading to the drive, but the next moment I reined her in
abruptly as a figure loomed up out of the mist in the centre
of the roadway directly ahead. She shied in alarm, whirling
skittishly in a circle, in and out of the hedgerow and then
across the lane, ending under an overhanging tree. A twig
whipped my cheek and stole my hat. I struggled to retain my
balance as she danced. I spoke sharply to her, pulled at the
reins, and brought her once more under control, out from
under the tree, and thence to a halt on the path. I was
breathing hard. I was quite shaken.

I heard the rattle of the cob's hoofs on the stones and Rufus's anxious call: "Miss Janet!" But my eyes were on the man on his knees in the centre of the lane.

"Are you hurt?" I cried urgently. He rose to his feet and stood, swaying a little, before me. I saw dimly the shape of a man at least a head taller than myself, with a dark visage and stern features. Heavy brows drew across a high forehead, and brilliant dark eyes looked into mine. The face was one etched in my memory.

"Father?" I said, bewildered.

I drew my hand across my eyes.

CHAPTER SIX

The Kestrel Flies

I discerned in the course of the morning that Thornfield Hall was a changed place.

❧ JANE EYRE ❧

*I*T WAS NOT, OF course, my father.

"Are you hurt?" I repeated.

"No, no. But you? How did you fare?"

The voice was deep and anxious, like—yet unlike—that well-loved voice of my father's, a gentleman's cultivated voice; this was no Yorkshire farmer. The stranger stared at me as if I were from another world, and I stared back as bewildered as he.

"Miss Janet? Art thee safe an' zound?" came Rufus's gruff voice from behind the stranger.

I dismounted, rubbing my face, which smarted from my encounter with the tree (my cheek would be marked, I feared), and brushed some wet leaves from my habit. I looked for my hat. I could not find it.

"I am quite well," I said, my face turned from the stranger. "But you, Sir? Were you struck by my horse? I must apologize. I did not see you there in the centre of the track in time to avoid you." Despite my apology, I could not help a certain indignation colouring my voice. Surely he must have heard the sound of hoofs approaching in time to avoid the encounter? Certain pungent phrases of Albert's, not suited for polite conversation, crossed my mind.

"It is for me to apologize, Madam. I am unhurt. I was deep in thought, conferring with the moon. A foolish habit, the more to be regretted if it has caused you harm." He looked down at his hands, marred with dirt and dead leaves. He rubbed them together and then bent forward and brushed at the knees of his trousers. He reached for something on the ground by the hedge. "But it has not. So let us say no more."

Rufus was now holding Nimbus's reins. It seemed to me her large, liquid eyes met mine with a rueful regard. Rufus moved to assist me to remount, but the stranger was ahead of him. He proffered my hat, recovered from the hawthorn hedgerow, and then his hand for my foot as an aid to mounting. My boot was muddy, I noticed with some dismay, and it soiled his hand anew. I felt his strength, the steady pressure upward as I was lifted into the saddle. I adjusted my hat; the feather was quite ruined with mud and rain. I prepared to ride on, but something kept me where I was. Once more I viewed the stranger.

"You are on foot? May I know your business here, sir? Are you staying nearby?" This was no servant. I longed to ask his name.

"I come from Highcrest," said the stranger. "As, I suppose, do you."

"From Highcrest! Are you visiting Colonel Dent?"

"I am his secretary. Good night, Miss Rochester." And he slapped Nimbus's rump, and she broke into a trot.

❖ ❖ ❖

Colonel Dent was indeed angry. He faced me in his study, his lips compressed, his nostrils narrowed. White indentations showed at the corner of his mouth. When I entered the house from the stables, where I had made sure both Nimbus and Rufus would be cared for, I had intended to go at once to my room and put myself to rights before confronting him.

But he had met me in the hall and commanded my presence in a tone that would take no refusal. I felt reduced to a schoolgirl again. And now I stood before him, just inside the room, in my damp, muddy riding habit, my ruined hat, smelling strongly of horse. My hair was whipped by wind, matted by rain. I cut, I felt, a most inelegant figure. Pilot came to my side, sniffing at me anxiously. I patted him with one unheeding hand. My temper was rising.

"How dare you behave in this way," he said coldly. "What can have been your upbringing? Inconsiderate, insubordinate, grossly flouting convention in a way that I can only describe as unwomanly! Yes, unwomanly! We had no way of knowing where you were, if you were safe, as hour after hour went by. Our anxiety has been considerable. I would have you know, Miss Rochester, that such behaviour is not acceptable. Your own home may have been unconventional, your mother unused to the ways of Society, but whilst you live under my roof—and under my guardianship—you will conform to accepted standards of conduct. Look at you, your hair unkempt, your garments in disarray! You will *not* ride like a gypsy unescorted—unchaperoned!— through the neighbourhood. By gad, Miss Rochester, if you were my daughter, I should be tempted to take a horsewhip to your sides … !

"Enough!" I said. My face was warm; I knew I had flushed. So that was how the County had regarded my mother—she who was worth a dozen of them! I would permit no criticism of her. My hands trembled, and I clasped them firmly together; the Colonel should not see me shaken. (My father stood at my shoulder, *"Daughter, disguise fair nature with hard-favour'd rage."*)

I straightened. Secure in my knowledge of Mr. Briggs's primary guardianship, I spoke my mind. "You f-forget yourself, sir! Before you go on, Colonel, I should remind you that I am not a soldier in your regiment. Please c-control your temper and speak to me in a more seemly way. And never, *never,* let me hear you speak disparagingly of my mother! Your own manners I can only call into question on that point!"

He glared at me but reddened and changed his tack. He upbraided me for my rejection of Milly Allnut, for the wounding of her feelings, for my ingratitude in not appreciating the efforts he had made for my comfort. I had stood quiet under his harangue until his reference to my mother, for I felt my guilt in causing the household worry (particularly my poor Laura), but I was not prepared to remain silent on the subject of my maid; for there he was at fault, not I. And now my voice was calm and level.

"On that score, Sir, I am quite decided. My maid will join me here in two days time. Sir Hugo Calendar fully understands my wishes. I am sorry to have caused you anxiety, but my behaviour was brought about by a most extraordinary error on your part. You had no possible right to tell Mrs. Deveraux that Annie was not needed here. Why was it left to me to ensure that my maid knew of my wishes? Why did you inform Mrs. Deveraux that she need not dispatch my maid to me, although it was my specific request? By what right did you countermand my instructions? That was the reason for my visit to Thornfield, and you were the cause."

He spluttered, his face crimson. "*Your* instructions? How dare you? You will do as you are bid in this house, Miss Rochester. I will not be questioned in this way."

"And *I* will not be shouted at. I repeat, *my* instructions. I am grateful that you are sheltering me under your roof whilst my parents are abroad, but I should remind you that it is Mr. Briggs, not you, who has final authority over me, and that under my father's direction. I have informed Mrs. Deveraux that Annie Parrott is to be sent to Highcrest within two days. If she does not come, I shall fetch her. Now, if you will excuse me, I should like to change my damp clothes. Perhaps we shall speak more calmly together tomorrow. Good night, Colonel Dent."

As I turned from him, it seemed to me someone moved in the shadows by the window. Was another figure, tall and dark, standing there, beyond the reach of firelight or candle? I did not wait to see but left the Colonel glaring after me and hastened out of the study. Laura was waiting near the main staircase. My hands were shaking still, and I was breathing hard from determination and attempted self-control. Laura put her arms around me and held my stiff form close for one moment. "My dear, you must forgive him. We were so worried. The storm blew up, and you were gone."

I softened in a moment. "Laura, I had no wish to cause you anxiety. The weather was well enough when I started out. It deteriorated as I neared Thornfield. I could not turn back so near my destination. And, oh, Laura, it was so good to see my home again, even occupied as it was by strangers. But it is plain that the Colonel had no intention of restoring my maid to me. (There is some reason, I am sure, for his deliberate deception. I do not understand it). But let us go upstairs. I must change—and I have so much to tell you of Sir Hugo and his sister. It is all so strange!"

We hurried up the staircase, gloomy despite the flickering lights, and along the passageway, dim and shadowy. The drafts gently agitated the tapestries, and the figures depicted in them seemed to advance and retreat, as if to bar our way. A grim and haunted house the manor seemed to me at that moment. When I was warm and dry again and comfortable in my dressing gown, a maid brought me hot chocolate and macaroons, and, seated together in our pleasant sitting room before a welcome fire, Laura and I talked for some hours. I told her of Mrs. Deveraux's oddly changed behaviour, of her unreason, of Sir Hugo's show of authority over her, of my discovery of Colonel Dent's deception. Laura was responsive and understanding, her intelligence quick to take my points. When I was quiet, she began to talk.

"I think you are right, Janet, in your assessment of the Colonel's behaviour. It is strange indeed, but I feel he wants as few strangers here as possible. To you he was committed if chance delayed your parents' return. He promised your father, and his honour will not let him renege on that promise.

"Oh, all this may simply be an embittered man's eccentricity. Having lost his family, he wants as little change about him as possible. And he is a highly conventional man, accustomed to the discipline of the army and accustomed to command. But, Janet, I must observe that this is not a normal household. You and I use certain rooms, walk in certain parts of the park. We have been carefully guided. Half this house is barred to us. And I am sure that there are large stretches of the grounds hidden from us behind stone walls and locked gates. The servants are controlled by Mrs. Brotherhood. Most of them seem related—to each other, to the gamekeepers or the head groom, or to Mrs. Brotherhood herself. They are pleasant to us, but they do not chatter. They are a clan. I think that is why it was important to exclude your maid, who has her own relatives in the neighbourhood, her own clan, to whom she may gossip. It is all strange, strange. There is some mystery at Highcrest."

"Perhaps you are right," I said slowly. "My mind has been on Annie. But we can quite easily test what you suppose. Let us experiment in the days to come."

I had much to ponder tucked under my covers that night. Alone in bed, I thought to myself of how fond I was becoming of Laura. Telling her about Thornfield and the strange behaviour of Mrs. Deveraux had cleared my mind. I went over once again my battle with Colonel Dent. I was shaken by the intensity of my feelings. Standing up to him had been much harder than opposing Miss Nasmyth, but I had done so. I was almost glad that I had had her to practice on. And I felt, on the whole, considerable elation. I had made my point; I had not been browbeaten by the Colonel.

Annie was to join me. I had been inspired by thoughts of my mother (it was she I resembled, and she I strove to emulate in my behaviour), but I also owed a debt to my father. My blood and my character came from both sides. My father was not one to be overawed. He stood straight and tall in the face of the world. Eventually I curled up on my side and settled to sleep. But, as I drowsed, I remembered one thing. I had not told Laura of the stranger in the lane, the tall, dark man who had reminded me so strongly of my father. What illusion was that? Was there really a resemblance, or did I so long to see my father that any well-built, dark-haired man called him to mind? And was it he who had waited in the shadows of the Colonel's study? I disliked very much the thought of a witness to my battle with the Colonel. How harsh and strident I must have seemed to one who did not know the cause. But I was too tired to stay long awake.

The next day dawned bright. Small, white clouds strayed across the sky like sheep on the moors. Looking from my window, I saw a kestrel hover over the fir trees, wings fluttering so fast they barely seemed to stir—it was as if the air itself vibrated about the sparrow hawk—death in a form of precision and grace. I remembered the bird I had seen fly up from the apple orchard at Thornfield. Windhover. A charming name for a fierce but elegant hunter. The nesting rooks rose cawing to protest its dangerous presence. They flew at it *en masse* and drove it away. I wondered if it were the bird I had seen the day before.

I found myself full of energy, with more anticipation of the day than was my wont. My dressing completed, I ordered my hair. For some reason, I found myself taking particular care to arrange it becomingly. Realizing this, I stared impatiently into the mirror. Plain, I said to myself. Like my mother. What does my appearance matter, as long as I am neat? I called to Laura, and we made our way downstairs together. There were voices coming from the study. The door was open, and we paused as we passed on our way to the breakfast room. The Colonel stood by the window, and with him was a newcomer, tall, dark, distractingly familiar in build. The Colonel looked around at the sound of our voices. He met my gaze and frowned; then, with conscious effort, he smoothed his brow, harrumphed under his breath, coughed a little, and came forward.

"Miss Rochester, Miss Alleyn. My secretary, of whom I told you, has returned from his journeyings. May I introduce Mr. Landless? Roderick, here are Miss Rochester and Miss Alleyn." His manner was quite different from the previous night. He seemed eager to be affable.

The stranger stepped forward. His eyes met mine with a keen and penetrating glance from under heavy black brows. His gaze reminded me again of the kestrel I had seen, that same keen, wild eye. He held out his hand.

"Miss Rochester," he said, bowing his head. And then, "Miss Alleyn."

His grip was firm and cool. When we moved together along the passage, Mr. Landless walked at my side, standing back to allow me to enter the breakfast room. We all sat down. The Colonel made no reference to our disagreement of the previous night. Mr. Landless made no reference to our earlier meeting—and nor did I. There was not much conversation as we ate and drank, but by the time we arose from the table—the Colonel and Mr. Landless to return to the study, Laura and I to make our way to our sitting room—I knew the house had changed. Its guarded stillness was disturbed. A new element had entered Highcrest, a breath of wind from off the moors, cold and piercing and wild, like the cry of a hawk. I liked it better.

But though we now numbered four, there was little alteration in our daily lives. Mr. Landless stayed mainly out of sight; he did not join Laura and me in our pastimes. I knew at times he worked in the library, but I did not think he was always indoors. Some mornings I saw him ride out on a handsome black gelding. He rode well. I watched him with pleasure, admiring his flat back, the powerful muscles in his thighs, the light touch of his hands on the reins. But more often, when I took my own rides, his horse was in the stables; there was not much, indeed, to take him to Hay. Once a week he rode to Millcote on business. Where he was when he remained at Highcrest, I did not know. Out of our sight, at any rate. And he was not gregarious when he joined us in the evening. At meals, he added little to the conversation.

"Indeed," I said to Laura. "He is no great addition to our circle. I hoped for better from the Colonel's first mention of him. He will speak if spoken to, but he volunteers little on his own."

"Perhaps not in speech. But he looks much, though he says little. He looks at *you*, Janet."

It was true that when, at table, I raised my eyes, I often found him looking at me with something of my father's sardonic gaze. I found it disturbing. His voice was deep; when he spoke, it was to the point. I wished it were possible to draw him out. There must be subjects to which he would respond. But I felt shy in his presence, as tongue-tied as if my years in London had never happened.

Halfway through Wednesday morning, as Laura and I were sitting on the terrace, a cart drove around to the side of the Manor. As I looked, a small, agile figure hopped down from the seat beside the driver, who lifted a box from behind him and lowered it to the ground. It was Annie.

I ran across the grass to her side, and when she turned to greet me, I hugged her. She was part of my old life, of Thornfield. I was so glad to see her. She was rosy and bright-eyed from her drive. She waved cheerfully after the departing groom, who seemed reluctant to leave her. He called some parting quip as he departed, and I saw her smile and tuck the smile away. He was not anyone I recognized. I looked at Annie, who glanced down, hiding her eyes. A dimple quivered at the corner of her mouth. My childhood companion had grown into something of a coquette.

And here was one more addition to the life of Highcrest Manor, and one who made a marked difference. Annie had a ready wit and was a lively conversationalist. Where she went there was laughter. She sang as she tidied my room and ordered my clothing. She approved very much of my London gowns, smoothing the silk and admiring the drape of bodice and fullness of skirt. ("Seven yards, Miss Janet? Oh, Lordy me!")

"You've grown up, Miss Janet, you have an' all. A real London young lady, you are now. I'm right pleased to see ut. Your mam liked to dress you in such Sunday meeting dresses, like a young orphling. But now you're right handsome!"

"Oh, Annie. You're more Irish than Yorkshire with your flattery."

She took to Laura at once and would willingly have maided her as well as me, but, in the name of peace in the household, I suggested Laura continue to employ Milly Allnut. With great tact, Annie soon made a friend of Milly. I would hear the sound of soft chatter in my dressing room and little bursts of laughter. And from almost the first day, we received information about the running of the house-hold and relations below stairs. Annie was afraid of no one. She was not pert nor argumentative with the other servants, but, she told me, when it came to being given instructions by Mrs. Brotherhood on where she could go and what she could do, she had replied that she would do her best, but in the end she took her orders from me and answered to me and me only. One strict instruction related to the East Wing. It was not in use. No one went there, she was told, and it was under lock and key.

"And so ut is. I tried t' door, Miss Janet, on t' ground floor near t' kitchens, and ut was locked, right enough. But that no one goes there, that's not so! I seen Ramsbotham comin' out, carrying a bundle o' cloths. And powerful cross he was t' see me! Sent me about me business, sharpish."

There was one thing I learned from Annie that I had not fully comprehended before. The comfort, nay, luxury, we found at Highcrest that was in such contrast to the castle-like design of the old building with its grim stone walls and long cold passages—all the rich carpets and drapery, the tapestry hangings that softened the walls and defied the drafts, the charming china ornaments, Dresden and Worcester, and Chinese lamps and bowls, the busts and statues that ornamented the niches in the halls—came there with Mrs. Dent. Our pretty bedrooms were of her furnishing. Our cosy sitting room had been her boudoir. (Something I missed from my London sojourn—there was no gas lighting. This newfangled luxury had not yet reached all such isolated houses, however large and important. Candlelight and oil lamps were still the order of the day in brackets and cande-labra and in our nighttime holders.) The Colonel's family had owned Highcrest for generations, but with the passing of time, their income had decreased. The army did not make its officers wealthy; the colonels and even generals among the Dent ancestors were honourable men—some heroic—but they were not rich. Mrs. Dent had been the only daughter of a wealthy wine importer; she was a considerable heiress. But she had had but one child, her son Nigel, and his death had been a great blow to them both. However, one of Annie's titbits of gossip surprised me. She had overheard Mrs. Brotherhood talking with Ramsbotham. Highcrest Manor was not entailed. Although it had long descended from eldest son to eldest son, the entail had been broken by Colonel Dent before his marriage, when financial hardship had driven them to sell a fringe property.

Nigel Dent was dead these two years. He had had no heir. Who then would inherit the Manor on Colonel Dent's death? There were no close relations. It might be expected that the servants would have ideas on this subject, but Annie's artless questions had been received with disfavour. It was not their business to wonder about such things, said Mrs. Brotherhood. Annie was to hold her tongue and go about her business.

I could not help but add this to my mental questions concerning Mr. Landless. What was he to the Colonel, and why did he so strongly resemble my father? I pressed Annie to sound the other maids on his background. Had he lived long at Highcrest? Who were his parents? Where was his home? But she could find out little. Milly Allnut told her Mr. Landless had arrived from abroad and became the Colonel's secretary some two years previously. Before that, she thought, as a young man, he had been an occasional visitor, a friend of Nigel Dent's. She had known him by sight. But Milly was young, only seventeen. She had had little contact with the dwellers at the Manor before she was employed as my maid.

It was my *father* he resembled, not Oliver. Where Oliver was a softened version of his parent, this man was hard. I remembered my mother's description of my father when she had first met him. She had spoken of his granite-hewn features and his massive head, of the unconscious pride in his port, and of such a look of complete indifference to his own external appearance. She called him sardonic, harsh. She might have been describing my new companion.

But I am running on too fast and leading my hounds. It was at this time that, at long last, I had news of my parents. A stranger came to Highcrest. The day was hot, the third in a series of humid, heavy days, the kind that end in storm, when the house was a refuge from the pressure of the heat. But we needed exercise. Laura and I returned from a gentle walk in the grounds, our steps languid, our heads protected by broad-brimmed straw hats and also, in Laura's case, by a very pretty white parasol, trimmed with scallops of *broderie anglaise*, to find that someone was closeted with Colonel Dent. Ramsbotham informed us that it was the Colonel's wish that we join him as soon as possible. We ran upstairs to remove our hats and smooth our hair, then made our way to the Colonel's study. He stood at the window and, facing him, a man was seated, a burly man with greying hair and beard and weather-beaten face, dressed in navy serge. A man of the sea. My heart contracted in my breast.

"Miss Rochester—Janet, my dear. This is Captain Harcourt of the merchant sailing ship, *Bristol Castle*. He has news for you. Sit down, my dear. It is best that you sit down. I fear you may be distressed. The news is not good."

"Oh, pray, tell me, sir. What news can you give me of my father and mother? Did they sail on your ship?"

The captain had risen at my entrance. Now he reddened under his dark-tanned skin at my intensity. "I regret they did not, Miss Rochester. T' news I bring is secondhand. Your parents sailed on my sister vessel, t' *Chatham Queen*, out of Singapore, these four or five months ago. But t' *Queen*, she did not make port. Some lascar seamen were picked up in t' China Sea and told a tale of typhoon and mountainous seas. T' ship was wrecked with all hands."

The blood drained from my cheeks. I rose from my chair and took two urgent turns about the room. Mr. Landless, entering the room at that point, stopped dead in the doorway, staring at me.

My brain began to work again. "But the seamen—they survived? They were in a lifeboat? How came that? Did they know of other boats launched before the wreck? What of the passengers?"

"They were cast into t' sea when the ship capsized—some four or five o' them—but struck out towards t' wreckage. When found, they were adrift on a mast and part of t' rigging. They had collected timbers and struts afloat and managed to rope them together in a makeshift raft and thus survive, though without food or water, and were near dead from thirst when rescued. Their only food was fish. They claimed, however, that at least two boats were launched, and passengers were given first claim. They did not see what happened next. When the seas subsided, they were alone."

"The lifeboats—on any well-regulated ship, they would have been stocked with food and water?"

"Indeed, yes. Captain Fisher, he of t' *Chatham Queen*, he were a fine seaman. There were two dozen passengers aboard t' *Queen*, according to t' passenger lists. If t' boats were launched and did not capsize, they would stand a better chance than t' poor lascars on t' raft."

"Miss Rochester, you have suffered a shock. Please, sit down again, and let me pour you a little Madeira." Mr. Landless urged me into a chair, and I sipped the proffered drink and found it did me good. A little warmth stole into my cheeks and fingers. Laura took my hand.

"You say, Captain Harcourt, that this happened five months ago? There is no more recent news?"

"Nowt that I know, but I have been at sea myself. I have just returned to England. I am a Yorkshire man and would come t' give you my news in person when I heard of your whereabouts from Mr. Briggs. Captain Fisher was my good friend. I assure you, I have enquiries abroad for any news, as has the shipping company. There are many islands in those parts on which they might make landfall, but they are scattered, isolated, not on any regular shipping route. They might well be safe on shore but hard put t' get news to English-speaking ports. You must not give way t' despair, young lady."

I thought of my father, my brother. Both were strong, vigorous men of considerable ability. And my mother, so steadfast, so determined. If they were together, if they had survived the storm, she would keep them alive by sheer strength of will. A picture flashed into my mind of my mother, her nose burned by the sun, her hair in disarray, strands streaming in the breeze, her skirts kilted up, standing barefoot on wet sand, organizing her menfolk! It was a good thought, almost humorous, restorative to my mind. But then my dreams came back to me, my father reaching out to me from the sea! Oh, how could I bear life without him?

I made my excuses and went to my room. I could not eat. For long hours I stood at my window, staring at the black clouds roiling on the horizon over the distant moors, uneasy, threatening, echoing the dark thoughts in my mind. Even as I watched, I heard the first rumbles of thunder. The great god Thor was driving his chariot across the sky and brandishing his hammer. Where, oh where, was Vulcan, my father, the smith of the gods? Surely one such god should protect another? Oh, my mind was reeling! I saw lightning tear with a jagged flame through the blackness of the cloud, and then the thunder crashed into my brain, nearer, louder, as the storm approached. Again and again the thunder rolled and then at last came the rain in torrents, hissing on the hot leads and streaming down the sloping roofs. A coolness stole into my room, a fresher, sweeter breeze made its presence felt. I took deep breaths and let my thoughts grow still.

I stayed alone through the evening, rejecting all company and spending a night tossing and turning, partly dreaming, partly waking; the next day I left a note under Laura's door, stole out early, and went straight to the stables. I rode on the moors, alone but for Pilot, for several hours, until physical exhaustion dulled the pain in my mind. I returned then to Highcrest, let Laura cosset me, and the

next day took my place again in the affairs of the household. I made it plain I did not wish to conjecture on my family's fate. The Colonel and Mr. Landless respected my wishes. Only Laura saw me weep, and her gentle caresses and talk of hope were filled with comfort.

One thing I must mention, one strange thing. The night after Captain Harcourt's visit—that desperate night of the storm in which I sank into troubled sleep and roused again to weep into my pillow and then sleep once more—I woke once for a different cause. Some sound disturbed my light slumber, and I started up in my bed, crying out my father's name as if he knocked at my door. Then, almost at once, I remembered Pilot, who slept across my threshold and sometimes rattled the door as he scratched or kicked out in his dreams. But as I listened, a sound came, quite unfamiliar. I heard a low voice, a laugh; "Pilot," a voice whispered, and then another, deeper voice said, "Shhhhh," after which came the sound of footsteps, a quick patter, patter. Little steps, like a child's, running, retreating down the passage. I slid from my bed with its rumpled sheets and damp pillow, lit my candle, and went to my door. Slowly, nervously, I opened it. Pilot was there, standing, staring intently down the passage. He turned his head to greet me and his tail, already wagging, moved faster. I could see nothing, no one. "Pilot?" I asked. I took the few steps to his side and patted his neck, and he licked my hand but still stood, alert. His hackles were not raised. He was not disturbed, just interested. For a moment more I stood with him and stared into the darkness. Then, sighing, I returned to my bedroom. My feet were bare and, just outside my door, brushed against something unfamiliar. I stooped and picked up a ball: a pretty, childish thing made of loops and braids of coloured yarn. A toy. Had someone given it to Pilot? Where had it come from?

I stumbled back to bed, not knowing whether I woke or dreamt. In the pale light of dawn, lying limp and tormented in my bed, filled with remorseless memory, I recalled this odd incident and felt sure it was a dream. I must have dreamt of childhood in an effort to escape the bitter present.

CHAPTER SEVEN

Sir Hugo, at Home and Abroad

They were discussing the stranger; they both called him a
"beautiful man."

⁂ JANE EYRE ⁂

*W*HEN I ROSE, I found the ball where I had dropped it by my bed. I stared at it in perplexity. Such a silly little thing it was. A child's plaything, no more, no less. Yet it was disconcerting in its incongruity. I tucked it out of sight into a drawer, beneath my chemises.

Later I wrote an entry in my diary, and one day asked Annie if anyone talked of ghosts in the Manor—in particular, the ghost of a child. Unfortunately, Mrs. Brotherhood overheard Annie questioning Milly on the subject and scolded her soundly. No, there were no ghosts at the Manor. She was a foolish, chattering ninny and should be about her work. And Milly should watch her step and not be pulled into foolish gossip about her betters; her father would know how to deal with her, if she did not mind her ways. Did she want to lose her position? Milly, said Annie, was quite upset and would not talk; she kept to herself for several days, all of which, instead of damping my interest (and that of Annie), only made us wonder. What was there to occasion such an upset?

At breakfast a day or so after Captain Harcourt's visit, the Colonel eyed my simple muslin dress (a quiet sage green, it was) and asked, with many a "humph" and cough, whether I had considered the suitability of wearing mourning for my parents. I was considerably taken aback. A feeling almost of panic caught at my throat.

"No, Sir! Indeed, I have not. My parents are not dead! They are missing—lost at sea—they are *not dead!*"

Laura put her hand on my arm.

"Indeed, Colonel Dent, I do not think the most stringent convention would demand mourning in such a case. Since some seamen were saved—men who had not even achieved a lifeboat—surely Miss Rochester has every reason for hope. As the captain made plain to us, there are dozens of islands scattered in those seas, far from any shipping route. We must wait in patience for much stronger evidence of the true fate of Janet's parents."

The Colonel looked his dourest, but Mr. Landless came in unexpectedly on my side.

"We must surely all do our best, Colonel, to encourage Miss Rochester to hope, and the wearing of black would cast the strongest spirits down. I have the oddest feeling that she should do better to wear cherry ribbons in her hair to attract the attention of any moorland sprite or wight who might wish her well and aid her fortunes."

I gave him a grateful smile and thought his visage softened slightly as he acknowledged my look.

I talked with Laura afterwards on that grim subject as we sat on the terrace. "There can be no disrespect, Laura, in my feelings, which tell me so strongly my parents, my dear brother, are alive! To mourn for them now, when they may be struggling with the elements to live, to find perhaps basic food and shelter—who can tell their circumstances?—would seem to me quite wrong, as if I had ceased to hope for their safety. I do not wish to anger the Colonel. He has expressed his sympathy most feelingly. But I must go my own way in this. My family lives! I will not, I cannot, wear black for the living."

My life returned to its accustomed routine. I walked, I rode, I spent quiet hours with Laura, reading or at music. It was a week later that we received a visit from Sir Hugo Calendar. It was late morning, and Laura and I were practising some songs on the grand piano in the drawing room. I played, and she sang some pretty Scottish airs, simple and fresh. The music soothed me. It was always pleasant to hear her voice with her slight Highland accent, and I noticed Colonel Dent pause in the doorway to listen for a while before disappearing once more in the direction of his study. The June sun streamed into the east-facing drawing room and lit up her dark honey hair and softly tinted complexion as she stood with one hand on the piano, the gold locket she always wore at her bosom stirred by her deep breathing, her face rapt. One curl fell onto her forehead. She was wearing a simple blue lawn morning dress fitted to her slim waist, the folds of the bell skirt falling to her feet; it became her well. I was wearing my sage green muslin. Laura was singing *"Ye banks and braes o' bonnie doon, How can ye bloom sae fresh and fair?"* with a plaintive note in her sweet voice, when Ramsbotham arrived to announce Sir Hugo. Our music had drowned the sound of his knock.

He apologized for intruding and looked searchingly at Laura, whom he had not met. I was pleased to introduce them. I had spoken of him to Laura more than once, and I was glad she could now clothe his imagined form in reality. He was looking his elegant self, in a black riding jacket, dove grey riding breeches, and beautifully polished top boots. His stock was crisply white and edged with lace. A yellow rosebud was tucked into his buttonhole. He came over to the window to shake our hands, and a ray of sunlight from the window illuminated his features. I was conscious of seeing him more clearly than I had ever done. At our first two meetings, I had viewed him as one of a pair with his sister—a "pair of matched greys," one would have said, had they been horses. At Thornfield, the atmosphere, the undercurrent of tension, of disagreement, had coloured my view of him as the dominant figure of the two. Now I regarded his physiognomy, displayed so clearly by the sun. He was indeed a handsome man. His complexion was pale and even, tinted but little by exposure to the weather, yet lined, it would seem, by that exposure. I did not know his age; between thirty-five and forty, I imagined. His nose was long and aquiline, his face was narrow, and the vertical lines running down his face, between his eyes and from arch of elegant nostril to chin circumnavigated a rather long upper lip, elongating his whole appearance. Yet they did not make him seem old, merely idiosyncratic. His chin—a decided chin—was cleft. His eyes, his most noticeable feature, were a clear, cool grey set off by short, dark lashes. His hair was a dull gold (though dull was not the right word for anything about Sir Hugo Calendar), perhaps the color of a polished coin. Intelligence was there in every feature, a cautious, thoughtful intelligence but hard and, to some degree, arrogant. He was short-tempered, perhaps: those lines between his eyes spoke of frowns. A complicated man, Sir Hugo, and interesting, but perhaps not kindly. Not open. And not someone to be taken lightly.

"Pray, do not stop," he said, indicating the piano after his introduction to Laura. "I listened to your song as I entered the hall. It was quite charming."

Laura blushed a little and glanced at me for a lead. "Perhaps one more song?" I suggested. "My Love Is Like a Red, Red Rose?" This was a long time favourite with Laura. But she shook her head. She flicked through the music before us and placed one sheet before me. I was playing the introduction before I took in the name of the piece, a simple Scottish folk song—"I Know Where I'm Going." It was a favourite with us both, but I wondered briefly at her choice at that time. Her voice rose true and clear in the refrain:

Some call him black,
but I call him bonnie.
He's the one for me,
my handsome, winsome Johnny.

Why, I wondered, had she chosen to sing in praise of a dark man when one so fair stood before her? As she came to an end and my fingers stilled on the keys, the silence was broken by light applause coming from the doorway. Roderick Landless stood just inside the entrance. Away from the window, the light was dim; though he was in shadow, I saw Sir Hugo stiffen.

"Thank you, sir," said Laura, dropping a curtsey in his direction.

"Of course, you know Mr. Landless?" I said to Sir Hugo, a slight question in my voice.

"Of course," he said. And his voice was echoed by the deeper voice from the door. "Of course," said Roderick Landless, "Sir Hugo." He bowed slightly and turned away.

"Don't go, Mr. Landless," broke in Laura. She spoke quickly and impulsively. "Colonel Dent tells me that you are a fine singer yourself. I have had my turn. Won't you now allow us to hear you?"

He advanced into the room and stood by the piano. He turned some sheets of music in his hand. But he shook his dark head. "Some evening, perhaps, Miss Alleyn. I have come in in all my dirt. I must change and make myself presentable before luncheon."

"We shall keep you to your word," I said. I was a little piqued at Laura's remark. I could not remember her mentioning his singing to me, and certainly I had been absent when the Colonel spoke of it. Had they then discussed him? I felt a small resentment that she should know more about our mysterious companion than I did myself. I found myself regarding the two men, both now lit by the sun, one so fair, tall, lean, and austere; the other black of hair and eye (*"some call him black"*), somewhat taller and much heavier in build, with a visage that seemed carved by harsh climes. But intelligent. Yes, here again one could not but be aware of a forceful, impetuous intelligence. I suppose there were persons who would have found Mr. Landless an ugly man, particularly in contrast to Sir Hugo's Nordic elegance, but I found myself repeating the words of Laura's song in my mind, " ... *but I call him bonnie.*"

I shook myself mentally, urging my mind to discipline. I remembered my manners and invited Sir Hugo to join us for luncheon. He accepted with what I could only term alacrity. Mr. Landless left the room, and we conversed for a few minutes before we moved to the dining room. Then the Colonel and Mr. Landless joined us, and Ramsbotham came bearing wine. Sir Hugo took up the conversation. He had come, he said, as he sipped a glass of wine, to make quite sure that all was settled with my maid. The words hung in the air a brief moment as I wondered if the Colonel would respond. But he said nothing, and I hastened into the breach to express my thanks for Annie's prompt arrival.

"You must know," I said, to soften the moment, "she and I are old playfellows. We grew up together. Her mother was my nurse. It is part of coming home to have her with me once more."

Sir Hugo enquired after my family, and I was forced to explain our recent news. My story was unadorned, a flat statement of such facts as we knew. He exclaimed with some dismay, but it was not a subject I wished to dwell upon. I answered his questions in monosyllables, reiterating that there was room for hope, and as soon as possible, I turned the subject. I asked about the gardens at Thornfield, speaking of my father's close interest, and the conversation took a safer turn, becoming general as first Laura, then Mr. Landless, spoke of gardens. Sir Hugo commented on our interest and, indeed, that of my father, which was displayed in so distinguished a fashion at Thornfield. In the north of England, he said, gardening was not as a rule a great interest, unlike in the south. My companions agreed. The books I had seen in the Colonel's library briefly crossed my mind, but my attention was engaged by the conversation. The softer clime, perhaps the more leisured life, encouraged the decorative arts, was the Colonel's opinion. But as the meal progressed and cold meats were replaced by fruit and cakes, Sir Hugo began to concentrate more on me. Was I riding regularly, he asked? Had I still my pretty mare? Did I ride on the moors?

"Has Miss Rochester ever told you, Colonel, of our first meeting? In Hyde Park? A horse belonging to her party had bolted, throwing the rider, and then took off across the park. Miss Rochester chased it down and caught it single-handed. My sister and I chanced to be observers of this gallant ride, and I was much impressed. At that time, of course, I had no reason to suppose there was any connection between us." He laughed at me over his wineglass. I lowered my eyes and stared at the table, knowing I had flushed and disliking the concentrated attention of the three men sitting there.

"Miss Rochester has always struck me as intrepid," said Mr. Landless. The Colonel grunted. If called upon to make a truthful comment, I think he would have said he could not approve of my making myself conspicuous in public.

Perhaps sensing my discomfort, Sir Hugo changed the subject. He enquired about my childhood at Thornfield, and asked about my favourite places and pastimes. He peeled a peach, and then, his chin on his hand, he lowered his voice and spoke across the table more intimately to me while Laura conversed with the Colonel and Mr. Landless.

"You must know, Miss Rochester, that, having seen you in your own house, I must now feel your presence at all times. Your light step descends the staircase, the rustle of your skirts precedes me into the dining room, your candle ascends the stairs at the end of the day. I feel some guilt that I am usurping your home."

I was considerably taken aback. I tried to laugh. "Sir Hugo—no. Please, do not say such things. You embarrass me by such statements. And you frighten me. Am I a ghost, haunting my family home while I am still alive?" (My heart contracted as I thought of other ghosts that might now wander the corridors of Thornfield. It was not a thought on which I wished to dwell.) "You are my father's tenant, and we are grateful to have such a good one."

"I feel a strong need to see you at home again, Miss Rochester. What, may I ask, are your—or your guardian's—plans for your future life? In the light of your unfortunate news—though this, we must hope, will soon be replaced by news more welcome—are you to stay with the good Colonel indefinitely?" He raised his voice and directed his enquiry pointedly to the Colonel. "I am enquiring into the future of my tenancy, Colonel Dent. Shall Miss Rochester wish to return to Thornfield—her inheritance, I presume—in the foreseeable future?"

The Colonel's face was quite without expression. "Mr. Rochester's plans for his daughter were laid well before his departure and covered all contingencies," he said. "For the present, she remains at Highcrest, where I may afford her any protection she needs." Sir Hugo's thrust had been parried; his blade had met with no counterthrust. The Colonel offered no further detail of my father's plans on my behalf. Sir Hugo's curiosity as to my inheritance—for such it had been—was still unanswered. (I remembered our meeting in London, in Miss Temple's room. There, too, he had attempted to learn about my fortune. Perhaps it was a normal social ploy?) But all he learned from Colonel Dent was that I should go on living at Highcrest and was well defended.

"I am happy indeed to continue my tenancy. But although you are not yet to take possession of your estate," said Sir Hugo smoothly, "perhaps I may still be so fortunate as to see you soon again *in* your own home? My sister and I should like to invite you all to take dinner with us." And on this last remark he spoke more loudly, nodding to Laura and Mr. Landless to make sure they knew they were included. There was a moment's silence. The Colonel's eyes were on his wineglass. When he spoke, it was with a shake of his head. "Thank you, Sir Hugo, but I seldom dine from home. The young people, however, I am sure will be pleased to oblige you. They are but little in society."

Sir Hugo left soon after, and Laura and I walked out through the grounds for our daily constitutional. The heat wave had passed. The day was warm enough, with some cloud hiding the sun from time to time. The rooks had finished hatching their eggs, and the fledglings were learning to fly.

We walked beneath the trees. One of the stable cats ran past us, its pregnant belly low to the ground, a prize dangling from its mouth. We recognized the partly fledged body of a nestling rook, which must have toppled from a nest. Laura shuddered and turned away. I spoke of our visitor, but she was not forthcoming. She mentioned Sir Hugo only when I enquired pointedly for her opinion, and I heard her with some dismay.

"Janet, my dear. I find him a most distinguished man. But—I hardly dare to say it—there is something there, something about him—not his looks, not his manner—that reminds me of my uncle. Some evasion, some lack of oral response, some assessment in his eye. What it is, I cannot tell, but I can only be wary of him."

I pressed her for a more elaborate comment, but she shook her head and looked distressed. So I changed the subject and questioned her on the subject of Mr. Landless's singing. The Colonel had told her, she said, that Mr. Landless had a fine *baritone*. As a boy, he had sung in the choir of his public school, and Mrs. Dent had much enjoyed his singing on his visits to Highcrest. As he grew older, after his young voice broke, it had deepened and matured into a *baritone*.

I was reminded yet again of my father, whose strong *bass* voice had often beguiled our evenings at Thornfield. I remembered, with sudden nostalgia, that he would never have my mother accompany him. Her fingers were not skilled enough; he always accompanied himself. There was some remembrance here, some tender moment between them to which he referred. They both would laugh and exchange glances. Now

I tucked the information away in the special, curtained recess of my mind where Mr. Landless had taken up residence—an attic, I imagined it, half empty, some few boxes and footlockers lying about as yet unpacked, papers and books piled on the seat of an old armchair. And now, a music box.

I looked forward to hearing him sing.

The days passed. I went through life in something of a dream, a dream with nightmarish overtones, walking, riding, sitting with Laura, writing in my journal, determinedly keeping myself well-occupied, and attempting—tentatively, warily, as if I were stalking some shy animal (some great stag or golden eagle)—to distract myself by moving nearer to Mr. Landless, gaining something of his confidence, and learning more of him. Too open an approach, and he would toss his antler'd head and shy away or would fly up from the earth with a harsh cry and much flapping of powerful wings and make for the open sky. Too much hesitation, and I should never close the gap. And yet somehow I felt he welcomed my quiet advances. Soon he would come to my outstretched hand. Sometimes, standing at my window and gazing over the trees at the far horizon, I thought about the practicalities of life. Women are seldom in control of their fates. Life for most of them unfolds in a steady succession of events: birth, child-hood, marriage, childbirth, death. If they are not *chosen* in marriage, there is little they can do to affect their lives. They face a straight road, for better, for worse. But sometimes—yes, sometimes—there is a bend in that road, a break, a fork, the unexpected (something in me rejoiced at the unexpected).

And, willy-nilly, their destination is changed. If my parents had stayed in England and I with them (or if they had returned in two years as they had planned), what should have been my destination? Should I have met Roderick Landless? What was he to me? Was my road still flat, or had it become a hill down which I was plunging with some abandon? What lay beyond the curve in the road?

About ten days after Sir Hugo's visit, we received a card from Mrs. Deveraux, asking us all to dinner and to music afterwards. The Colonel declined on the grounds of health (though he was as active and energetic as ever); the rest of us accepted. It was not an evening of unmixed pleasure, even though I was glad to be at Thornfield and happy to show the house to Laura, to direct her attention to my favourite rooms and aspects and to some of the portraits of my family still hanging in their accustomed spots; in particular, one good portrait of my father, in the library. My heart contracted as I gazed at it. She regarded it for some moments, then turned to meet my eyes. There was a question in hers that I was not prepared to deal with at that moment. I had never mentioned to her the likeness between Mr. Landless and my father. I led her away. I should have liked to take her all over the house and grounds but kept my raptures under control, reminding myself that I was but a guest. It was not easy for me to visit my old home as an outsider, soaked as it was in memories of my family, who were so far from me, whose fate was unknown. In any case, the group was not in all ways compatible. My knowledge that Laura had taken Sir Hugo in some aversion put me on edge; my knowledge that he and Mr. Landless seemed at odds was not encouraging. My own feelings were too mixed to counteract the feelings of others. I found Sir Hugo attractive but disconcerting. I did not understand him. And I knew that Mrs. Deveraux and I, however we might seem, were not friends.

Her manners throughout the evening, however, were charming. She was dressed in mauve silk, with ruffles of lace at her throat and crystal beads at her ears and her neck; she looked and smelled delicious—of lilac, I thought. I wore the steel-blue shot-silk dress I had worn in London; Laura wore blue also, her favourite light shade of summer sky with a lace stole, since the evening was cool. Mrs. Deveraux commiserated with me on the bad news about my parents. She said all that was suitable, but I hastened to turn the subject. She took care to make Laura welcome. As we conversed before dinner, Mrs. Deveraux's manner towards Mr. Landless echoed Sir Hugo's manner to me; she seemed to want to single him out and keep him to herself. I noticed, however, even while she made graceful conversation and warmed Mr. Landless with glances from her fine eyes, she glanced from time to time at her brother, as if to attract his attention, perhaps wanting to be sure of his approval. But Sir Hugo's eyes were veiled. He seemed to avoid meeting her looks. Oh, but perhaps my imagination was overwrought, excited, almost fevered—just as I was by my presence in that house. There was a third man present, making the number even. I turned my attention to him. This was the Hon. Adolphus Ingram, elder brother of my old acquaintance, Isabella.

It was he, I remembered, who had selected the regrettable young horse, Beau.

He was a languid young man with limp, dark hair drooping over his forehead and a long moustache drooping over his mouth. The mouth itself was full and red. His eyes were a clouded brown, not large; his eyelids drooped in sympathy with his locks, and his manner, though giving lip service to the dictates of polite society, was bored to the point of insolence. Sir Hugo quizzed him in a manner as ambivalent as his own, and Mrs. Deveraux flirted with him, seemingly trying to provoke some sign of interest but not succeeding to any great extent. He took my hand at our introduction and brought it almost to his lips. I was relieved that he refrained. I had been imagining the wet softness of his mouth and schooling myself not to shrink. His eyes looked me over with some care before he murmured "Charmed!" Laura's hand he did kiss at length, in a way I thought presumptuous and unnecessary, then he dropped it without a word. Mr. Landless and he did not shake hands. They nodded curtly to each other, one no more aloof than the other. I saw the Hon. Adolphus's eyes narrow as Mr. Landless turned from him. He did not look pleased. No relative of Isabella's would meet with my unearned approval. I decided he was a true Ingram. No doubt he felt it was his prerogative to snub—but he disliked the reciprocation of such disdain.

Dinner was long, with many courses. I found the dishes overrich and took but small portions. There was a tension in the air between the diners that tautened my nerves and spoilt my appetite. I was pleased to see Sir Hugo making a point of including Laura in the conversation, but she was subdued and responded mainly in monosyllables. She, with her simplicity and quiet good looks, made a decided contrast to Mrs. Deveraux. Mrs. Deveraux gave the full value of her bright gaze to each man in turn. If she said rather more to Mr. Landless than to the others, it was not extreme, and doubtless a less careful watcher than I should not have noticed. Her conversation was deft; she had a tendency to flatter, but as hostess she did not neglect my presence or Laura's. She did it well; I had to give her credit. She was a sophisticated woman, a practiced hostess.

Towards the end of the meal, she turned to me with a query about Colonel Dent. How was his health? Was he at all lame? She had seen him on his horse and had not thought him handicapped; she wished to know him better. I felt manipulated. I reiterated his reluctance to go into Society, his preference for his own hearth. But I was a guest, and politeness induced me to mention, as casually as I could, the hope that the night's hospitality might be returned, that she and Sir Hugo might dine at Highcrest.

She sprang eagerly at the bait. "So kind. That would be most enjoyable, Miss Rochester. We leave for Scotland quite soon—a shooting lodge in the Highlands—but when we return? You must know that I have some slight acquaintance with Colonel Dent's son, Nigel. I was at a regimental ball in Cawnpore one time. I remember well my introduction to Captain Dent—and his wife."

I had heard little of Nigel Dent's wife. There was no portrait of her that I had seen in the living rooms at Highcrest. The marriage had been of short duration, I understood. The unfortunate couple had been trapped by an outbreak of cholera and had died in the second year of their marriage, leaving no child. Was there something in Mrs. Deveraux's speech, some ambivalence, as she spoke? It was surely not a matter of surprise that she had met Captain Dent in India. I imagined the English society was not overlarge; most members would know, or know of, the others. And yet I was surprised as much by her manner as by the words she used.

"The Colonel seldom mentions his son. He still feels his loss greatly. It would be unwise to introduce the subject, I believe."

"Indeed, Miss Rochester? Ah, but I understand his feelings."

"Alicia," broke in Sir Hugo. "I think it would be wise not to disturb the Colonel. His memories must be painful to him. Let the past bury the past."

"Naturally, Hugo, I should be discreet. I should not wish to cause the Colonel grief for the world."

Once again, there seemed more to her remark than the actual words. The subject changed. Shortly afterwards, Mrs. Deveraux rose and led Laura and myself first to her boudoir and then to the sitting room on the first floor, which had been my mother's retreat. It gave me something of a pang to see it filled with bright silks and cushions and ornaments of oriental design, though I was charmed by some Persian paintings of birds and flowers and robed women. My brother's miniature was gone. Put carefully away, she assured me when I queried her. When we returned to the drawing room, we waited only for the men to join us and then moved to the music room. In each room, she displayed the changes she had made and talked in a lively, amusing manner of the origin of some of her draperies and artwork. Her every movement was graceful and her voice sweet, but I found myself becoming more and more reluctant to speak. It was left to Laura to exclaim and examine.

In a burst of savage imagination, I saw myself bundling up all these intruding artefacts and casting them forth with their owner. My home, my home! My mother's room. My father's house!

When the men joined us there, Mrs. Deveraux was the first to take her place on the bench of the grand piano. She played a Chopin mazurka with ability and some vivacity. Then she sang a Puccini aria of lovers parted by fate; she had been well taught, her voice was a true rich *mezzo-soprano*, her performance dramatic. My malaise turned to pleasure. The evening gained in enjoyment; music had a great appeal for me. I missed the London concerts. Then it was Laura's turn to sing, and I accompanied her. She sang a simple ballad. Her voice and manner were quite different from Mrs. Deveraux's: sweet, gentle, melodious, with true (not dramatic) feeling. The applause was sincere, and I noticed the Hon. Adolphus, despite (or perhaps because of) the wine he had downed at the dinner table, looked now wide awake—and almost intelligent.

At Mrs. Deveraux's urging, her brother joined her for a duet. Sir Hugo was a *tenor*, competent but not exceptional. They were obviously accustomed to singing together; their performance was smooth. The Hon. Adolphus claimed he did not sing, but Mr. Landless was now requested to pay for his supper. He demurred but, on Laura's joining with her host and hostess to persuade him, consented. Although I longed to hear him, I held my peace. From among Mrs. Deveraux's music, he extracted a sheet. But then he turned to me.

"Miss Rochester," he said, quite formally, bowing to me from where he stood, "May I ask you to accompany me? I know the strength of your performance."

I was disconcerted. I wished merely to stay in the background and listen. But meeting those black eyes and hearing as always in his speech that echo of my father's voice, I complied. I looked at the music. The tune was by Tchaikovsky, the words by Goethe. The song was named "None But the Lonely Heart."

None but the lonely heart
Can know my sadness.
Alone am I and far
From joy and gladness.
My senses fail,
A burning fire devours me …
None but the lonely heart
Can know my sadness.

His voice was deep and true, the song poignant. I knew the poem, though not the music. I was caught up by the words, which echoed my deepest feelings. My fingers executed their duty mechanically while my heart wept inwardly for all that I might have lost—"*none but the lonely heart can know my sadness.*" These last words hung in the air after the piano had died away. Oh, how true, how true, I thought. Was he, too, an isolate, an onlooker as I was at the dance of life?

A half hour later, as the evening drew to a close, he sang again a duet with Laura of an English country favourite, "Barbara Allen," lightening in some sense the mood of the evening, though the song told of a heartless beauty whose lover dies for want of a kind word.

Laura's clear voice blended in a descant with Mr. Landless's *baritone*. The two voices curled smoothly around each other. I listened in enchanted silence.

Soon after, we made our farewells. All three of us were quiet on the journey home.

CHAPTER EIGHT

The Dark of the Night and the Light of the Day

"Jane, will you have a flower?"

He gathered a half-blown rose . . .

◁ JANE EYRE ▷

*D*AYS AND WEEKS WENT by, scarcely distinguishable. I moved with unthinking precision through such tasks as I had.

I did not sleep well. My sleeping habits changed with the coming of Captain Harcourt and his ill tidings. I woke often in the small hours and lay unsleeping, listening to the silence as the minutes ticked by. My thoughts ran in circles, around and around. "*Drowned. Lost at sea.* Oh, my fath …" Lost, but *not* drowned, I told myself. *Not necessarily drowned.* Hope on. Sometimes I rose and lit my candle and read the small hours away. The great dark house was, as a rule, silent as a sepulchre at night, and there was little to disturb me until bird song and servant activity stirred the morning echoes. Sometimes an owl hooted, a nightjar called harshly. A rabbit caught by a stoat or fox gave a desperate squeal. I was aware that Colonel Dent went to bed late, but his bedroom was in the main section of the house, close to the grand staircase; he did not affect the tenants in the West Wing. Mr. Landless's room was nearest the East Wing. Pilot slept, as always, on a mat at my bedroom door. Sometimes I woke to hear him stretch and scratch, rhythmically drumming on the panels of the oak door; once or twice I thought I woke to voices, but when I listened, there was nothing. I heard no more laughs or small footfalls.

I find from my journal that it was some four or five weeks later that I was again disturbed at night. Pilot barked at my door, and a soft voice shushed him. He barked again, not aggressively; it was what I should call his friendly bark.

This was not at all usual at night, and I went to him, throwing a shawl hastily about my shoulders.

When I opened my door, I did not at first descry him. I called in a low voice. I had no wish to disturb Laura. A half moon peering through the windows gave pale light to the scene. I heard the grandfather clock in the hall beneath strike two as I explored the passage to right and left. The tapestries were moving with a life more robust than any draft could impart. I called again, and Pilot appeared from behind the nearest hanging, poking out his head and peering at me in a way too young for his age and dignity. Not that Pilot was old—some seven years—but puppyhood was long behind him. Now he seemed playful; he wagged his tail at me and pranced a short way along the passage, looking back at me, then gazing into the darkness. I snapped my fingers at him, bidding him return, but he did not obey. I went up to him, put my hand on his collar, and let him pull me towards the grand staircase. Did something move in the shadows ahead of me; did some pale draperies stir? Surely there was movement? I stood still, listening, waiting. I was puzzled but not afraid, not with Pilot by my side.

Pilot tugged at my hand, eager to continue, and I walked on, conscious of the ancient smell of stone and dust, of the drafts rising from the main hall stirring the tapestry, of the roughness of the matting beneath my bare feet. This way led to the East Wing. I had an eerie sense of being perhaps not quite alone. And an alien scent impinged on my nostrils, faint but insistent. Surely not incense? Was some ghostly nun at large in Highcrest Manor? Then, at the end of the passage ahead of me, the entrance to the East Wing, I heard a door close. It was quite distinct; there could be no doubt. I stopped dead. Had I really seen a figure at that last moment, small and bent, dark-haired and robed in white, disappearing through the door? Pilot whined and tugged. He was not alarmed; he did not growl, and the hair on his neck stayed smooth. Quickening my pace, I made my way to the door. It was closed. It was locked. Pilot whined again and scrabbled at the threshold.

"Hush, Pilot," I said. "We must go back."

I turned, pulling at his collar, and at that moment a door along the passage opened abruptly. Mr. Landless stood there, wearing a dark red velvet dressing gown pulled loosely over his nightshirt. His neckband was open over his chest; his hair was tousled. He held a lighted candle in a pewter candlestick. We stared at each other with equal surprise and embarrassment.

"Miss Rochester!" he cried. "What has happened? Are you ill?"

"No, oh no," I said. "I am so sorry to disturb you. Pilot was restless. We thought we heard a noise, he and I, someone moving ... I was investigating."

"The servants have been long abed," he said in a matter-of-fact tone, adjusting his collar. "Perhaps Pilot encountered a mouse?"

I was suddenly conscious of my thin lawn nightgown under the shawl—I had not stopped to pull on my own robe.

And my hair hung in its long, thick nighttime braid over my shoulder—his eyes lingered on it, then fell to my feet.

"You will take cold," he said all of a sudden, his deep voice low, a little unsteady. "Your feet are bare."

I blushed. I seemed to feel his gaze warm on my feet. I looked up and met his eyes. My heart felt tight in my breast. Then the clock struck the quarter hour. I shivered, sharply aware that I was standing, in the small hours of the night, alone and in my nightgown with Mr. Landless.

"Forgive me, I did not m-mean to awaken you," I stammered, pulling my eyes from his. "Come, Pilot."

And I turned and fled back to my room. Pilot collapsed on the floor at my door with a deep and tragic sigh, which I could only echo as I shut myself into my bedroom and clambered once more into bed, only to lie awake, running the scene once more through my mind, feeling Mr. Landless's gaze once more on my bare feet.

My mother had done her best to erase all vanity from my nature, yet I could not but be aware that my feet were slim and shapely. (Paulina had praised them; her own were marred by bunions. I was thankful that my mother's strictures had denied me tight, fashionable boots as a girl.)

One night, as I lay awake thinking over this happening (for it lingered oddly in my mind), it occurred to me that these nighttime incidents echoed strangely those of which my mother had written in *her* journal. When she was first living at Thornfield, as governess, she had heard on occasion a strange disturbing laugh. Eventually the presence of a

madwoman living in the attic was revealed to my mother. All
the servants had known about this but were sworn to secrecy.
What no one had known was that she was, in fact, Mrs.
Rochester, my father's first wife.

This strange, old story filled my mind. Surely there could
not be someone similarly hidden away here, creeping out at
night? But then I remembered Pilot. I felt a strong reliance in
Pilot's judgment, foolish perhaps, but then he was, after all,
part of my past. Whatever—whoever—it was, to him it was
a friend, a playmate, even. Was it one of the maids who liked
to explore at night? This did not seem likely, given Mrs.
Brotherhood's stern management of the household. But who
else? Who hid in the locked and shuttered East Wing?

And then there was the question of the laugh: that first
innocent, childish chuckle. Just as I was sinking into sleep, a
memory jarred me. What was it Laura had said weeks before
about Annie and the servants, the reluctance to let in
strangers, the high walls and locked gates? "There is some
mystery at Highcrest Manor." We had intended to investigate, but over the weeks and with the interest of Mr. Landless's arrival, we had lost sight of our purpose. But it seemed
it was true after all. And my midnight intruders were part of
it. I slept at last, tired out by my puzzlings.

I told Laura of the sounds in the night and my glimpse of
someone entering the East Wing, but I did not mention my
nighttime encounter with Mr. Landless. I was reluctant to
discuss this meeting with her. I felt I had been immodest and
feared she might reproach me. However, she and I continued

to explore the grounds, eyeing the flint walls and locked gates with frustration. The Colonel and I had long resumed amicable relations; he showed me great consideration over my parents' shipwreck. I wrote to Mr. Briggs and he to me, and I knew I had entered the contingency phase of his instructions. But I was, as I already knew, to remain at High-crest Manor until my twenty-first birthday. (And never did I let myself lose hope that my parents would return. I knew I could trust Mr. Briggs to make every endeavour to gain information from the Indies.) The Colonel and I dealt well enough, but he seemed to find it easier to talk to Laura. She liked him, I knew. Laura and I grew closer; she was the sister I had never had. Mr. Landless remained an enigma. He had retreated since our late night encounter. I still on occasion thought, alone in my bed, of his dark eyes and tumbled hair, of the smooth pale skin of his neck, protected from the sun, where it ran down to meet his chest, and of the low pitch of his voice. And I felt again the warmth of his gaze on my feet. But I recalled, as best I could, my mother's strictures and exerted self-discipline.

Life was, in most ways, uneventful. But not completely. I found new interest in studying my companions. And, as I grew accustomed to Roderick Landless's presence, I grew braver.

One day in the library I found, among Mrs. Dent's collection, a book by an author known only by name to me, the Russian Pushkin in an English translation. The book's story was told in poetry. It was fat, battered, much read, it seemed, and the title was *Eugene Onegin*. It told a story of a shy young girl who falls in love with an older man—a guest in her house, a man of the world, almost a stranger. Ardent, unused to the ways of Society, she declares her love in a letter written from her heart. I read her words with an empathy I had seldom before felt for the written word: "*My soul had heard your voice ring clear,*" she wrote. "*I stirred at your gaze, so strange, so gleaming,*" then, "*all in a blaze, I said: it's he!*" She tells him, "*My heart awaits you: you can turn it to life and hope with just a glance.*" Onegin rejects her with some condescension, treating her as a child.

The story resounded deep inside me. I read on eagerly, my sympathies engaged. When Mr. Landless entered the library and seated himself at the desk, I looked up with a start, jerked out of my inner world. He did not seem to notice me, and I continued where I was, the book loose in my hands, watching him. He settled himself at his desk and began to write in a big ledgerlike book, keeping some sort of record. Around him, the desk was strewn with open books. I found myself frowning as I regarded him across the room. He was an enigma, his likeness to my father a riddle I could not make out.

"You examine me, Miss Rochester," the quiet, deep voice cut into my reverie. "Do you admire my person?"

Was there a hint of laughter in those dark, intense eyes? I felt I was being mocked. Colour sprang hot to my cheeks, and my reply was curt. "You resemble someone I know. It puzzles me." I closed my book—I would show it to Laura and finish it later—and turned back to the shelves, finding myself by the collection of gardening books. There were gaps in the collection now, and I guessed that the missing books were those surrounding Mr. Landless.

"May I enquire the name of that someone?"

"I think not." I changed the subject abruptly. "Are you interested in gardening, Mr. Landless? I recognize some of your collection of books. My father also owns them." Even as I spoke, I realized my mind had played a trick on me; I had not changed the subject after all. My father was still to the fore of my thoughts.

"Your father is very important to you, Miss Rochester, is he not?"

The unexpectedness of his query shook my self-control. Tears stung my gaze. I blinked them hurriedly away. "He has always been my great and dear friend," I said.

Mr. Landless smiled at me. The smile changed his whole face. There was no mockery now. "You are lucky indeed," he said, and his sincerity was obvious. "And you are right. I *am* interested in gardening. Perhaps you too have read some of these books?"

"Yes," I said. "Some." And then, with newfound bravery inspired by his kindness, I asked him a question. "Is this an active occupation of yours, Mr. Landless? My father used to say that this is the age of gardening. But I see no new design at Highcrest. And no flowers or flowering shrubs. I hunger for colour as I walk the grounds. Do you perhaps experiment behind stone walls?"

There was silence for a slow moment or two. "Yes, you have guessed right, Miss Rochester. I take an active interest in gardening. I find it most rewarding. The Colonel and I have experimental gardens within closed walls. His interest is not, perhaps, as deep as mine. But he encourages me. The wind is so strong and the climate so bleak in this part of Yorkshire, close as we are to the moors, that it is necessary to create a more sheltered situation for tender plants."

"And are they private as well as sheltered? I should be most interested to see your work, your experiments, if that did not displease you."

"This is now your home, Miss Rochester, your own sheltered situation—for the winds of the world blow coldly on you; you are cut off from your parents, your rightful protectors, and in need of tender care. I am sure Colonel Dent would wish me to show you anything within reason."

Within reason! That was an odd stipulation. (His reference to my need for tender care also struck me as odd from such a detached man. I should think about it later.) But I had made an advance and was anxious not to lose any advantage. "I should indeed like to see your garden, Mr. Landless. It would interest me greatly—and Laura, too, Miss Alleyn, would be delighted. I hope you have flowers. There is, as I have said, a marked absence of colour in the Highcrest grounds."

He closed his ledger and stood up. "If you should care to join me?"

"With pleasure, Mr. Landless. I shall fetch Laura."

I used a scrap of paper as a bookmark and laid my poem on the library table; then I went swiftly from the library in search of Laura. I had left her in our sitting room, trying over a song. She was no longer there and not in her bedroom. Downstairs again I looked in the drawing room and out on the terrace. Laura was not to be seen. Then, as I walked along the passage, I heard voices from the Colonel's study. He was seated at his desk, seemingly cleaning a shotgun, but his cloth and rod were in front of him, his hands idle. All his attention was on Laura, seated before him. She ceased to speak as I entered. She gazed up at him with animation. They both looked at me, as I entered, with similar expressions. They seemed disconcerted. I was much struck. I knew the Colonel admired Laura. She was more to his taste than I, always neat in her attire, her fair hair smooth, her voice gentle. She would never deserve his reprimand for being "unwomanly." And she, having no reason to resent his authority, did not find it hard to be at ease in his company. Her father had been such another gruff old gentleman, she said. For the first time, I wondered if a deeper attraction would develop. He was some thirty years her senior, but it would be a fine thing for Laura from a practical point of view. And I was learning to think of the practical.

"Forgive my interruption, Colonel," I said. "Mr. Landless has offered to show us his flower gardens. Laura, I think you would be interested?"

Laura's face lit up. "I should indeed," she said. "Perhaps we may continue our conversation later, Colonel Dent? I hope so."

He inclined his head, taking up his ramrod. He did not frown, but his face was watchful.

"What were you discussing so earnestly," I asked, as we traversed the passage to a side door.

"Life in India. The Colonel's stories are most interesting."

"Stories of battles? Of army life?"

"Of army life, yes, but the small facts of everyday life. Of encampment, but also of houses and servants, so many servants. People born to that pitiless sun, that debilitating heat, have little stamina, he says, so many must be employed to do what one or two would do in England. It is the custom. He speaks with great affection of his soldiers—Pathans, he calls them— but he regards them, these short, dark-skinned men, as children over whom he needed to watch with a fatherly eye. Yes, that is how he sees himself, as a father, dealing out law and justice to those inferior to himself.

"And he talks of the clothes the English must wear: helmets to block the sun, puttees wrapped around their legs to guard against snakes. And food. Exotic fruit—mangos, mangosteens, kumquats, rambutans—such strange names. Chutneys and curries that set one's throat on fire. And screens at windows against stinging insects, mosquito nets draped over beds at night. There is much fever to guard against. Strange customs, Janet. And the wildlife! Elephants used as mounts for travel, tigers to beware of on those journeys, monkeys that scream and chatter and come close to the houses to steal. Scorpions! Imagine, Janet, and centipedes lurking in the shadows in one's shoes; one must shake them out each morning before thrusting in one's toes. And snakes, even in the house! Snakes in one's bathroom. Imagine that!"

Yes, I thought. That would interest Laura. For all her intellect, she was a domesticated woman, accomplished with her needle, appreciative of everything that made a comfortable home in England or abroad. She had not my restlessness, my need for action, for keen exercise and employment. She was indeed a womanly woman, and that presumably was what a man admired and sought—allied, of course, with a sufficiency of comeliness to please his eye. For some reason I sighed, then I brightened as we joined Mr. Landless on the terrace. He looked very much alive that morning, standing, like my father, a head taller than I, his black, curling hair shining in the sunshine and ruffled by the breeze, his dark eyes glinting. He led us across the lawns and through the shrubbery to a wooden door we had often noted (had indeed tried to open), hinged and barred with iron, in one of the ubiquitous flint stone walls.

He unlocked the door with a large iron key from a bunch that had been dragging down one of the many pockets of his Norfolk jacket and stood back to let us enter.

We entered another world.

It was late June, that month of roses, and perfume came in gusts to greet us. Roses bloomed everywhere, sheltered from the wind, protected from storms, in every shade of pink to deepest crimson, some single, some with layer on layer of petals like a multitude of silken petticoats. Some were white, many were yellow, deepening to peach. *Gloire de Dijon, Maréchal Niel, Cromoisi Supérieur, Stanwell Perpetual*... Mr. Landless named them one by one. Some were from Persia, some from China, some from Japan. Some were indigenous to Yorkshire— simple, single roses these, fiercely scented. They bloomed on bushes and on walls, climbing over arches that led on through other internal walls to other cultivated beds. The scent was dizzying, and so too, surprisingly, was the sound—of bees busy at their work in those perfumed hearts of paradise. My head swam. I took Laura's arm; for a moment, I thought I might faint in that enclosed, magical place, alone with my friend and this man who resembled my lost father, who was, like him, larger than life, and who bent his intent gaze on me, eager, it seemed, for my reaction, my approval.

We exclaimed, we were enraptured, we bent our heads to breath in the soul-disturbing scent. Laura lifted a radiant face.

"You are a magician, Mr. Landless. You have conjured a southern paradise out of your northern fastness."

"Roses are a hardy race, Miss Alleyn. With proper care, pruned and mulched, they survive the long northern winters, the sharp northern frosts. Think of the Wars of the Roses and the wild rose of Lancashire. They belong as much to the rugged north as to the more indulgent south. They grow here readily enough, even in the hedgerows. It is the wind from the moors that batters them, tears them apart, blows their petals to the four corners of the earth before one is ready to part with them. So I protect them."

I had been silent in my appreciation. He turned now from Laura to me. "And you, Miss Rochester? Do you share your companion's raptures? Do my roses appeal to your warrior spirit as they do to her gentle heart?" His eyes met mine.

I was startled and provoked. Once again I thought he mocked me. But was that really how he saw me, contrasted with Laura, as a warrior, combatant and defiant? Unfeminine? Wild and reckless? I made haste to defend myself in speech.

"They are superb, Mr. Landless. And unexpected. If I was silent, it was because my raptures took time to express themselves in words. My appreciation was immediate and inward." I took a deep breath. "But I fear you overrate my strength to call me 'warrior.' No *Boadicea*, I. My parents encouraged me to walk and ride, as well as to read and learn and study music, so I might face the world on my own feet, with a head held high. I am willing to leave the physical battles to men while reserving my right to defend what is mine."

"To defend what is yours. That I can well believe, Miss Rochester. You are proud. You would not willingly give up a birthright."

I turned from his searching eyes. He put me on the defensive. I did not understand him. There seemed some hidden meaning in his words. Once again I was faced with the mystery: Who was he? What did the word "birthright" mean to him, whose name was "Landless?" For the first time, I allowed myself consciously to wonder, was he—surely he must be—kin to the Rochesters, and therefore my relation? But a robin landed on the wall and eyed us with a cocked head. I smiled to see it. There were small birds rustling among the violas and pansies that grew around the feet of the roses. Butterflies, as well as bees, flickered from flower to flower. It was indeed an earthly paradise. Man, with his problems, was the intruder.

I pondered later over his assessment of me. Was it based on our first encounter? Or perhaps my opposition to Colonel

Dent? I remembered thinking, while Colonel Dent upbraided me, that someone else was in the room. Had he watched there in the shadows? Did they discuss me? Did he, like the Colonel, find me "unwomanly?" Did all men value the conformable in woman, the meek and biddable? But then, thinking of Laura, I remembered her determination, her willingness to change her own life, her defiance of her uncle. She, no more than I, was to be judged by outward appearances, by first impressions. The man who deemed her docile would be wrong. We were neither of us meek and biddable, but nor was I an Amazon out to make war on mankind.

After that introduction, we joined Mr. Landless many times as he worked in his gardens, directing the gardeners in their labours but also himself joining in manual endeavours with some enjoyment when he thought fit. He was a different man working in his rose garden, his hair tousled, perhaps a smudge of earth on his cheek. He did not look nearly so grim. Laura liked to learn the names of the roses, and he seemed to find pleasure in teaching her. Sometimes she brought her needlework. I took up my old hobby of sketches from nature. Sprays of rosebuds and pansies blossomed under my pencil, and thorny twigs took eccentric shape. Fragments of stone wall, enhanced by entwined roses and clematis, were captured in my sketchbook. He admired my work and encouraged me to draw his roses, saying the sketches would be of use to him in his record keeping. I was pleased indeed at his praise.

Those were enchanted days. The sun shone. The gardens grew daily in beauty and we in health, spending so much of our time out-of-doors in the good Yorkshire air. We talked a little, not much; we were all occupied. We laughed together. Laura and I felt we knew him better. My fears for my parents receded a little with this pleasant companionship.

One day I sat near him, sketching, as he trained a climbing rose against a wall, pruning and tying the thorny branches to staples he hammered into the mortar. Laura had returned to the house, needing more silk for her embroidery. I was lost in a daydream of my parents, returned and with me in that sunlit afternoon, all of us together, my new friends and my old, and I started and dropped my pencil when he spoke to me.

"You told me once, Miss Rochester, that your father was your dear friend. An unusual wording that stayed in my mind, orphan that I am. What kind of man was he, your father?"

Like you, I thought. I temporized. "A strong man," I said, "in mind and body. He liked to work, as you do, with his hand—for he has but one. The other was injured in a fire and had to be amputated. He is widely read, despite his weakened sight. My mother read to him each day. In his youth he has travelled widely, and he had many interests. But he would also join my brother and me in our activities. He rode well, and it was he who taught me, when I was young, to love horses."

"And your mother?"

"She is very different, not so robust. But energetic and enterprising. She is difficult to describe; there is no one like her."

"She was his second wife, I have been given to understand?"

"Yes." So he knew something of my parents' history.

"But he had no children by his first wife?"

"No." Was my manner too curt? I wanted suddenly to acquaint Mr. Landless with something of the flavour of my parents' marriage. "They are all in all to each other, my mother and father. They are seldom apart. I think my mother would follow my father through hell itself, if he were dispatched to that fiery pit. And he would brave any danger to keep her safe. That is why ..." I faltered suddenly. My feelings threatened to overcome me. "That is why I am sure they are together, wherever they are. One could not live without the other."

There were tears in my eyes. I looked down at my sketch of the flint wall and the roses. I blinked.

"You draw a remarkable picture, Miss Rochester." I looked up, and his eyes dropped to my sketchbook. "I envy you your parents. And I envy them their devotion." There was something harsh in his voice, a constriction of the throat perhaps? Or had I in some way disturbed him?

Laura came through the archway and rejoined us. Mr. Landless picked up his pruning shears and moved away. Our conversation was at an end.

❖ ❖ ❖

But still, Laura and I decided, conferring in our sitting room, all was not yet revealed to us. The rose gardens were now open, as were the kitchen gardens, with fruit trees espaliered on the old flint walls and raspberries and red currants growing in protected beds, as well as vegetables. We saw the glasshouses and experimental seedbeds and sheds. But we did not wander there unaccompanied. We could not be sure we had seen all.

I must confess I often thought about Roderick Landless when I was alone. More and more, he intruded on my thoughts. He came insistently into my mind, my daydreams, my dreams at night. But he was a stranger still. I remembered Paulina when she spoke of her feelings for Evelyn Trent, of whom she knew so little. I had kept my reaction to myself, but I had wondered at the way she endowed him with every virtue on the strength of regular features, a pleasant smile, good manners. I had felt in some way superior. Now, what of me? How much did I know of Roderick Landless that went beyond appearances to allow him so to engage my thoughts? He was intelligent. He was well read. He liked to be occupied. He rejoiced in hard manual work, which he did not need to do, just as my father did. They both had strength and energy that demanded to be used in ways not considered appropriate for a gentleman. Mr. Landless was creative in his gardening, in the plants he propagated. He loved colour and scent and form. He was silent; away from his roses, his moods were sometimes grim.

All this certainly amounted to something. But I knew little of his inner character—could he be counted a good man? And in whose sense (for certainly my mother's views and my father's would differ on this point)? Was he generous? Had he humour? How much did this mean to me?

One day, as I fetched Nimbus from the stables for my daily ride, I found Mr. Landless there in his riding clothes. We visited the moors together. We talked little, but when I suggested he join me again, he accepted. And this became a habit.

The weeks went by. July unfolded, and then it was August. Sir Hugo and his sister were in Scotland, we heard, for the grouse shooting. They had not yet paid the return visit that was their due.

There was no fresh news of my parents.

One late morning, Laura and I lingered together in the drawing room. She had been arranging flowers and was moving her vases from place to place to see where each looked best. The June roses were over, the late bloomers not yet out, but Mr. Landless had brought her lupines, carnations, delphiniums, and other summer blooms. He was standing by the piano, idly fingering the keys while I gave most of my attention to Laura, when Colonel Dent entered the library dressed for riding.

"Ah, there you are, Rory," he said. "I ran into an old acquaintance of yours in Millcote. Isabella Ingram. She is back from London and was riding with her brother. She made haste to enquire after you—you were always a favourite." He smiled in an indulgent fashion, not at all like himself, I thought. "A charming girl," he went on. "Eh, Roderick? Grown to be quite a beauty. Wilful as ever. Her horse was too strong for her; she needed her brother's hand on the reins when a dog barked or a cart rumbled."

I laughed. I was reminded strongly of the day in Hyde Park.

"Oh, are you there, Janet? Miss Ingram also wished to be remembered to you. She said you met in town. She talks of holding a ball at Ingram Park within the month, for her eighteenth birthday. Her mother is introducing her to Society. I gather she will be sending you both an invitation."

"They are not a family for which I have much respect. Young Ingram is a wastrel," said Mr. Landless repressively, his mouth a grim line.

"She will be an heiress, so they say. Lord Ingram has made money overseas."

Mr. Landless shrugged. The Colonel gave him a quick hard look, started to speak, coughed, and changed the subject. He began to talk of harvesting on the Home Farm.

I stayed silent. I had no wish to reencounter Isabella Ingram, and I could not believe she was anxious for my company. But the subject that exercised my mind was Isabella's acquaintanceship with Roderick Landless. He, a favourite of hers? And the Colonel reminding him of Isabella's expectations? All this startled me. But of course, he must be acquainted with the County families.

And did other people, then, note and comment on his likeness to my father? Here was something else for me to ponder in those dark and wakeful nights.

CHAPTER NINE

A Ball at Ingram Park

The long cloud of gentlemen . . . mixed with the rainbow line of ladies.

⊰ VILLETTE ⊱

THE INVITATION CARDS FOR Isabella Ingram's birthday ball were lettered in gold: the *pleasure of my company* was requested for a date two weeks ahead. There was a card for the Colonel and one for Mr. Landless. Laura was not included. This last I regretted, but it was not unexpected—she was, after all, an employee and not therefore considered an equal by local Society. I did not expect to find much enjoyment at Ingram Park, and Laura's company would have been compensation. Besides, I was always anxious to have her known by a wider range of society. Her ladylike appearance, personal attractions, and sweet voice needed to be more widely exposed; I thought I would enjoy finding her a suitable husband. This urge gave me some secret amusement; she was older than I, yet I felt towards her as if I were a matchmaking mama.

She herself was not dismayed at her exclusion. She was used to the ways of Society.

Annie was delighted that an opportunity had come for me to wear one of my fashionable London-made gowns. I often found her airing them and smoothing them with her fingers, delighting in the feel of silk against her skin. I had decided long since that if a suitable occasion occurred—a betrothal, perhaps? —I should make her a present of one of them. (I had seen her often talking and laughing with Albert Higgins. But Milly Allnut also seemed to enjoy his company. Albert, the Cockney, was freer in his approach to the opposite sex and a livelier conversationalist than the reticent Yorkshire-born stable hands.) Now I had her take them out of the wardrobe, and one by one I held them against me. In the end, I decided on the sea-green watered silk, a subtle blending of blues and greens with a shine of silver in the folds where they caught the light. It was cut low in front, a fashion that no longer embarrassed me. The bodice was swathed at the nipped-in waist and decorated with seed pearls; the skirt was full, the fullness swept mainly to the back in the newest London style; a short train trailed me. I was glad it was no longer necessary to wear a full crinoline "cage" of whalebone with straps over the shoulders. Paulina had shown me one her mother had worn only a few years earlier. My dress demanded a farthingale petticoat: a boned half cage, attached at the waist, over which went two other petticoats of taffeta, which rustled appealingly. The hem of the skirt was caught up in scallops, low in front, higher behind, showing the deep, pleated ruffle of my underskirt in a stiff pearl-coloured silk. An edging of the same pleated silk decorated the *décolleté* neckline. With this I should wear my mother's pearl necklace, and a brooch made of a circlet of pearls would ornament my hair. I had no plan to change my hairstyle, but this was taken out of my hands. Annie began experimenting with my hair, saying that my simple everyday style was not suitable for so grand an ensemble. She had, she told me, aglow with pride, paid close attention to the methods of Jeanne-Marie, Mrs. Deveraux's haughty French maid, and by judicious flattery and meek offers of help had persuaded that aloof personage to teach her some of the tricks of her trade. She swept my hair up off my neck in bands and braids and chignons, trying several effects before she decided on the one she claimed suited me best. Laura, too, took great interest in my adornment.

Ingram Park was some ten miles from the Manor. We were expected there at nine o'clock, and at a quarter to eight I came downstairs, a black velvet cloak draped over my bare shoulders. It was indeed a splendid night; the moon was full, the air balmy, and the perfume from the night-scented stock, pinks and mignonette in the little flower bed Mr. Landless had, at our persuasion, planted in front of the wall leading to the rose garden, wafted through the open front door into the hall. Laura and Annie had pored over me as if I were the latest member of a harem being arrayed for the pleasure of the Sultan! I felt strongly that my mother would have disapproved, and yet, when all was done and I was guided to my place in front of the cheval mirror, I could not help most desperately wishing that she—and my father—were there to see me, rescued from that unknown fate, restored to life and me—*but oh, they were not dead, they were not dead* ... Two years before, I was but a school-girl. They never did see me in full regalia, dressed for a ball. Would they even have recognized me? Would my father be proud of his bluestocking, outré daughter, civilized and groomed? Would my mother approve, even smile at me, rejoicing in my grown-up self? *They* would not expect me to be dressed in black. Tears filled my eyes, but I blinked them away. This was no time for such self-indulgence.

My summer at the Manor, with my daily rides, walks with Laura, and work in the gardens (despite my attempts to protect my complexion from the sun), had left my fair skin a warmer ivory and had flushed my cheeks with rose. My light-brown hair, gilded by that same sun with a touch of gold, was brushed till it shone like satin. Annie had not tried to eradicate my waves and curls. She piled my hair high, with a braided chignon at the back of my head and in front a collection of soft curls and waves, like (I felt) the decoration on an iced cake, above a small curled fringe. The style was sufficiently different from my daily wear to cause me to hold my head high in automatic compensation for the gentle, unaccustomed weight. My pearl brooch was centred above my brow; my pearl necklace glimmered against my skin. Laura had insisted on lending me three slender gold bangles for my left wrist, worn over my long ivory gloves, and, on my right hand, I wore my mother's emerald ring. My appearance startled me. This haughty damsel, all pearl and sea-foam like Hans Christian Andersen's "Little Mermaid," was a stranger, for my skin took on the glow of mother-of-pearl and my eyes lost their shadow and echoed my dress.

"Oh, Miss Janet. You look a right beauty!" said Annie, sitting back on her heels on the carpet and clasping her hands in self-congratulation as she arranged the folds of my skirt.

Laura said nothing. She just smiled at me and kissed my cheek.

And now I swept downstairs, quite taken out of my normal self and parading as to the manner born. There was perhaps a touch of defiance in my attitude; would the Colonel look at me with disapproval? The two men waiting below, in their formal black and white, with ruffled shirts and patent-leather evening slippers, stared up at me. The Colonel was about to smoke a cigar. He held it between his fingers, his lips parted as if he were about to insert it but had lost his way. Mr. Landless was in shadow. He moved abruptly, and I saw his black eyes gleam in the massed light of the candelabra. For a moment he held my gaze, and then he began to insert his fingers into his gloves and found suddenly that this task was all absorbing.

The carriage was at the door. I could hear the horses stamp and snort. We made our way outside. I sat next to Colonel Dent, managed my skirts, and tried to command my thoughts. Mr. Landless sat opposite me. I had no great expectation of pleasure from the evening. To dance a little, to talk a little—with Sir Hugo, possibly, and his sister—not to be too conspic-uously a wallflower. I did not expect to like the Ingrams.

We were a little late, and the reception rooms were full of people. We greeted our hosts. Lord and Lady Ingram stared at me in haughty surprise. Isabella, in virginal white satin and lace, her skirt a huge bell and with diamonds at her throat and ears, smiled sweetly and told me I had changed. Her eyes moved on immediately from my face to Mr. Landless. "You, too, have become a stranger. You must not be so," she said in dulcet tones.

Most of those present I did not recognize. Mr. and Mrs. Eshton, down from Scotland and staying with one of their married daughters, were present with that daughter, her husband, and her eldest children. Sir George and Lady Lynn and their family, sons Frederick and Henry, with their wives and older offspring, were familiar, and we exchanged greetings. The news of my parents' shipwreck was, of course, known in the County. The Eshtons took time to sympathize with me, and I warmed to their kindness. Lady Lynn, as stout and as haughty as ever, condescended to pat my hand. Colonel Dent began to introduce me to those who came to greet him—he, of course, was recognized by all. I saw some surprise—a raised eyebrow here, a pursed mouth there—as my identity became known. A dowager, plump with the artificial importance of inherited wealth, raked me with her lorgnette. (I heard one acid comment: "The Rochester gel? And at a ball? Not even half-mournin'! Typical of the family!") Several men frankly stared. Sir Hugo and Mrs. Deveraux came up to speak with me.

The dancing began, and my hand was requested at once by Henry Lynn. To my surprise, a steady stream of partners came my way. Early on, Sir Hugo claimed me. We waltzed, and he danced expertly, a notable partner. He talked to me of Thornfield, of the fine workmanship and noble architecture, and he asked about the historic Thornfield, some two hundred-years-old, which had burned to the ground. He talked well, and he interested me. Indeed, he seemed to have come armed with subjects that would engage my attention, praising our butler Barley and the staff. He held me firmly but not overclose; I was constrained to follow his movements, but his person did not intrude on me. I was always on guard with Sir Hugo, though I knew not why. His every move and statement seemed worked out in advance, and now I felt sure he exerted exactly as much pressure on my waist as would control me but not alarm me. The dance was pleasant, but I could not relax with Sir Hugo.

Other partners followed, but most of all I was waiting for one, and one alone, and eventually he came, moving easily through the people surrounding me, making his presence felt. Mr. Landless bowed over my hand then led me onto the floor. The dance was a mazurka. I had learned it but had never danced it in public. The music was insistent, the rhythm demanding; my blood pulsed in time with its beat. I turned and swayed at his command, my skirt billowing behind me. There was a deep pleasure at surrendering to his will, which had been quite absent in my reaction to Sir Hugo. A memory surfaced in my mind of my old forbidden fantasy of being held in my father's arms at night as my mother was, closely, closely. I felt the blood rise to my cheeks. I forced myself to stay in the present and, unexpectedly, I began to enjoy myself, mind and body, wholly, in a way that rarely happened in my life—oh, sometimes on my wilder rides—watcher that I was, I was not often a partaker.

I ate supper with my own party, with some additions in the form of young men. The conversation was lively, though my part in it was small. Quite some fuss was made of me by others. Mrs. Deveraux spoke openly of the evening as *my* social introduction as much as Isabella's. She was looking sumptuous in violet satin, and a diamond tiara flashed brilliantly in her hair. An amethyst and diamond necklace circled her throat, and her earrings matched the necklace. A handsome diamond ring sparkled on her right hand. But despite her almost regal appearance, she was not aloof but was at her most persuasive, as charming in her speech as in her looks. She insisted on introducing me to every man who hovered in sight, much like a matchmaking mama. Oh, she puzzled me, that woman, with her changing moods and manners. She was much sought after by the older men present. One of my earlier partners had spoken of her, calling her "the Viking princess" and "the ice maiden." He admired from a distance, he said; he was too nervous to approach her.

When the dancing began again, my hand was in demand. I became aware of something akin to rivalry between Sir Hugo and Mr. Landless in their requests for my company. Isabella intruded herself on my party, arranging the country dances so that she and her partner were next to me and mine. She made laughing, teasing remarks that invited Mr. Landless's complicity in memories from which I was excluded. At one in the morning, she requested a certain waltz from the band of the Light Horse, which was playing that evening. She returned to us, holding out her hands, demanding Mr. Landless's partnership. "This we have danced before," she said, lifting her eyes to him, all fluttering lashes, honeyed tongue. "The Blue Danube."

"Then I regret that I am already engaged," he said. She flushed deeply. I believe Paul Eshton requested her hand; I ceased to think of her. The music began, and Mr. Landless swung me onto the floor to the strains of the popular waltz imported from Vienna a year or so before. As I circled in Roderick Landless's strong arms, I saw Isabella pass by. Her eyes met mine with what I could only deem a glance of hatred. A shiver brushed like an icy finger down the nape of my neck. But Roderick's eyes were my world. His warm hand was holding mine, and his arm encircled my waist. The music caught us up and flung us unheeding into the lilting passion of its rhythm.

Some fifteen minutes later, we stood by the open terrace door, thankful for the cooling effect of the light night breeze. An apricot moon, looking as if it would fill a reaching hand like a ripe fruit, beamed at us from just above the horizon. "Goddess of the night," said Roderick, just audible above the beating of my heart. I was still exhilarated from that last wild dance. "A true harvest moon," I responded, glancing at him, but his eyes were not on the horizon; they were on me. His face was very grave, not at all flirtatious. We stayed that way, looking into each other's eyes. His hands were on my arms, and he turned me towards him. The moment caught itself up into some timeless space, some other world far away from this earth. I could not speak; I could not look away. I was as still beneath his hands as my mother had been when I watched my father caress her.

A voice jarred us out of our intimate silence; Isabella Ingram's voice. Shrubbery encroached on each side of the terrace, directing the gaze towards the far vista. Narrow paths wound among the bushes. She was not visible, but her voice carried clearly.

"I can assure you, he is much admired, Sir Hugo, among the damsels of the village."

"But not by you?"

"Oh, he is very entertaining. We always include him in our gatherings—he dances well, plays cards, rides, and shoots. But he is not, shall I say, quite one of us. *Un peu farouche?* So we pull the strings, and he springs into life for our entertainment. And then he goes back in his box." She laughed, a thin, tinkling trill like a cracked soprano bell.

"His family is not of the best? Is he not related to Colonel Dent?" A trickle of cigar smoke, pungent and familiar, reached us from the shrubbery.

"Why no, indeed. Colonel Dent has taken pity on him, they say. And I believe he is very good at his—er—situation. But his father is not known, though it is not hard to guess where the connection lies."

"You must enlighten me, Miss Ingram. To what connection do you refer?"

"You are Mr. Rochester's tenant, are you not, Sir Hugo, at Thornfield? Did you not meet Mr. Rochester before he left England? He is, of course, well-known in the County. Well-known indeed!" Her laugh trickled out. "Mr. Rochester's *ancestry* is impeccable. It is his *life* that has provided us all with rather scandalous entertainment over the years—or so they say." She dissembled hastily. "I, of course, am far too young to know the truth firsthand—this was all of twenty, twenty-five years ago. He married a lunatic from the West Indies, so the story goes—oh, this was before I was born—and kept her walled up in secret at Thornfield. It was for her money, all for money. No one knew he was married. My Aunt Blanche—Lady Bartlett, you know—had a tendre for him; he is very rich, after all; but luckily, she had refused his advances. She felt all was not as it should be. Then, it seemed, he planned to marry a governess! The neighbourhood was all agog! But for some reason all was exposed—at the very altar, so rumour has it. Like some Gothic novel of the day! Later, the house burned down, and the madwoman was killed. Oh, scandalous indeed! And then he married the governess—Miss Rochester's mother. She was not acknowledged, of course, for years. But, as I say, Mr. Rochester is so very rich and has a great deal of influence—these things are glossed over in the end.

"But when Mr. Landless came to live at Highcrest Manor, all the old scandal revived. For, as I am sure you must recognize if you ever met Mr. Rochester, it is quite obvious that Mr. Landless is his by-blow! The likeness is quite striking. It is, as I say, just like a romantic novel, is it not? Miss Janet must watch what she is about."

And that shallow, silvery laugh filled the air once more.

The hands on my forearms had tightened painfully with the twisted relating of the old story. I was rigid beneath their touch. Then we were moving quickly back through the terrace doors, into the house, and on to the ballroom.

"May I bring you something to drink, Miss Rochester? Some fruit cup or lemonade?"

"Please."

He walked away from me across the room. I watched him go. He did not return.

For once in my life I wanted, quite desperately, to reach out to my mother. There was no one there—no older woman, no mother substitute—to whom I could turn as a friend, in whom I could confide. Laura was at Highcrest; Mrs. Deveraux I did not trust. I was still warm from dancing, yet my skin was suddenly cold, damp with perspiration. A blindfold had been wrenched from my eyes. Yes, from the first I had known him to be of my own blood, so like as he was to my dear father. Yet I had not pushed to define that relationship. Oh, what was I to do? How could I live? For I loved him, dear Reader. That, too, was very plain to me now. I could deny it no longer. For weeks I had lived in a dream, responding to his voice, to his presence, missing him when he was not there. My body was alive as it had never been. We worked in his gardens, side by side; I played the piano, he sang; we rode side by side on the moors. He was not talkative; but then, neither was I. We were, it seemed, becoming true companions. And now tonight, in that wild and wonderful waltz, when I allowed my barriers to fall as I gazed into his eyes and he had pressed me against him … and afterwards, as we stood so close together on the terrace, as his eyes held mine, I thought my love was returned, that he was about to speak.

The last hour at Ingram Park was blurred to me. My hand was requested in dance after dance by Lord Ingram, by the Hon. Adolphus, by Basil Lynne, by the Hon. Theodore

FitzWhalen, by Sir Hugo. It was all one. Mr. Landless—Roderick—did not come near me. If I spoke in answer to my partners' remarks, I have no recollection of what I said. I danced with mechanical precision, an automaton. Then the music came to an end, farewells were said, and I was draped in my cloak and ushered into the carriage by Colonel Dent. Roderick Landless sat opposite me, gazing out of the window. His face was cold and stern; he did not speak. I was aware of nothing but the painful beating of my heart. I lay back in one corner of the carriage and closed my eyes. Colonel Dent accepted that I was tired; he did not try to talk to me. Only when he had helped me down at Highcrest Manor and escorted me into the house did he turn to me and say, quite gently, "My dear, I was proud of you tonight. You did your family great credit."

I managed to smile and thank him before I ran upstairs to my room. Annie was there with hot milk. She took down my hair from its careful pins and helped me undress, and then I sent her away and sat sipping my milk by the window. Only a few hours remained before dawn. The luscious apricot moon had gone, and so had the magic. I heard a fox bark in the parkland, and some apprehensive duck let out a quack, quack, quack. At last I climbed into bed and curled myself into a tight ball. I was so tired, I slept almost at once and did not wake until Annie brought my chocolate at noon.

Laura came to speak with me, smiling and happy.

"The Colonel was so complimentary, Janet. I was quite surprised at his eloquence. You were the belle of the ball, he says. The County was taken by storm."

"Oh, no, he exaggerates."

"I am quite sure he does not! Did you not enjoy yourself? Was not your dress the prettiest there?"

"Laura—I cannot talk about it. Something happened. Let me be quiet today. I will try to tell you later. I am sorry, Laura."

She wondered, but she accepted my wish for reticence. It was strange that my need for a confidante had passed. But I was back in my shell. The Colonel, unused to fashionable late hours, stayed out of sight in his study. Mr. Landless was not to be seen, and I was thankful. How to meet him, how to greet him, I did not know. When I thought how close we had come to an embrace, my mind filled with dread. This relationship, of all things, was forbidden. I remembered my young dreams of my father; they, too, had been forbidden, but there had been no reality behind them. They were fantasies merely, and I had put them aside. But this, but this ...

The day was hot, and we stayed indoors. Later, a breeze got up, and at three o'clock, I went down to the stables, and Albert saddled Nimbus for me. He was ready to accompany me, but I bade him stay, as if I were merely going to ride in the park. "Pilot will be my guard," I said. But once out of sight of the house, I set off for the moors, the dog happily bounding at my side.

By that time, clouds were shrouding the sun, and the breeze was cool. I rode for an hour, letting Nimbus have her head and galloping across the heather. I wanted to be tired again, so tired I could not think. Pilot was tireless. He loved the moors and covered more ground than I, running in circles as he did, putting up lapwings, which flew away, giving their high, sad call—weep, weep, weep—or being distracted by a hare or grouse. He dug furiously among the tough, dry roots of heather and bracken for rabbits but always returned, dusty and stuck about with dead leaves, to keep pace with me once more. At last, wary of the thunderheads building on the horizon, the clouds piled black behind the purple of the heather, I came down the track once more towards the park, and it was then that a second horseman emerged from the trees and blocked my path.

CHAPTER TEN

Revelation

"I'll put a case to you . . ."

JANE EYRE

$\mathcal{I}$T WAS MR. LANDLESS. A pulse hammered in my throat. I gazed at him in silence.

"Miss Rochester, will you hear me out? I have a story to tell."

I could not refuse him. Just inside the wood, in a dim, leaf-shadowed glade, we found a fallen tree. We left the horses to graze together nearby and sat ourselves down on the trunk, not close. A space lay between us, mind and body.

He removed his hat and laid it on the tree. He was silent for some moments, playing with a spray of leaves, which he stripped, one by one, from a twig. Then he began.

"The first dwelling place that I remember was in the village of Morton, some ten miles from Highcrest. I lived there with my mother, Mrs. Gray, Verbena Gray, and our housekeeper, Mrs. Brewster, who was also my nurse. My mother, I came to understand, was a widow. She was a sweet and gentle woman, sad-eyed and soft-voiced, seemingly permanently subdued by the vicissitudes of fate. Her eyes were a faded blue, and her hair a dull gold, as if the energy, the bloom of youth, had left it. But beautiful still, yes, a great beauty in her melancholy way. An Italian painter would have chosen her as a model for the Madonna. But I was a robust lad, very different from her, a gypsy, with my black hair and my skin brown from the sun. I controlled myself in my mother's presence, muffled my exuberance. Mrs. Brewster hushed me as if my person and my ways were too loud, too rough, for my mother's spiritual delicacy. Yet I loved her dearly and felt protective towards her, and, by the time I was six, I had appointed myself her champion. But too long by her side and I ached to run and shout—and even laugh. I never heard my mother laugh. Her spirits were not high, and I imagine she had never been vigorous. I do not associate extremes with her, of wild happiness or of fierce pain. Yes, a gentle soul. Once away from her presence, I ran wild in the village and spent hours roaming the moors.

"I understood that my father was dead—vaguely I thought him a soldier. My mother had a regular income, a comfortable income. We were not poor. I never questioned from whence it came. When I was six, the local vicar began to teach me to read and write and calculate, but he also taught me some Latin and Greek. I was quick to learn, and he was kind to me; he was a good man and a fine scholar.

"When I was ten, I was sent away to a small preparatory boarding school in Dorset, a school for the sons of impecunious gentlemen, I believe. I was not unhappy there, but I made no friends. I seemed set apart. The other boys sensed something unusual about me, something wild and strange. I was tall for my age and accustomed to being by myself, accustomed to silence. With my dark hair and eyes and my olive skin, I seemed to come from a different tribe than those rosy-faced, snub-nosed, fair-haired young cubs. The Romany, they called me, and it was not meant in a friendly fashion. But never to my face. That they did not dare.

"At twelve I was sent for from school because of my mother's illness. She died of a decline soon after my return.

Mrs. Brewster took charge of me. She had many conferences with the Vicar and another gentleman, a Mr. Crampfurl, whom I was told was a lawyer. I did not return to Dorset but went with Mrs. Brewster to Hay—she wished to be near her sister, Mrs. Brotherhood, the housekeeper at Highcrest. Then it was that I first saw the Manor. Soon I was sent away to school again, this time to Winchester, where I received a gentleman's education. When I came home, it was to the Manor, where I stayed with Mrs. Brotherhood—Mrs. Brewster was by that time crippled with arthritis—and played with Nigel Dent. It was when I went to Winchester that I was told my name was really Landless, Roderick Gray Landless. From Winchester I went to Oxford.

"Oxford exposed me to many things other than mental stimulation. I met the full force of upper-class snobbery. Pedigree was of great importance, and mine I could not produce. I am not a man to acquiesce meekly in the stupidity of society's dictates. I made good friends, and I made bad enemies. I fought more than once. It was then I faced Colonel Dent, demanding to know the truth of my parentage, the origins of the Trust from which my money came. He told me he was 'not at liberty to say,' that he had been sworn to secrecy. I held my peace. It is only now that the subject has returned, with overwhelming importance.

"It was suggested I travel. I made my way across France and Italy, taking my time, and then journeyed to the Mediterranean and thence to North Africa, to the orange groves of Jaffa and the vineyards of Palestine. And there, in foreign lands, I learned horticulture. I did well; I came to own my own vineyard. All this was at the instigation of Colonel Dent and Mr. Crampfurl. I could, I suppose, have refused to go abroad, but travel appealed to me, and there was nowhere I called home, and no one to miss me. And horticulture I enjoyed. Colonel Dent called me back two years ago, after Nigel died in Cawnpore. I had made my own life in Palestine, but I could not refuse him. I owed him much. He appointed me his secretary and agent and encouraged me to experiment with roses as a substitute for my vineyard."

"And your father, who was he? In whose name was the money left in trust for you? Was he indeed named 'Landless?'" I persisted.

"I have no father," was the dour reply.

"Colonel Dent can put no name to him?"

He did not respond.

It occurred to me that if Mr. Landless had lived at the Manor for some years, it was likely he had met my father. I struggled to form the sentence; my throat closed up as I tried to speak.

"Do you know my father? Did you meet Mr. Rochester here at Highcrest? He made his arrangements with the Colonel over two years ago."

"Mr. Rochester had left the County before my return." He hesitated, in his turn reluctant to speak. Then, "Rumours had reached me, on my return to Yorkshire, of a likeness between me and the Rochester family; *friends* made sure of that. But when you came to Highcrest, although I was keenly interested to meet one of the family, I could see no resemblance. I watched you often, at the dining table, at the piano. Colonel Dent tells me you take after your mother."

I could only concur. I had been imagining a meeting between the two men, both so tall and grim, so much a match. I could not speak. But I must. Silence served no purpose.

"Are you my father's son? Are you my brother? Speak, please, I must know the truth."

He looked down at me, his eyes shadowed by drooping, leafy branches. I saw his mouth tighten, the flash of his bright pupils as his eyes half closed as if in pain.

"Janet—my bright, steadfast Janet, my warrior maid—I cannot tell you. I do not know."

We returned to Highcrest in silence. We parted and went our separate ways. I was deeply distressed. My mind was a tangle of past and present. There seemed no future.

One thought I had. Mrs. Gray—Verbena Gray, the beautiful but subdued and faded fair-haired lady described by Mr. Landless—if she had been my father's mistress, she was no likely match for him. By what charm would she have ensnared him? I knew of his Continental mistresses from my mother's journal—the opera singer, the docile German, the Italian countess, the French dancer. All handsome, distinctive, filling some need. He had taken no English mistress to my mother's knowledge; there was danger in a liaison close to home, especially with a woman of good reputation. His somewhat odd code of honour would not allow it. Moreover, he was seldom at Thornfield for long; it was a place he shunned. And then he had fallen in love with my mother. No beauty, she, but an individual, a personality, strong and original, with a directness, an integrity, that had made her refuse to take him as her protector, desperately though she loved him.

Mrs. Gray fitted into none of these categories. No, something in this story did not ring true. There was more to know, I was sure. Who was Verbena Gray, and what was her parentage? Colonel Dent must know, but if Roderick Landless had not persuaded the truth from him, how could I intrude? Mr. Crampfurl, I thought. The unknown lawyer. Mr. Crampfurl may be the key. And surely my friend Mr. Briggs was the one to enquire on my behalf. I was deeply troubled at the thought of invading Roderick's privacy. Yet, if he were indeed my brother, I needed to know. Oh, how I needed to know! I was not acting as an inquisitive child but as a woman, concerned for my own sake, as well as for his.

CHAPTER ELEVEN
Winter

"You are cold, because you are alone: no contact strikes the fire from you."

⊰ JANE EYRE ⊱

*T*HERE FOLLOWED A DARK time, dear Reader, when my fears for myself were added to my fears for my family.

What was to become of me? If my beliefs had been those of the Church of England, I should have seen the Pit opening at my feet, hell yawning hot and sulphurous in my path. But my father raised me to be rational. We make our own hell in this life, he said. A loving God would not indulge in torment. Appalling as was the thought that I should fall in love with my half brother, sense and intellect told me this was not proven. I could not see my father allowing a son of his to be raised in the neighbourhood without acknowledgment, providing for him financially but ignoring him personally, and keeping his existence a secret from my mother. I could not believe this was my father's way. He had, after all, accepted responsibility for Adele Varens, his ward, doubtful though he was as to her parentage.

But the warmth had gone out of my days. No more pleasant comradeship, no sketching in the walled gardens while he directed his gardeners and plunged his own hands into the rich mulch. Mr. Landless (for so I now rigidly called him) returned to his own walled silence. I stayed away from places where he might be. I practiced on my piano for hours every day; I made reading lists, and Laura and I worked our way through them; and I rode (my cure for all ailments of the spirit)—*not* with him, but accompanied only by Albert—longer and harder than before. I lost weight. My dresses hung loose on me. There seemed more hours in each day; the days seemed unending.

Laura comforted but did not question me. Sometimes I wondered at the appropriateness of her sympathy, puzzled over her depths of understanding. Had she, too, been "crossed in love," as the poets called it? Or (I winced away from the thought) did she, too, love Roderick Landless? She always responded to him warmly. I knew she had discussed him with the Colonel. We had known him for only a few short months, and yet it seemed he had always been part of our lives. He was such a strong male presence, the only eligible man we saw with any regularity. Propinquity was important. I watched, on occasion, the maids with the manservants—each had her preference. And both Annie and Milly flirted with Albert Higgins, though I also thought one of the Yorkshire grooms was an admirer of Milly's.

Before Mr. Landless came, I had tossed idly in my mind the idea that the Colonel's "secretary" might be a suitable candidate for Laura's hand. But then I had not expected the unknown man would resemble, so fatally, my lost father. Laura had admired him from the first but had always spoken as if he were *my* admirer—long before I had come to think so. If he and I were locked in a forbidden relationship—if he were indeed my brother—what better than to have him come to love Laura, almost a sister and very dear to me? Why should tears sting my eyes at the thought?

Autumn came and passed. September was glorious, warm and hazy, with yellow oak leaves carpeting the ground and flame and orange maples adding spice to the scene. The scent of rain, fallen leaves, bracken, and wood smoke filled the air, intoxicating. I watched a fox one day making his elegant, black-footed way through the undergrowth. He saw me but did not find me important. I rejoiced that the hunt did not invade our land.

At night I tossed and turned. I was troubled with dreams. Night after night, I hunted through the grey stone passages of Highcrest Manor, following a will-o'-the-wisp, a dancing, elusive child spirit that laughed and led me on around corner after corner, only to vanish before my eyes behind a closed door, but not the door into the East Wing. Instead, the door belonged to Mr. Landless, and it was locked and barred against me with iron, like one of the gates in the old flint walls. I woke, feverish, my pillow damp with perspiration.

October grew steadily colder. I stood at my window and watched the leaves falling from the trees, drifting away like my dreams. I remembered in my childhood piling dead leaves high and competing with Oliver to run through the leafy mounds and scatter them once more to the winds. There was a satisfying scrunch each time we flattened the leaves underfoot. The first rainstorms lashed the last of the leaves down to the ground. The trees' bare branches held up supplicating arms to the grey and heedless sky. Then frosts rimed the lawns and bushes. Each twig was filmed with ice.

Isabella Ingram and her brother issued invitations for us to join riding parties and, when the season opened, the local hunt. I believe my unsociable behaviour was put down to the loss of my parents. Annie brought me news that the shipwreck was widely known, and their deaths taken for granted.

Whether I wore black or not, I was regarded as in mourning. I do not believe Mr. Landless took advantage of these social openings, either; I did not ask him, and he did not volunteer the information.

After days of silence, I found relief in telling Laura what I had overheard at the ball. I watched her as I spoke of Mr. Landless; she kept her eyes lowered, but when she raised them, though she looked at me with sympathy, I found no evidence of her own feelings. She had guessed, I found, of my feelings for Mr. Landless and had been happy for me; earlier still, she repeated, she had suspected his feeling for me. (Quite early on, she said, she had watched the way his eyes sought me out as we sat at table or in the drawing room. This amused me. I knew now that he had been searching for a family likeness, not giving way to admiration.) She liked him, she said (and her voice was steady), and had watched benevolently, hoping for a fairy-tale "happy ending." The portrait of my father I had shown her that night at Thornfield had puzzled her, but she did not know my father and could not tell how close the likeness was; she had never dreamt of the possibility of a relationship between Mr. Landless and me. She was aghast at the abyss this opened up, but she remained convinced there must be some other explanation. She was naturally hopeful. My parents would return, she said. All would be explained. I must have patience and not despair. I tried to match her quiet assurance, but the light had gone out of my days. The Grimm Brothers' princess with the sliver of ice in her heart had replaced Hans Christian Andersen's little mermaid.

In the main, I was reassured about Laura's own feelings. A failed love affair there might be in her past, and one day she would tell me. One thing I noticed: she always wore a locket on a chain at her neck. I had glimpsed it many times. Now, on occasion, I saw her fondle that locket, smooth it with her hand, hold it close in her palm. Had she done so in the past? But my own pain held most of my attention.

Laura, at mealtimes, would try to find topics that would draw us both safely into the conversation, but she rarely met with success. Mr. Landless would talk to her on household matters or blameless topics such as the weather. He showed to her, or so it seemed to me, a gentler side than I had ever seen. The Colonel also softened his tongue and his gaze as he addressed Laura. As for Mr. Landless and myself, the Colonel surveyed us both with a shrewd and bitter eye, as cold as the hoarfrost on the moors. His gaze flicked from one of us to the other, without movement of his head, but he made no comment on our silence and withdrawals. If he had ever been a warm and friendly man, those days were long gone, killed, I presumed, by the death of his wife and his heir.

Day by day, weather permitting, my rides took me farther afield. Nimbus thrived on the frosty weather. She was York-shire bred. Her coat thickened. She would stamp her hoofs and toss her head in eagerness, her breath steaming in the chill air, and then gallop the moors with her mane and tail streaming in the careless wind. Albert rode at my heels. He, too, was thriving on his Yorkshire life.

More than once I met Sir Hugo, riding a handsome, rat-tailed grey. Once Mrs. Deveraux was with him, but on that occasion he rode with circumspection, and she sat on her demure, dappled mare, poised in her sidesaddle, upright and elegant in a dark blue habit with velvet collar, her hat, fashionably small and decorated with three of her favourite peacock plumes, perched on the front of her head. I wondered casually how she made it stay on and whether it would have stayed in position had she ventured to ride *ventre-á-terre*. When alone, Sir Hugo would join me in my gallops. Soon it became obvious from his timing that he sought me out. I did not welcome him, but neither did I refuse his company. At first we rode in silence, and I believe if he wondered at my scanty conversation, he blamed it on my continued melancholy at the lack of any news of my parents' whereabouts.

Albert made a silent third to our *tête-à-têtes*, riding slightly to the rear. The Colonel insisted on his presence, and I found him comforting. There was nothing secretive or subtle about Albert. He had filled out, even grown an inch or two, on good Yorkshire food and robust exercise. He was no older than I but much more worldly-wise in his London urchin way. He was happy in his job, so he told me. I knew he sent money back regularly to his mother.

One thing was certain. I became accustomed to Sir Hugo. I could no longer turn to Mr. Landless, but Sir Hugo now seemed more approachable, and I had need of a male figure in my life, a gap the Colonel could not fill. The Colonel lived his life by rigid rules. There were things one did, things one did not do. He allowed no exceptions to this rule and, I believe, continued to view my refusal to wear mourning clothes with a censorious eye. I did not fit his concept of lady-like behaviour. But that was the least of my worries.

As my decision was, I wrote early to Mr. Briggs, asking him what he knew of Roderick Landless and about any stories of Rochester relatives living in Yorkshire. I mentioned the lawyer Mr. Crampfurl and the sad lady Verbena Grey. He acknowledged my letter quite briefly and said he would make enquiries. Most of his letter concerned the widespread feelers he had instigated among copra traders, pearl fishers, and fishermen in the China Sea and Singapore Straits, in his search for news of my parents. And the Missions, he thought, might be a source of information. In contrast to this careful listing of the search for survivors of the shipwreck, his response to my query seemed curt. A second letter, sent two weeks later, was acknowledged by his clerk. Mr. Briggs, it seemed, was unwell and was keeping to his bed.

As the weeks went by, Sir Hugo and I began to converse, jobbing side by side across the frostbitten moors and down the narrow, flinty lanes. He called at Highcrest and sat with Laura while I played or listened while she sang. We talked about Scotland, where Sir Hugo owned a shooting lodge and where Laura had been raised, about Yorkshire's history, which my father had taught me, and about Europe, which he knew, and we did not. We dined at Thornfield on more than one occasion, the Colonel reluctantly accompanying us, since Mr. Landless was persistent in refusing. I waited for Mrs. Deveraux to claim acquaintance with Nigel Dent, but she refrained. Twice they dined with us, but on each occasion, Mr. Landless was away in Manchester.

Laura became more at ease with Sir Hugo, but her feelings did not change. She did not trust him, and she saw him as my suitor. I laughed at this at first, then came slowly to believe it true. Sir Hugo became more concentrated in his attentions. His looks, his conversation, sought to involve me. He brought me small gifts: crab apples from a particular Thornfield tree, a caraway seed cake from Mrs. Barley's kitchen, an old favourite baked "especially for me," nothing remarkable, nothing to attract anyone else's notice, but establishing a personal bond.

Annie went to visit her mother and came back primed with gossip. She kept quiet until we were alone, then told me what another maid had overheard: Mrs. Deveraux and Sir Hugo, arguing over the possibility of his marriage. *She* seemed much upset; nay, in quite a passion, said Annie. My name was not mentioned, but "Who else could ut be, Miss Janet? T' ole neighbourhood knows he's a courtin' of thee. And thee all alone, like, with tha Pa in furrin parts."

She did not disapprove. She thought Sir Hugo a handsome gentleman, though Mrs. Deveraux was not liked. "Aye, a fine and dandy temper she's got on her," said Annie, "She box't my ears, onct, when I werr helping her change her dress. Her hair tangled on a fast'ning. My cheek werr still scarlet next morn."

One rainy afternoon in November, Laura chose to nurse a slight cold in her room. I left her tucked up in bed, with a shawl around her shoulders and a volume of Browning in her hand. I sought solitary diversion in our sitting room—playing a scale, changing the order of the ornaments on the carved overmantel, adding a log to the fire (and sending up a shower of sparks). The house was silent, the light already fading. Outside the weather was *wuthering*, as the Yorkshire people say: cold, wet, windy, the wind full of sleet coming from all directions, no comfort to be found. I gazed out of a window over the tops of the tormented trees and imagined the sheep on the moors with their long bony heads like medieval saints, their fleece thick with lanolin, beaded with rain, and stuck about with burrs and thistle heads, following the bellwether in search of shelter under the sprawling gorse bushes or hawthorn hedgerows, bare now of leaves, where they would stand, their backs to the wind, huddled close together for protection. (There is no comfort outdoors or in, I thought.) Casting about for amusement, I came across a fat, well-worn volume tucked away on a bottom shelf by one of the maids (I presumed) and forgotten by myself. The book was the one I had discovered that magic day Mr. Landless (*Roderick!*) had shown us his secret gardens, opening, I felt, his mind as well as the iron-barred gate. *Eugene Onegin* was the title. That day was one that shone bright in my memory.

But surely, I thought, I had left the book in the library? How came it here?

I sank into a chair and turned the pages idly, looking for my place, and a paper fluttered loose and came to rest on the carpet. I picked it up and was caught by my own name in black and spiky handwriting—

Janet
My Maiden of the Moors,
so tall and proud—
born to the freedom of the purple heather,
the driving wind, the drenching rain,
the piercing cold of winter weather,
the unexpected brilliance of the sun,
the frowning cloud.

Go thy ways. Fight
the good fight for Honour, Duty,
Truth and Beauty—
all that's right.

Thy battles won,
come home to me, my Moorland Maid,
single-hearted, unafraid,
all searching done.

I sat very still, my heart beating steadily in my bosom. Some of the words (*the driving wind, the drenching rain*) echoed the noise of the storm outside the window. But all I could think of was the end:

Thy battles won,
come home to me, my Moorland Maid,
single-hearted, unafraid,
all searching done.

I rolled up the page, carried it upstairs with me, and laid it carefully in my dressing table drawer, smoothing it flat beneath my gloves and handkerchiefs and lavender sachet. When was it written, I wondered? When was it placed in our sitting room? What were his sentiments now?

Winter closed over Yorkshire, snow fell, and lakes and streams were fringed with ever-widening ice. The summer migrants were gone, but Laura and I spread crumbs and grain and suet in special places for those birds remaining. We hid and watched as sparrows, starlings, hawfinches, chaffinches, a rare greenfinch, jackdaws, a thrush, a blackbird, and a robin, even a rabbit and a squirrel, came shyly to sample our wares. Flocks of quail came from open land, and we doubled our supply of food. Wood pigeons flew down from bare branches. The squirrels might have their own stocks of nuts hidden away, but they seemed quite pleased to vary their diet with bread crumbs and wheat and rapeseed when they chose to come out of hibernation on milder winter days.

Deer came down from the moors (sometimes we glimpsed them from the house), and they too approached our picnic table. We did not see them there; they came at dusk or early morning, but they were betrayed by the sharp, curved prints as of elegant little high-heeled slippers left in the crisp snow among the bird scratches and paw marks.

The big, gaunt house, so like a fortress, was hard to heat. Laura and I wore mittens as we moved about. Log fires roared well into the night in the fireplaces of the principal rooms, but outside the rooms, one plunged into cold. The passages were always icy and always drafty. The manservants worked constantly, renewing supplies, and the gardeners sawed and chopped in the cobbled yard behind the kitchen and washhouse. Featherbeds and pillows kept us warm at night, and the chill was taken from our icy linen sheets each bedtime by careful application of the copper warming pans.

Pilot's big old wicker basket, with its curving hood, was brought up from the cellar and placed in the bend of the passage near my bedroom door. It brought with it a chain of memories. The Pilot of my infancy had occupied it. Pilot had his own blankets, somewhat tattered and smelly but much loved. He wound himself up in them, turning around and around until he had made a dog-sized nest, and then flopping down with a groan and a satisfying creak of basketwork.

I thought, idly, that perhaps Pilot needed a mate. It would be pleasant to have puppies, black and white like their father, romping in the stable straw. But spring would be a better time for young life.

❖ ❖ ❖

Annie brought a strange tale one day from the servants' quarters.

"Mrs. Brotherhood, she werr in a pother, Miss Janet. We mun keep 'em warm, she said to Mr. Ramsbotham, her face all puckered and worrited. Poor critters, we mun keep 'em warm. Who, Mrs. Brotherhood, I asked, all innocent like, knowing she'd use my head for washin'. Be off with you, she said. You sly thing. Poking and prying and forgetting your place. You'll come to no good! And then she looked at Mr. Ramsbotham and changed her tack. There's a leak in t' kitchen maids' bedroom, she said. Icicles hanging 'round t' window frames. And she sent old Jonas off with kettles o' boiling water and stone water jugs. T' whole kitchen smells for days on end o' that foreign food t' Colonel likes. Curry! She cooked a great batch of et."

"What do you think is going on, then, Annie?"

"It be t' ghostie again, Miss Janet. Aye, t' ghostie in t' East Wing. As sure as eggs is eggs."

CHAPTER TWELVE

It Came Upon a Midnight Clear

During all my first sleep, I was following the windings of an unknown road . . . rain pelted me; I was burdened with the charge of a little child.

❧ JANE EYRE ❧

$\mathscr{C}$HRISTMAS WAS FAST APPROACHING. I consulted Mrs. Brotherhood on the Colonel's customs.

As I might have guessed, he liked hearty traditional fare and traditional celebration. My mother's customs were more frugal; she disliked the idea of celebrating the birth of Christ by overindulgence. My father liked the carol singers and the old stories, the holly and mistletoe, and the great yule log in the fireplace. But the Colonel insisted on a baron of beef at the master's table, a whole bullock's leg for the servants' hall. Preparations began in November. Plum puddings and mincemeat and two large Christmas cakes were made then by Mrs. Hobbes, the cook. At sixteen, I had not paid much attention to housekeeping for a large household. I took it for granted, and my mama did not insist. I was far more likely to have my nose in a book than my fingers in a mixing bowl. But Laura, coming from a less prosperous household, had taken an active part in the cooking, as well as in such artistic pastimes as the decoration of the principal rooms. We invaded the kitchens together.

At the Manor, we found the kitchen maids spent days stoning and washing large quantities of dried fruit. Each raisin and sultana had first to be cut open and the stones removed by hand, and then, with the currants, they were rinsed in sieves in three changes of water to remove any grit. Almonds were blanched and peeled. Some were dipped whole into melted sugar, and these were set aside; the others were slivered for addition to the fruit. The hard sugar centres were removed from the halves of candied citrus—orange, lemon, and citron—which were then sliced and chopped. I noticed the sugar was put carefully to one side. When I was very young, Mrs. Barley, the cook at Thornfield, had saved the sugar for Annie and me. I wondered which of the young maids at Highcrest (one or two were no more than thirteen or fourteen) would receive this bounty. The cake and pudding mixtures and mincemeat were liberally laced with brandy. Mrs. Hobbes explained that the cakes would be baked in a slow oven, left to cool overnight, and then wrapped and stored in brandy-soaked cloths. The week before Christmas, the cake tops would be covered by a half-inch layer of march-pane, made by Mrs. Hobbes from ground almonds, sugar, and white of egg pounded together, the resulting paste rolled out smoothly with a marble rolling pin. Over the marchpane went a smooth coat of royal icing, which was decorated with a piped ornamental border and crisscross patterns. The puddings would be steamed for several hours, then put aside in the pantry to mature and await the final cooking on Christmas Day. The mincemeat would eventually be made into pies, large and small, and served on Boxing Day to those employed about the grounds and, of course, to such parties of carol singers as might make their way to the Manor. It all added up to a considerable amount of work. Mrs. Hobbes, in particular, worked from dawn to dusk.

Mrs. Brotherhood looked askance at Laura and me intruding on the kitchen premises; she did not consider it seemly. But Laura talked to Mrs. Hobbes about "black bun," the traditional Scottish dish served on New Year's Day—a pudding black with dried fruit cooked in a casing of pastry. Mrs. Hobbes knew it well; they exchanged recipes and beamed approval at each other. Having acquired a friend in the cook (the undisputed queen of the kitchens), we were accorded a welcome whenever we made an appearance. And when all ingredients had been mixed together and the great bowl of sticky, spicy pudding mixture was ready for transfer to basins and cloths, a maid was sent to call us to the kitchen for our "good luck" stir and wish. The mixture was so thick with fruit that it was an effort to move the wooden spoon through the uncooked pudding. We made our silent wishes and licked our sticky fingers. The whole kitchen was aromatic with cinnamon, nutmeg, allspice, brown sugar, and brandy. I drew in great breaths of Christmas and felt more cheerful than I had for some time.

The gardeners brought in baskets of nuts—chestnuts for roasting at the open fires, walnuts and hazelnuts for dessert. They cut great boughs of holly, ruddy with berries. Bunches of mistletoe were gathered from the home woods and tied with red velvet ribbons. Laura and I supervised the decoration of the great hall and staircase.

No news had come from the shipping company. But that was better than definite knowledge and the abandonment of hope. I put my trust in imaginings and thought of my family keeping Christmas on a tropical island with breadfruit, papaya, and bananas. Whatever my inner spirits, I owed it to my companions to show a cheerful face over the holidays. And there were tasks to keep me busy. The selection of gifts for the household fell to me and entailed several visits to Millcote and Manchester. Laura and I practiced our favourite carols. It was perhaps an inconsistency, but my lack of feeling for religion had never stopped my enjoyment of religious music, and I loved singing. In London, Miss Temple had taken us to Westminster Abbey and St. Paul's Cathedral to hear the choirs and famous organists. Making a joyful noise (for whatever purpose) seemed to me a worthwhile end in itself; it had appealed to my father. And Christmas, with its intertwined Christian and pagan symbols, whether it celebrated the birth of Christ or saluted the passing of the seasons from winter's icy grasp towards the waking and rebirth of spring, was a welcome (perhaps a necessary) interruption to the long, cold winter.

The whole household was abustle. Every room was furbished, polished, and garnished until the very holly berries admired their reflections in the surfaces of the furniture, the shine of the stair treads. Shut in as we often were by inclement weather, we sought other means of exercising. Laura began to teach me the basic steps of Scottish country dancing, and when we could, we gathered in Annie and Milly to make a set in our little sitting room. We learned a dance or two, first practicing in pairs while Laura or I played Mrs. Dent's piano, then singing the tune while we all four danced. I could not help but enjoy myself; indeed, we laughed as often as we sang.

One afternoon in mid-December, we practiced dancing Petronella. Annie had told me in confidence that they were teaching some of the other young servants, and Albert and his fellow groom, Yorkshire-born Reuben Misselthwaite, son of the coachman, were joining in the fun. They hoped to persuade Mr. Ramsbotham to add a Scottish dance or two to the country dances at the servants' ball. We were just finishing the set, and Laura and I, partnering each other, made one last triumphant *pas de deux*, twirling together before the open door and finishing each with a grand curtsey. We were disconcerted to meet with applause and looked up to find Mr. Landless, for once released from his grim rigidity, smiling at us from the doorway.

"Bravo, ladies," he said. "A charming picture."

Annie and Millie took one look at him and rushed away, flushed and giggling happily, to plunge down the back stairway and take up the duties they had been ignoring. Laura and I rose in some embarrassment. She smiled at him and turned away, tucking up her dishevelled hair with both hands as she walked into the sitting room, but I stayed where I was. I could not let this moment pass. Surely we could be friends?

"Mr. Landless—please don't go. It is hard indeed to share this house with you and play the stranger. May we not be friends, whatever our ... relationship? Can we not live here in peace and kindness, as companions, for whether or not we are ... brother and sister ... we are, it seems, related. I have need of kinship, with my family lost to me somewhere in the wide, wide world. It is Christmas. Pray, let us be friends."

I held out my hand. His smile had faded as I spoke. For a moment he met my eyes earnestly; he hesitated. Then he took my hand in a firm, brief clasp.

"It shall be as you wish, Miss Rochester. Winter is bleak enough on the Yorkshire moors without importing that bleakness into the house. I shall be proud to claim ... companionship."

And so we were friends of a sort once more. We began to talk, stiltedly at first, but then with more ease. We had, after all, many interests in common. And if there was still a deep reserve, if fingers about to brush moved hastily apart, and if our eyes did not linger but met and winced away from hurt, outwardly, at least, there was tranquillity. I slept the better for it.

Two weeks before Christmas, there was a thaw. The snow melted; the land was sodden; the brooks and rivers filled to overflowing. The white coverlet was ripped from the park and the trees reappeared, bare-boned and gaunt. More wood was cut and brought in. Visits to town were paid. But after several days, the weather changed again for the worse. A storm settled in. Day after day, rain and hail thrummed on roof and terrace, cascaded down the battlements, and turned the gravel paths into tumbling mountain streams. I missed my walks and rides, but I have never minded rain. It stirs my imagination during the day and lulls me at night. Despite the enforced imprisonment, I slept soundly. Laura and I, fidgety with lack of exercise despite our dancing, walked the passages from West Wing to East Wing, and one afternoon mounted the stairs to the third floor, which was little used these days when few if any guests were expected at the Manor. We explored some of the small, wainscoted rooms, fitted out with furniture unchanged since the days of the Jacobeans: great carven chests and chairs fit for trolls. The beds were heavily curtained with tapestry (smelling strongly of the dust of history) or even shut in with doors of oak, like dark little rooms within rooms.

"Delightful for children's games," said Laura, closing a door behind her and brushing dust from her fingers.

"As long as one did not get left behind," I added, imagining some panic-stricken child banging on such a door with no one left to hear. "Do you remember the story 'Under the Mistletoe Bough'? Oliver told it to me and frightened me."

Laura stopped so suddenly I bumped into her. "Janet," she said. "Do you remember, months ago, telling me you thought you heard a child at night, a child who laughed and ran in the passage?"

"Yes, indeed."

"I am a sound sleeper," she continued, almost apologetic in her glance at me. "It takes a lot to waken me once I sleep. But last night I did awake—somewhere a shutter banged— and once awake I thought I heard a voice, a small high voice of someone talking near my door. You are braver than I. I did not go outside to see. And I soon slept once more and forgot, till this moment, what I had heard. Was it a dream? What is it that we hear?"

For answer, I led the way downstairs and into my bedroom. I hunted in my drawer and found the coloured ball I had hidden long ago. "There," I said. "I found this outside my door. Do dreams—or ghosts—play with toys?"

We were called to take afternoon tea with the Colonel and put our thoughts of ghosts—and hidden children—aside. I thought of them again as I prepared for bed. The barometer fell again. Frost followed frost, and the ground was iron hard. The rain turned once more to snow. A blizzard blew; the wind howled like a lonely wolf prowling about the chimneys. I thought of all people out at night—in England and in foreign parts—cold and wet and unprotected, hungry, poor, and needy, and I sent my good wishes forth on that fierce wind.

Snuggled in my feather bed, my quilt tucked about my ears, I drifted warm and safe into sleep. How long I slept, I do not know. I woke to hear a tapping at my door. The fire in my bedroom, little more than ash, still gave a faint and ruddy glow. I pulled on my robe and thrust my feet into slippers. I lit my candle. It was no night to be unprepared. And then I opened my door.

Laura stood there, a finger to her lips. She looked like a woodland elf, a hooded robe of dark green woollen half hiding her sunny hair. Her eyes were big with excitement. She caught my arm and pulled me to the turn in the passage, where Pilot's basket sat. His face peered out from under the basketwork. He did not move. He sprawled at ease and, close up against his black-and-white furred body, nestled in the blankets, a second body lay.

A small, brown face, a long, black braid, a slender arm the colour of creamy coffee. A silky, scarlet robe, edged with golden braid, partly covered by a white knitted shawl. A bare foot with an anklet of gold hung over the basket's edge. Pilot licked that tender brown ankle. His tail, gently wagging, stirred the blanket.

We crouched side by side, Laura and I, our eyes wide with questions. I reached out and touched the little foot. It was icy cold. Then Laura looked beyond me. She stood.

A figure emerged from the shadows of the passage. It was a woman: small, bent, less than five feet in height, brown-skinned like the child but darker, with bright shining black eyes and a face wrinkled like a nut. She, too, had a long braid falling over her shoulder to her waist. She was bundled with clothing. Around her legs I caught a glimpse of white, some flimsy robe trailing to the floor, but she was so covered over with shawls and woollen wrappers that her upper body seemed bulky and out of proportion to her thin arms and ankles. Her head, her shoulders, were huddled in wool. Wrinkled woollen stockings covered her feet, which were thrust into flat leather sandals. She stood still, a gnomelike creature from another world, watching us, and we watched her. A strong scent of incense ebbed from her; I recognized it. This was my ghost. Then she darted closer and sank to her knees besides Pilot's basket. Urgently she shook the little arm.

"Parvati," she said, her voice high and frightened, giving little glances at us and away. "Parvati!"

The child stirred. "Pilot," said a small, sweet voice. "Ayah, I stay with Pilot!" She opened her eyes and, seeing us, shrank back in fear, holding tightly to Pilot's neck.

Laura recovered first. She knelt by the side of the basket. "You are cold," she said. "This is no place for you.

You will take a chill. Come, little one. Parvati? Is that your name? My name is Laura. Will you come with me to the fire and warm yourself?"

The child considered her gravely. She still held onto Pilot, but she sat up. "Lau-ra?" she repeated.

The little woman darted forward. "Not good, not good," she said, pronouncing the words carefully. She was frowning and looking anxious. "The Sahib not like. Come with Ayah, Parvati. You are naughtee child!"

"Let us get her warm, first," said Laura in a decided voice. She reached out and picked up the slender form. The child clung for a moment to Pilot's curly coat, then surrendered and allowed herself to be carried. I saw her arms slide around Laura's neck. We entered Laura's bedroom, where the ashes glowed dully. I ran to poke them into flames, adding wood slowly, piece by piece, from the log basket until it was well established. Laura pulled the quilt and blankets from her bed and we made a nest on the rug before the fire and sat ourselves down, our little visitor in our midst. Pilot stood in the doorway, his eyes anxious, his ears drooping.

I remembered there was still some cocoa in the stone jug in my fireplace. I ran to fetch it and had a sudden memory. When I returned to Laura's room, I was carrying not just the drink but the coloured ball I had found months before.

The child smiled when she saw it and reached out an eager hand. The ayah, still agitated but obedient to our wishes, crouched behind us. "Who is she," whispered Laura. "Why is she living here, hidden? An Indian child? I don't understand."

"I can perhaps guess," I said. My thoughts were coming together: Mrs. Deveraux's odd manner when she spoke of Nigel Dent. Her pointed mention of meeting his wife (yet later she had not spoken of this in front of Colonel Dent). The lack of any pictured version of that wife. The possible reason for the Colonel's secrecy: Had Nigel Dent married an Indian woman; had his father denied his marriage? Then, had both husband and wife died of cholera, leaving this child? It made a sad, distorted sense. Poor, foolish, lonely man, I thought, to deny himself a grandchild—this beautiful little girl—from pride and prejudice.

Laura and I shared my bed that night. We left Parvati with her ayah in Laura's room. Laura, in firm decisive tones, had told the ayah to remain there, where it was warm. We did not think it wise for them to return, in the early hours of that night of bitter cold, to the East Wing. The child seemed about four but more slender than an English child of similar age would be. We feared for her, this child of the tropic sun, in this inclement English house.

And there indeed we found them next morning. While Laura stayed with Parvati, I dressed quickly and made my way downstairs somewhat earlier than was my custom. I hoped to find the Colonel alone. He often sat in his study before breakfast, rigid in his heavy leather armchair, staring out the window at the leafless, icebound shrubbery. He was there that day, but Mr. Landless sat with him.

They rose as I entered.

"Colonel," I said. "Good morning. I have some interesting news. There is a child in Laura's room. A sweet and pretty child. We hear her name is Parvati. I think she must be your granddaughter. It shall, of course, be as you wish—but I shall think you harsh indeed if you rob us of her company."

The Colonel's face was a study. He had made an odd noise, half gasp, half grunt, and fell back in his seat as he listened to me. All at once his face looked haggard, defeated.

"No one else need know of this, no outsider, if you still do not wish it. But we are part of your household. You cannot shut us out. And it is the Christmas season, when a child should be greeted with love and tenderness. Laura loves children. She will have much pleasure in tending her and teaching her. And the child is obviously lonely. She comes in search of Pilot—her playmate—in the middle of the night. We found her last night curled up in Pilot's basket for warmth. More than once, we have heard her and even gone in search of her."

My eyes met Mr. Landless's at that point. I knew he, as well as I, was remembering one of those times.

"She wears Indian dress, which is charming but not suited to our English winter. It must be cold in the East Wing and certainly when she roams the passages at night. She will catch pneumonia. And while she stays with her ayah, she learns little English. Is that fair to her? She will remain an outsider. If you show the world how proud you are of her—and she is beautiful—she will more readily find acceptance in this foreign land. And you will have the pleasure of her company."

The Colonel's hand clutched his chest. He was breathing heavily. Mr. Landless brought him a glass of wine. "Sit still, sir, if you will. Sip this slowly. Rest. You will soon be better. And this disclosure is a happy one. I have suggested, many times, that Miss Rochester and Miss Alleyn would be good for the child."

I left the Colonel in Mr. Landless's hands. I had urgent errands. The child must be fed. I visited the breakfast room and helped myself to porridge and milk, apples, bread, and preserves. I was not sure what Parvati would like to eat. Presumably the ayah ate curry, which explained why Annie so often smelled it cooking. Back in my bedroom I found Laura already cutting up a flannel nightgown for Parvati to wear.

"We must make her some clothes as quickly as possible," she said with enthusiasm. The child sat on the bed, laughing and stroking Laura's fair hair with one hand. Her ayah knelt on the floor. She was smiling a little, but she looked apprehensive.

"I have broken the news to the Colonel," I said. "I think she is his granddaughter, Laura. Nigel Dent must have taken an Indian wife, and the Colonel, stubborn man, would not acknowledge her. He is upset, but I told him we will love her and should love to care for her. Mr. Landless supported me— I think the Colonel will come around. After all, it is Christmas. It will be wonderful to have a child with us."

I could only think this the nicest thing that had happened for some considerable time.

CHAPTER THIRTEEN

Carved in Stone

Resurgam.

᚛ JANE EYRE ᚜

$\mathcal{O}$N CHRISTMAS DAY, WE visited the Church at Hay. The Colonel was not a regular churchgoer and had not insisted on our attendance. Laura was a Presbyterian and content to leave the Church of England to its own devices. But the Christmas Day service was as much a social event as a religious duty, and it was the Colonel's custom to attend. The Reverend Cedric Martindale was presiding. (Mr. Pimlico-Smythe, my mother's *bête noire*, had retired some years before.) We left Parvati with her ayah (whose name, we found, was Mattie), and two lively willing helpers in Annie and Milly, in the sitting room on the ground floor we had made over for her daytime use. Pilot was always a welcome playmate. She clung to him and walked by his side, as I had once walked with an earlier Pilot, his father.

It was bitterly cold. The snow was caked hard on the roads, making driving perilous. There were carriages ahead of us lining up to deposit their burdens as close as possible to the door of the flint stone Norman church for the eleven o'clock service. They would return in an hour to collect their passengers; it was far too cold for the horses to stand and wait. The organ rang out in a medley of carols through the open door. "Hark! The Herald Angels Sing," "Christians, Awake, Salute the Happy Morn," "The Holly and the Ivy," and my own favourite, "I Saw Three Ships Come Sailing By." Worshippers were at their grandest in velvets and furs and cashmere. Ready, I thought, to be worshipped in their turn by such of the townsfolk as were able to crowd inside; but they, of course, were also dressed in their best and were interested mainly in themselves. I saw Lord and Lady Ingram sweep up the aisle to their family pew. The Dent family also had a pew, though it was seldom occupied.

Laura was wearing blue-grey merino, with a full skirt and long-sleeved jacket with a flaring basque; her matching bonnet was edged with fur. An elegant stole of grey Shetland wool, which she had worked herself in a lacy pattern, gave extra warmth to her shoulders. She carried a grey squirrel muff, which had been my Christmas present to her. I wore dark blue-green trimmed with black Persian lamb. The Colonel and Mr. Landless followed us into the oak pew. Even approaching midday, the sky was overcast (there would be more snow before nightfall), but the church was bright with holly and candlelight, all the brass and copper was polished to a dazzling glow, and a bouquet of lilies from someone's hothouse sat on the altar. The stone building was cold, with only human breath to warm the air. I saw many a nose red with cold and heard many a cough and snuffle. Some people had brought hot bricks for their feet.

I must confess, I did not pay deep attention to the sermon, which was on the need for charity and humility on that day of all days. The subject did not seem relevant to the prosperity amassed on the oaken benches, but perhaps individuals went forth refreshed and ready to bestow bounty on their under-lings. My mind wandered to that day long past, when my mother had ushered my brother and me from the church, leaving Mr. Pimlico-Smythe affronted. I wondered what had been his comments—to his family perhaps—afterwards. Did his wife assent to his views (she had five children), or did she hold her peace, reserving her true thoughts to herself?

And then my thoughts drifted to the little girl, safe and warm at the Manor, enjoying such playthings as we had been able to collect in the last week. Some of Nigel Dent's old toys had been rescued from an attic and repainted and refurbished for his daughter: a cart and horse with a real horsehair tail; a Noah's Ark with quite a number of animals minus only an occasional horn or leg; a bat and ball. In just a week, she had learned a number of words and phrases, which she used with an air of accomplishment. Laura and Annie between them had made her several warm dresses in bright colours. She enjoyed being dressed and undressed, with the attention of three adults concentrated on her. And the full-skirted dresses pleased her. She swirled around the room in a very English manner, while her ayah tried to quiet her. But Laura took her hands and danced with her, encouraging her to laugh and pleased to find her energetic. She did indeed seem to be less languid.

She needed shoes and stockings and a coat and bonnet for outdoors.

Sir Hugo and his sister did not appear. I had heard they were in London for the holiday, yet I found myself looking for them. I realized I missed him. I had become accustomed to his company, his constant interest in my family, verging on curiosity, his flattering attentions. I told myself he was my connection with Thornfield, but I did not examine my feelings too strictly.

The service came to a close, the last loud and joyful "Oh, Come Let us Adore Him" rang out, Mr. Martindale said a final blessing, and we began to make our way towards the door. We could not move quickly; the aisle was jammed, and everyone had a word to say to everyone else. I made my bow to my acquaintances, curtsied briefly to Lord and Lady Ingram, exchanged a shallow smile with Isabella, who was wearing sables, and then edged my way to the side of the nave while Colonel Dent was trapped in conversation with the Ingrams. While I waited, I read the memorials engraved on the walls to various local notables and the presiding clergymen of long gone years. With mild interest, I identified such names as I could. There, looking quite newly etched, was enshrined Mr. Pimlico-Smythe. So he was dead. I did not grieve. And, in panels above his, were his predecessors, the Rev. the Hon. Basil Wortley-Clarke, the Rt. Rev. Aubrey Gray Hawksley, the Rev. John Arthur Senior.

None of these names were familiar to me. I traced the engraving idly with one gloved fingertip. My black suede glove came away dusty.

Laura tugged at my arm. The Colonel was moving closer to the entrance but was still blocked by the chattering throng.

"Why do we not make our way to the side door, Janet?"

Her remark caught Mr. Landless's ear. "Why not indeed, Miss Alleyn," he said, and spoke in a low voice to the Colonel.

They made their way through the pews and we moved down the side aisle, turning to wave politely to a few last calls for our attention. A little conviviality went a long way with the Colonel, and Laura and I were anxious to go home to Parvati.

We emerged from the church into an icy blast that drove the air from our lungs and left us gasping for breath. Our carriage was one of a long line coming up the drive. Mr. Landless guided Laura and me with all due haste across the snow-covered sward, which crunched under our feet, and found us shelter in the doorway of an ancient mausoleum, close by the low flint wall that bordered the graveyard. While he strode out towards our carriage, waving to attract the coachman's attention, we stamped the snow from our boots and looked around us. The stone door of the mausoleum was engraved with elaborate lettering; more than one generation lay inside. It took me a little while to decipher the old-fashioned script, with its flourishes and curlicues, but I persevered, and I found that the name was once again Hawksley, like the name engraved on the church wall, beginning with Aloysius Reginald Gray Hawksley and, a line below, Gennifer Abigail Hawksley, beloved wife; then Reginald Aloysius Gray Hawksley and Alizon Mary Hawksley, beloved wife. And again, below that, Aubrey Gray Hawksley and Verbena Hawksley, beloved wife.

Verbena. Verbena Gray. It was not a usual name. I felt the shock of recognition.

Were these people Roderick's forebears? Was he descended, on the distaff side, from a former Vicar of Hay?

We were stiff with cold, our fingers and toes numb, by the time we were assisted into the carriage. We huddled together, Laura and I, sharing a robe lined with bear fur. It was a slow and cold journey, the horses stepping carefully yet still sliding occasionally on snow-covered stones and patches of ice, despite the coachman's care. He clucked to them encouragingly. Yet there was a warmth in my mind, a feeling of discovery. At last, I thought, I have found a thread. If I pulled, perhaps the mystery would now unravel.

CHAPTER FOURTEEN

Wings of the Storm

The storm broke, streamed, thundered, blazed . . .

❧ JANE EYRE ☙

*I*N THE NEW YEAR, when the hard work that underlay the Christmas festivities was at an end, I contrived an opportunity to speak with Mrs. Brotherhood alone. She had softened towards me since Parvati's presence became known and had, in fact, even spoken to me of her anxiety over the child and her relief that there was no longer need for secrecy within the house. I had seen the rooms in the East Wing that were reserved for Parvati and her ayah. The floors were layered with carpets and the heavy drapes that masked the windows and walls did their best to shut out the drafts. A fireplace in one room had been made into a primitive cooking stove with a spit for roasting and a cradle to hang a pot. The rooms were close and stuffy with no free entry of air and redolent of the exotic scents of incense sticks, saffron, and turmeric. The whole effect was of enclosure, a cave, claustrophobic and muffling. It seemed to me the child had been treated like some exotic pet. No wonder that she, constantly guarded, longed to run and play and escaped at night, while her ayah slept, to romp with Pilot in the lonely passages.

"Aye, we did our best to keep her comfortable and happy, Miss Janet, we did 'n' all. She wanted for nowt but freedom. But 'twere a worritsome thing, tryin' to keep tongues from waggin' as t' Colonel ordered. It preyed on my mind."

Now, meeting Mrs. Brotherhood one day in the passage near the upstairs sitting room, I invited her inside. I asked her to sit, but she would not. She stood fair and square on her feet, a strong-willed country woman with a pugnacious nose and double chin, her fingers holding tightly to the chain around her waist to which her jangle of keys was attached. She did not smile, but waited for me to speak. Not rejecting me, but perhaps a little wary. I wondered why.

"Mrs. Brotherhood," I said. "You have lived here many years, I believe."

"Yes, indeed, Miss. That be true enough. All my life. My father was t' coachman here, before Misselthwaite's time." (Brotherhood, I knew, was her maiden name; she had not been married. "Mrs." was a long-accepted honorific for a housekeeper.)

"Then you must have known the Rev. Mr. Hawksley— Aubrey Gray Hawksley. I saw his plaque on the wall of the Church at Hay and on the old mausoleum in the graveyard."

Her eyes met mine briefly, then found the floor. "Oh, aye, Miss. T' awksley name goes back to Norman times, so they say. A dour 'n' rigid man, he was. A reg'lar Hell-Fire parson, they called him." Her nostrils flared, and her mouth pursed with something other than approval.

"Did he have a family? Did he—by any chance—have a daughter?"

Her face stilled. She was silent.

"Mrs. Brotherhood, it is important that I know. Was he the father of Verbena 'Gray,' and was she the mother of Mr. Landless, Roderick Gray Landless? Your sister, Mrs. Brewster, was his nurse. I cannot believe you do not know. You must not think that I am prying. Mr. Landless told me of his mother himself."

"'Twerr so long ago, Miss. 'Twerr such a terrible disgrace. Parson werr so angry. She werr his darling, his 'pure soul.' He cut her off, he would not listen, he drove her out. Aye, there's some will call that Christian love. Seems more like hate to me. He preached on t' sin for which there werr no forgiveness. He would not see her or hear her name. Her mam died soon after. Poor sweet lady, it broke her heart. My sister worked at t' Rectory, she nursed little Miss Verbena—a right pretty bit of a thing she was, with golden hair like an angel, but weakly, hard to rear—and when the parson drove her away, my sister followed her and found her wandering in t' snow. She would have died there but for my sister. *She* found her shelter."

"But the man, Mrs. Brotherhood. Who was the man, the father of her child?"

"Mr. Landless asked me that, Miss Janet, you may be sure, long since. I can't tell you more than I told him. My sister never would tell me, Miss. Aye, she kept a close mouth, did Nellie. Nowt would she ever tell me."

It was a grave disappointment. I had hoped for better things from my Christmas discovery. But Roderick's mother had been a lady. And it was unlikely that her lover had been anything other than a gentleman. The Rochesters, the Ingrams, the Dents, the Eshtons. The names of the local gentry ran through my mind. Once more I wrote to Mr. Briggs, hoping I found him fully recovered from his illness. I told him all I had learned about Verbena Gray and again asked for his assistance.

The New Year made its presence felt in a series of snow-storms. All through January and well into February we were confined mainly to the house. Riding was out of the question, except for dire necessity.

Laura and I found our entertainment with the newest member of our circle. We both began to teach her English: I through nursery rhymes and simple poems and stories, Laura through songs. I drew and cut out a quantity of letters and numbers. These we painted bright colours. We encouraged her to draw and paint, and this she much enjoyed. We played as much as we taught. Albert, at Annie's instigation, carved the handles for a skipping rope made of clothesline. Millie made a rag doll. Parvati was a mixture of docility and wild energy when nothing could keep her still. Then we dressed her warmly and ran with her along the passages, playing tag and hide-and-seek. She was only five and not very strong. She soon tired and then liked to share a chair with Laura or curl on the floor with Pilot. Pilot she adored. Her life had not been healthy, continually hushed, confined, and controlled by the need to avoid discovery.

Food was a problem, at first. She was accustomed to the vegetable curries her ayah cooked. We felt she should get used to English food as well. But she would not drink milk nor eat porridge. She would eat bread and cake and loved Mrs. Hobbes's marrow and ginger jam and blackberry preserves. Laura had the happy thought of topping her porridge with jam or treacle, and this she came to like. Soups she would take: lentil, split pea, and mulligatawny.

Meat she would not eat, nor cheese, and at that time of year there was no fresh fish.

Another problem was Mattie. Although she welcomed a life in which she no longer had to hide, she resented sharing her authority over the child with us and did not like to see Parvati dressed in English clothes and eating English food. She took refuge in her native tongue, refusing to understand our requests, though her English was adequate. Laura was very good with her.

"Janet, she must be very frightened. Without the child she is lost. If we take the child from her, we take away her importance, her reason for being here. What else can she do? She is half a world away from her home, in a cold and hostile land."

This I could understand, but I also thought that, slowly but steadily, we must wean the child from her. Mattie saw no reason for Parvati to learn to read and write or to run and skip and play rough-and-tumble English games. To dance, yes, that was good, but in the Indian manner. Already Parvati could take slow and graceful steps, her arms above her head, her wrists and hands moving in intricate gestures, the bangles on her wrists and ankles jangling. But it was certain that in India, Mattie would not have been left so long in sole control of the girl. Captain Dent's household had been run on English lines.

Laura was better with Parvati than I—more patient, ready to devote long hours to the child—and Parvati responded with affection. I tired sooner and retired to read or play the piano. My spirits were not high. The lack of exercise took its physical toll on me, and the lack of news dulled my mind. I had heard nothing from Mr. Briggs since the news of his illness. He was not young. My apprehensions were aroused.

Where was Mr. Landless all this time? We saw little of him during the day. He worked in the library and with his cuttings and seeds in the glasshouses; he made charts of rose strains he was hybridizing and maps of his walled gardens and flower beds. He strode through the park in weathers I dared not face, his fur-lined cloak blowing behind him, accompanied often by Pilot, who needed considerable exercise. In the evenings, he would join us in the drawing room, sometimes willing to sing, more often reading quietly in some corner seat. From time to time, I would notice him watching us with Parvati. He was gentle with the child but kept himself aloof. She was not shy with him, however. It was plain she had come to know him quite well in her secluded days. And I found I was right about the walled gardens. There were enclosures Laura and I still had not seen, where Parvati had been able to play in safety.

The Colonel seldom came near us while we played with Parvati. He still insisted she was not to be discussed outside the house. He let us have our way in caring for her, but his mind was closed against her. But for those bitter winter weeks, we scarcely saw a soul outside the household.

In mid-February there came again a thaw. The earth threw off its blanket of snow and revealed its shivering shape once more. The countryside was sodden. There was flooding in the valleys and, until some of the water had drained off into the pebble-bedded streams, the rivers and bogs, as it made its way to the sea; there was no riding. But at last I was able to venture out on Nimbus, who felt as I did: fidgety and impatient with lack of exercise. She greeted me with a gallant show of rearing and prancing.

"Take 'er slow, Miss," cautioned Albert, himself having all he could do to keep his own sturdy cob from galloping away with him. I grinned at him in an unladylike way, and we set off happily up the twisty lanes towards the moors.

It was perhaps inevitable that we should meet Sir Hugo. He came to us across the brown and soggy heather at a fast gait. His grey was full of mettle, tossing his head and champing his bit, but he was kept under control by a strong hand. Steam rose from his haunches. Sir Hugo pulled to a stop in front of us and saluted me with his whip. His eyes held mine, excited and demanding.

"Well met, Miss Rochester! I have missed our rides these long, bleak weeks."

"I also," I said. "I long to gallop!"

"Then let us away!"

He wheeled, put his heels to his horse's sides, and led the way in an invigorating dash. The air was like wine in my lungs, and his company also went to my head just a little, a very little. To have so handsome and sophisticated a man seeking my favours could only flatter me. And I thought, why not? If one man is forbidden to me, why should I not enjoy the company of another?

We rode together by agreement two more afternoons. Then Sir Hugo left for London, and I rode alone. The thaw held. There came an afternoon when I was late starting out. The Eshtons had paid a call on the Colonel, delaying my departure. Laura thought I should not ride; the days were still short, and storm clouds were building, but a day without exercise and with a surfeit of polite conversation had irritated my spirits. Mr. Landless had ridden to Millcote the previous day and had stayed overnight. I changed quickly into my habit, added a warm cloak to my attire, hugged Laura, and made my way outside. There was a bitter cold edge to the wind that boded ill, but I would not be deterred. I had sent a servant to warn Albert to saddle the horses, and he met me in the stable yard.

"Don' look too promisin,' Miss," he said, pulling his hat well down over his scarlet-tipped ears as he looked askance at the sky.

"Then we must hurry," I said. He gave me a reproachful look, but I was already in the saddle, and I touched my whip to Nimbus's side. I heard the rattle of his hoofs behind me.

All sensible creatures were under cover on such a day—rabbits in their holes, snuggled together, squirrels curled up in their dreys, noses tucked under tails, birds roosting in the trees, heads under wings—but almost at once, we startled a kestrel up from the ground. A mouse dangled from its claws. It flew away towards the moors, and I watched it with pleasure. I always felt a kinship with the elegant winged hunter.

We hacked our way across the park and along the lanes, bypassing Hay. It was no day to invade the moorland. I had no expectation of seeing Sir Hugo; it was at least an hour later than my regular time. After we had ridden for twenty minutes and were made more reasonable by the insidious cold and the increasing cloud, I was ready to head back to Highcrest. Then, I heard a shot. And then another. And then we saw Sir Hugo emerging from behind a rocky outcrop isolated in a ploughed field.

He saluted me in his usual stylish fashion. He wore a heavy cloak lined with fur and his hat, in the Russian style, was also made of fur. His elegant cheekbones and the bridge of his thin nose looked reddened and roughened by the wind. I was aware that my own nose and cheeks were windburned and my hands stiff with cold inside my gloves. He pulled his horse across the track in front of me.

He wasted no time on civilities.

"Miss Rochester, I was hoping we should meet. I have made two trips in my endeavours. I have an important subject to discuss with you. My trip to London bore strange fruit."

I shivered as I sat on my horse. I was struck by the urgency in his manner, but I was too cold to be curious. I was conscious of Albert edging up behind me.

"Sir Hugo, this is hardly a day for conversation. The horses must not stand. Perhaps you should visit us at Highcrest quite soon if you have business to discuss."

I would have turned the mare, but Sir Hugo sat his horse stolidly in the way. I glanced at Albert. He was chafing his hands, which were blue-knuckled with cold. I had not realized he was not wearing gloves.

"Miss," said Albert urgently. "Miss, the storm is comin'."

I stared up at the sky. A great black cloud loomed over us. A spiteful wind was getting up, cold and knife-edged, gusting through the trees this way and that. Already I could feel the spit of rain against my face.

"We must ride fast, Miss Rochester. To Thornfield! Thornfield is the closer. Come, Miss Rochester. We must outrun the storm!"

Sir Hugo wheeled his own horse, slapping Nimbus on the rump as he passed, and the two horses leapt forward, Nimbus close behind the rat-tailed grey. It was as he dashed past me that I noticed the rifle affixed to his saddle and the limp bundle of feathers hanging behind. I had no time to consider. He was right that Thornfield was the closer. "Albert!" I called. And knew he would follow. Then we plunged downhill through the wood, nose to tail, a daredevil ride on the wings of the storm.

But even as I rode as if the devil were at my heels, my mind registered the barred markings I had seen on the dead bird at Sir Hugo's saddle. I knew those markings so well and had seen them so recently.

Sir Hugo had killed the kestrel.

Chapter Fifteen

The Honour of My Hand

"Tame or fierce, wild or subdued, you are mine."

❧ SHIRLEY ❧

$\mathscr{B}$Y THE TIME WE had connected with the road beyond Hay, the rain was pelting down, slanted by the wind so that it whipped my face with a thousand icy fingers. In better weather, I should have enjoyed our wild ride. But it was all I could do to stay in the saddle under the abuse of wind and water. When we entered the drive at Thornfield and made for the stables, I could only feel relief.

Micah, the young ostler, came running to greet us. Sir Hugo leapt down and held out his hand to help me dismount. Albert came closely after us, but as he made to dismount, Sir Hugo forbade him.

"No, no," he said, his voice raised against the howl of the wind. "You must return to Highcrest. Colonel Dent must not be caused anxiety as to Miss Rochester's whereabouts."

Albert was as cold and wet as we. I protested, pulling at Sir Hugo's arm. "Let him get warm first," I cried.

"Be off!" ordered Sir Hugo. "Tell Colonel Dent Miss Rochester will stay the night at Thornfield. Go! It is my order."

Albert turned the cob. Head down, shoulders hunched, he rode away.

"That was *wrong*," I said angrily, as we ran through the nearest door into the warmth and comfort of Thornfield. "Albert needed respite from the storm as much as we. There was no reason why he should not have warmed himself before returning."

"A servant is a servant, Miss Rochester. They are employed to *serve*. You are too tenderhearted. It is a mistake.

Depend on it, they do not expect softness and doubtless despise it."

I made no response. I was shocked and displeased. A footman came to take our coats, a man I did not know, and Barley followed.

"Show Miss Rochester to Mrs. Deveraux's room," he was told. "And instruct her maid to attend Miss Rochester."

I followed Barley upstairs. He returned my smile when we were alone but looked pinched and worried.

"Are you well, Barley?" I asked.

"Thank you, Miss Janet," he said. "I've nowt to complain of. Are you aware, Miss, that Mrs. Deveraux is away from Thornfield?" I stopped on the landing and stared at him. Why had Sir Hugo not told me this important piece of information? But with or without my hostess, I must dry my hair and change my clothes.

"Is Mrs. Parrott here, Barley?" I said, at the bedroom door.

He nodded and gave me a quick glance of comprehension. My chaperone in the eyes of Society might be absent, but I was certainly surrounded by friends. I changed under the supercilious gaze of Marie-Jeanne, but she found me a gown of dark green velvet that became me well. My hair was wet, and it took some time to dry and arrange it to her satisfaction. (I would not have insisted on such perfection.) When I was ready at last to join Sir Hugo, she disappeared with my habit and cloak.

There was little conversation during dinner, and indeed, I played little part in what talk there was, returning monosyllables to Sir Hugo's attempts to arouse me. He talked to me of London and a play he had seen the previous week. I was at my most stiff and formal. The new footman served us; Barley stood by the sideboard. I felt awkward in my borrowed plumes, as stiff and as socially unskilled as I had been when I first made Sir Hugo's acquaintance. But his manner was different. I was coming to believe he had been playing a part with me, that of the charming, urbane companion, and that he had now let it slide. The keen, cold, calculating intelligence that I had recognized long before was back in evidence.

At his direction, the tea tray was taken into the drawing room, where a brilliant fire blazed. I sipped my tea.

"Is Mrs. Deveraux gone for long? When do you expect her to return?"

"Tomorrow. My sister has been with friends in Derbyshire. We are good friends, but we must take our own paths from time to time. She makes her home with me until such time as I supply a mistress to govern my domain, a wife to rule my household. Then we shall part."

"It is your intention to marry, Sir Hugo?" I was trying to sustain conversation, but at once I wished I had held my tongue.

"It is, indeed, Miss Rochester. And perhaps you can guess whom it is I have chosen? Unconventional though this *tête-à-tête* may be, I am glad to have this chance to speak to you alone. I have been hoping for such an opportunity.

"Miss Rochester, I think you must know how much I admire you, how deeply I wish to honour and serve you. Miss Rochester,

Janet—for surely I may call you so—will you be my wife? Grant me the honour of your hand in marriage."

He had risen as he began to speak, and he now went down on one knee. I was startled and embarrassed.

"Sir Hugo, pray, rise. Please, do not … Get up, I beg you. Oh, this should not be happening! I cannot … I regret I cannot accept your most flattering offer." The words rushed out. My face was flushed. I wanted very much to be gone.

He rose with one graceful gesture and walked the length of the drawing room and back. He stood with one hand on the back of a winged armchair.

"I have told you I wished to speak to you. And not just for this purpose. Miss Rochester, I wonder if you are quite aware of your position? Your parents are lost to you, at best hidden from sight halfway around the world, at worst … One of your guardians, Colonel Dent, is an old man. The other, Mr. Briggs—yes, I know of the estimable Mr. Briggs, Miss Rochester—is ill of pneumonia in London. I took the liberty of calling on his place of business while I was in London recently and learned from his clerk that he was in a sad way.

"Quite soon you may find yourself a wealthy woman and unprotected, young as you are, inexperienced, with no close relative to guard you. Property is a man's business. You need a protector, Miss Rochester, a younger man, a man of influence and position. Let me be the man you turn to." He seated himself at my side and reached for my hand. But I shrank farther into the corner of the sofa.

"What took you to Mr. Briggs's office, Sir Hugo?"

He looked momentarily disconcerted. "I ... felt it necessary to find out what I could about your father's dispositions—your situation, Miss Rochester. Your rights. Your expectations. And Mr. Briggs is, of course, your father's agent in the leasing of Thornfield. I assumed he would also be your father's representative where you were concerned. I enquired of Miss Temple, and she was happy to confirm the correctness of my supposition.

"Miss Rochester, I think you cannot be aware of the danger in which you stand."

My temper was rising with his glib assumptions. I disliked his having interrogated Miss Temple (or, I wondered, had it been Miss Nasmyth?) "Danger, Sir Hugo? To what do you refer?"

"Danger to your inheritance, Miss Rochester. From your half brother. The man who calls himself *Landless*."

I started as if I were struck. "Danger? Mr. Landless is no danger to me. And I do not know that he is my half brother—and nor, I am sure, do you."

"He is widely considered in the neighbourhood to be such, Miss Rochester. And if you are left without a legal protector, what is to stop him from claiming Thornfield and all your inheritance?"

"He would do no such thing, I am assured of it. And even admitting that we may be related, as an illegitimate son, he would have no claim."

"But what if he were legitimate, Miss Rochester? Have you thought of that? What would then be your position if he claimed inheritance of Thornfield?"

I stared at him in disbelief. "How could that be? What is it you are implying, Sir Hugo? I do not understand you. My father was a married man until the death by misadventure of his unfortunate first wife. He could never have been married to Mrs. Gray, Verbena Gray, Mr. Landless's mother."

"Ah, yes, I have heard that story. You wrote to Mr. Briggs about it. He, I am sure, is discretion itself; but he was absent, on his sickbed. One of his clerks was happy to assist me in return for a gratuity.

"I must confess, I find it hard to believe in Mrs. Gray, Miss Rochester. What evidence have you of her existence— her reality as Mr. Landless's mother—other than his word— at best a child's memory? No, no, I tell you. He is the son of Bertha Mason Rochester."

Bile rose in my mouth. I swallowed hard. "This cannot be. This is some distorted figment of your own imagination. Bertha Rochester was mad long before her arrival in England. She was kept in confinement at Thornfield. She did not live as my father's wife."

"Forgive me, Miss Rochester. I must speak of things that are inappropriate for your youth and innocence. For you *are* very young. You can have no knowledge of the nature of men. Men are different from women, Miss Rochester. They have needs—desires—appetites—that women do not." His whole face tightened, narrowed, before my gaze; yet his mouth, though thin of lip, was moist and red. His eyes watched me with an urgency, a glittering eagerness, that made me glance quickly away, avoiding his stare. "*Most* women do not," he added, so quietly his words barely reached my ears. And then, more loudly, he said, "Your father was denied the comfort of a wife for many years. She was, I understand, a fine woman when he married her. She doubtless had lucid intervals. Is it so unlikely she bore him a child, which he could not acknowledge because his wife's very existence was a secret? A child that was farmed out to some willing lady in need perhaps of money, doubtless of gentle birth—Mrs. Verbena Gray? This seems to me far more likely than a liaison in the County of which no one was aware. Gossip, as you know, is hard to contain.

"You must listen to me, Miss Rochester ... Janet, dear Janet." His speech grew more rapid, more intense. "With your parents lost to you, this man may well claim your estate. He is a man with a grievance, disinherited. Does not the name he chose make this clear? I feel he is biding his time until he is sure your father will not return. He may think it a just revenge to claim your inheritance from you, you who have usurped his place at Thornfield. His grievance is doubtless deeply felt.

"I love you. I deeply admire you. Let me be your protector against this evil man."

I was filled with horror, but at the man who spoke, not at his picture of the man I loved (forbidden though that love might be) and not at a view of my father I could not possibly accept. I had striven to subdue my feelings for Roderick Landless; I had done my best to interest myself in Sir Hugo, and flattery and the pressure of his masculinity had undermined me. This had been foolish. He was right. I *was* inexperienced in the ways of men. But now my love and trust and deep commitment were once more aroused. What chance, after all, was there that I should marry a man who killed a kestrel?

"No," I said violently, shaking my head as if to expel his words from my mind. "No, you are wrong, Sir Hugo. This is not true of Mr. Landless. And it is not true of my father. And I say, once again, I cannot marry you. I am appalled that you know the contents of my private letter to Mr. Briggs; be sure he shall hear of this betrayal. He is *not* dead. He and the Colonel are my guardians; even if I wished, I cannot engage myself without their consent, and I have no such wish. Nor, by my father's instructions, may I marry before I am twenty-one. I am not unprotected! And now I must go home."

"Not yet, Miss Rochester. The storm has barely passed. You must—I insist—you must stay the night. And though I admire your optimism, I must repeat that it may well be that Mr. Briggs no longer lives. He is not young, and pneumonia is a bitter scourge. That would leave the Colonel your sole guardian. And, despite your father's wishes, it may be possible to persuade the Colonel that he would be advised to consent to your marriage. The Colonel has his vulnerabilities."

There came to my mind Mrs. Deveraux's insinuations in regard to Nigel Dent. If she had met the Captain's wife, she knew the Colonel's secret. Did Sir Hugo plan to make use of the Colonel's dread of scandal to force him to consent to my marriage?

I looked at Sir Hugo. No longer did he seem to me hand-some. His thin face held craft and calculation. His visage was predatory. My discomfort was extreme, but I tried not to show it. (*"Stiffen the sinews,"* said my father's voice in my ear.) I took refuge in convention. I rose and took some steps towards the door.

"I am tired, Sir Hugo. It has been a wearing day. Please excuse me. I wish to retire."

As I stood, so did he. He moved in front of me, smiling. "Why so hasty, Miss Rochester? You must know I greatly enjoy your company." He took my hands in his and pulled me towards him. I stiffened my wrists and jerked my hands free. He took a stride forward, and his hands closed painfully on my shoulders. "You are very young, my dear. But full of promise. Your lively mind and physical grace have long pleased me. Stay a while. Let me introduce you to some of the pleasures of maturity." He pulled me close to him and lifted one hand to my chin. I could feel the warmth of his body against mine, smell his wine-tinged breath. He bent his head towards mine, his eyes on my mouth. I turned my head. I tried to pull away, but he laughed and held me tighter.

"Your spirit pleases me. But you will have to learn to obey me, my dear. There will be time for that later. Your schooling will be most pleasurable."

The drawing room door slammed back on its hinges.

The noise set me free. I pulled myself out of Sir Hugo's grip and turned towards the door, expecting Barley. But it was Mrs. Deveraux who stood there, hatless, her hair sequined with rain, her cloak sliding from her shoulders. The lace frill at her grey velvet bosom rose and fell with her agitation. Sir Hugo's hands fell to his sides. I stepped back.

"Hugo, Hugo, what are you about?"

"My dear Alicia, what brings you back so early? You must know, you are *de trop*. May I suggest that you leave us? Miss Rochester and I have something to discuss in private."

Her voice rose. "Hugo, I will not have it. You cannot do this to us!"

"Alicia!" His voice cut through her mounting hysteria with an edge of ice. "You forget yourself." He seemed to recall my presence. "Forgive this unacceptable behaviour, my dear Miss Rochester. My sister is distraught. She is—sometimes— over excitable."

They stood face-to-face, she only an inch or two shorter than he, their profiles similar, their colouring matched.

"And if I am, who has made me so! How old was I when first you won my heart—and body?" Her poise, her calm control, were gone. She ignored me completely and looked at him with huge eyes welling with tears. Her lips trembled. Her form was as elegant as ever in its grey velvet gown. But her fair hair was coming loose from its combs, and her hands tore at the lace ruffles at her wrists.

"I think you must retire, Alicia. You are suffering from delusions. Miss Rochester will be alarmed by your behaviour; she does not know you as I know you. Take your laudanum drops, and you will be calm shortly. We can discuss this later."

"Retire? Retire? To my bedchamber? What memories shall I find there to calm my spirits, brother, and soothe my senses? Hugo, Hugo, my own, beloved brother, my twin soul, my demon lover, you cannot treat me thus."

She clutched at the lace at her throat as if suffocating, tearing it free from its stitches. I was stiff with horror, but I forced myself to move. Slowly, step-by-step, I backed away from the couple. Absorbed as they were in each other, they did not see me go. I passed through the open door into the hallway and found Barley there, listening, his comfortable, wrinkled face blank with consternation. I put a finger to my lips and tugged at his arm. We hurried down the passage, past the dining room, and through the green baize door that led to the kitchens.

Mrs. Parrott and Mrs. Barley rose from their seats at the table, their teacups still in their hands.

"Miss Janet!"

"I must go quickly. Sir Hugo will come after me. Oh, help me. I must have a cloak. I can't go out like this." I looked around me urgently, trying not to panic.

Mrs. Parrott scurried into the back kitchen, returning almost at once with a heavy-hooded cloak over her arm and a pair of boots in hand. They were, I guessed, garments used when the kitchen staff dashed out to the barn for eggs or milk.

"Take this, Miss Janet. Oh, my dearie dear, what would your poor mam say!"

There was no time for such discussion. I pulled the cloak around me, kicked off my borrowed slippers, and stuffed my feet into the boots. They were loose, but that was better than tight.

Then I was out the scullery door and making my way in the bitter dark, down the muddy path towards the stables. The oversized boots sucked and slopped with each step. It was no longer raining, and the wild wind had dropped. The roofs and the trees dripped steadily as I passed underneath. A diminishing moon gave but pale light behind ragged black clouds. But this was my territory. This was where I had spent my childhood. Ah, how far had I come since then? My feet moved of their own accord. I knew this place as I knew the back of my hand.

Lamplight shone inside the stable door. I pushed my way into the thick, comfortable warmth, which smelled of horse and hay. Two figures rose abruptly and stood staring at me. One was Reuben, the other Albert.

"Albert! Thank goodness. We must go, Albert, go with all speed. Sir Hugo will come after me, I am sure!"

"Steady, Miss Janet. We was expecting you. Reuben let me stay in the warm. The 'orses are saddled and ready to go. I'll soon 'ave you 'ome. Let's scarper!"

Reuben was leading Nimbus out from her stall as we spoke. Albert went for his horse Trusty. I took a moment to wrap myself more firmly in my borrowed cloak. Then Albert tossed me up into the saddle, and we were off, jogging our way down the service paths at the rear of Thornfield towards the road. Albert had grabbed a lamp, which he sheltered inside his coat. In the flickering light under the grabbing hands of the branches, we could not go faster than a walk. But already I felt a wave of relief pass over me as I put distance between me and that evil, avid man.

And then behind us, the sound carrying clearly in the momentary still of that deceptive winter night, came the slamming of a door.

A voice was raised in anger.

CHAPTER SIXTEEN

Protection

I was left there alone—winner of the field.

JANE EYRE

$\mathscr{T}$HE SHOUT WAS REPEATED. Other voices were added to the noise. Sir Hugo was at the stables and knew that I was gone.

We could not pause, we could only struggle on. It would take some minutes for Sir Hugo's grey to be saddled; that was the only advantage we had, that and my knowledge of Thornfield. The cold seeped inside my borrowed cloak and wrapped itself around me like a second skin. My velvet dress was soaked at hem and sleeve, and my feet, stuck in the overlarge, ramshackle boots, were already blocks of ice.

We reached the road, not much more than a lane. But even this, the tradesman's road, was marked with its blessed line of white stones. They glistened with moisture in the faint and intermittent moonlight. The rain held off. We began to make more speed. Albert fell behind me as I urged Nimbus to a trot. Nimble creature, she did her best. Where the lane was clear I urged her to gallop; in the shadows she trotted again. I knew the man pursuing me would be undeterred by consideration for his mount. He would choose a breakneck speed.

As we drew farther away from Thornfield, my fear of being trapped eased, and my mind was filled once more with the images of that appalling encounter I had witnessed between brother and sister—the "matched pair," as I had seen them—joined, it seemed, more closely than by appearance. A shudder not due to cold shook my upper body.

My absence of mind communicated itself to Nimbus, and she slowed her pace. "Miss, Miss!" cried Albert, at my heels. "A rider's comin' fast. Make 'aste, Miss Janet. Gallop!"

We stumbled and splashed our way along the lane, and there at last was the road to Hay! Twice as wide, twice as clear. The clouds withdrew for the moment, and we kicked our horses forward. The pounding of hoofs behind us was clearly to be heard. How many, I wondered? Who would aid Sir Hugo in this nefarious business?

We passed the church. The gargoyles leered from the old lead roof and spouted water from their gaping mouths, leaning down as if to pounce on us.

My hands were numb on the reins. It was all I could do to maintain my hold. The wind was getting up again, and the clouds strayed across the declining moon like the shadows of witches. A low-slung shape slunk across the lane ahead of us and Nimbus shied. I held her together with all my skill and forced her on. A hunting cat, a fox?

"Bloody 'ell!" yelled Albert, too close behind me. The cob stumbled, but Albert had him in hand.

The hunter was at our heels. The thudding hoofs were counterpoint to our own. "Ho, there! Stop!" cried Sir Hugo, his voice hoarse with anger. There were two or even three horses following us.

I had no whip. I struck Nimbus sharply with the flat of my hand on the shoulder. "Run, Nimbus. Run!" I told her. I felt her muscles gather themselves, and we sprang ahead. Behind us I heard the hoofbeats falter. I reined in, looked back, and saw that Albert had drawn up across the road.

"Get out of my way, you cur!" commanded Sir Hugo. "Miserable scum, take that! You shall not hinder me! *Get out of my way!*"

I heard a cry from Albert. I could only guess Sir Hugo had struck him with his whip. I would not leave him.

I slowed and wheeled around. "Albert!" I called.

"Go on, Miss. Go h'on, for Gawd's sake! Ride like the bleedin' wind!"

There was a crash of heavy bodies behind me as one horse tried to force its way past another. I heard an oath, thuds, another cry of pain.

I could not leave Albert to suffer for my sake. I looked about me for some weapon and found a branch half torn from a hawthorn tree by the storm. Brandishing it, I urged Nimbus around and back towards the fray, but at that moment I heard the pounding of hoofs coming up behind me from the Hay road. Someone shouted. We were surrounded.

And then the newcomer's horse drew level with mine, two brilliant eyes met my own, and a hand reached out for my reins, brushed my hand, and then reached up to touch my ice-cold cheek. Roderick Landless sat his horse beside me. Warmth seemed to spread from him.

"Janet, Janet, are you hurt? What happens here?

"Roderick! Thank God!" I cried, half sobbing with relief.

"It is Sir Hugo, he tried to keep me at Thornfield. He is beating Albert!"

The man and the horse were gone from my side, moving as one up the road to the struggling figures ahead. I followed, still clutching my branch.

"Hold there! Give way, sir. What folly is this?"

"Keep out of this, Landless," snarled a voice I barely recognized as Sir Hugo's, so distorted was it by anger and passion. "I warn you, do not interfere with your betters, you nameless bastard!"

I saw a whip raised high in the air above the struggling mass, but it barely started to descend. It was wrenched from the hand that held it and snapped in two.

"Albert, get behind me. Take your men and go, Sir Hugo!"

"We are three to your one, Landless. I repeat, do *not* interfere."

"Nay," said a voice, silent till then. "Nay, that bain't so. I'll have nowt to do with this, Sir 'ugo. I'm not ahurtin' of Miss Janet."

It was Rufus.

"Do as you're told, fool!"

"Nay, this bain't right. Nor for you neither, young Micah. T' meester's got no call to make you do wrong. There's nowt but one for you to mind, Meester Landless, sir. I'm away home, and young Micah's a-goin' with me."

A horse wheeled from the scrum and seemed to push a second horse ahead of it. There was a jostling in the road, and then the two trotted away, their steps fading.

Albert had managed, I know not how, to preserve his lantern under his coat through the roughhouse. He raised it now, and all three faces were illumined by its flickering wick. There was a dark slash across Albert's face from which slow blood oozed. Sir Hugo had lost his hat. His pale hair was in wild disorder, his face as white as the belly of a fish; his eyes glared. He did not look sane. Mr. Landless's face was a mask, rigid in its mix of determination and anger. He faced his assailant, broad of shoulder, stern of mien. Sir Hugo seemed to shrink in size before him.

"Are you mad, Sir, to try an abduction in the countryside of Yorkshire?"

"I know your game, you …" Sir Hugo spluttered and closed his mouth. "You need not think I'm beaten. You shall never have Miss Rochester's fortune!"

"You should go home, Sir Hugo. You are astray in your wits. You are not wanted here."

"Yes, go," I joined in. "Leave Thornfield. Leave Yorkshire. You are no longer welcome."

I wheeled Nimbus and started up the Hay road once more. I was still carrying my weapon, and now it seemed melodramatic. I tossed it into the hedgerow. My hand had been clenched so tightly around it, my fingers did not want to uncurl. All at once, I realized I was bitterly cold and tired in mind and body. I shivered uncontrollably and tried to rub some warmth into my hands and arms. Hoofs sounded behind me, quiet, sober hoofbeats no longer riding hell-for-leather. Mr. Landless came up beside me, with Albert close behind.

"Are you all right, Albert?" I asked over my shoulder.

"Yes, Miss. I'm right enough."

"Then let us go home as fast as we can."

A tight threesome, we trotted towards Highcrest.

❖ ❖ ❖

In the stable courtyard, Roderick had to lift me from my horse's back. I was so stiff with cold, I could barely move. When he placed me on my feet, I swayed. His arm came quickly around me. But before we left the horses, I reached out to Albert. In the lamplight, I could see one-half of his face was bruised, and that bruise bisected by a bloody welt. His hands were purple with cold and bleeding across the knuckles. He had, I guessed, landed a blow or two himself upon another body.

"Albert," I said. "I'll not forget what you did this day. Now let the others mind the horses. Get yourself warm and have your wounds attended to."

I rested my head against Roderick's chest and closed my eyes. My hands clung to his cloak, as if holding on to sanity. He lifted me and carried me along the covered way from the stables and through a side door into the Manor and so to warmth and safety. He climbed the stairs to my bedroom wing. There was no one in sight.

"Janet," he said. "My Janet." His mouth was against my hair.

There were no rules left that night, no moral prerogative to inhibit my feelings, my actions. I slid from his grasp to the floor and stood facing him, holding still in his arms. They closed firmly around me, and I lifted my face to his. His lips were cold as ice yet burned their way into my heart. I had long dreamt of his kiss; it was all and more than my dreams had promised. For the first time, I knew what it was to melt in a man's arms, to feel one with him, body and soul. He held me so while time stood still.

And then we drew apart. For a long moment, we looked into each other's eyes.

"All will come right, my love. Don't despair. Now I will find Laura and send your maid to you. You will catch cold, if you stay in those clothes. Take care, my love."

He turned and walked away from me to the grand staircase. I staggered into my bedchamber. A small fire burned there, and I crouched over it. After a while, I rose and went to my dressing table. My hair straggled around my pinched, white face. My borrowed velvet dress clung damply to my body. I pulled it off me with distaste. I wrapped a shawl about my shoulders and sat down on my dressing stool.

Annie came running into the room, a glass of hot milk and honey in her hands. She helped me out of my bedraggled garments and rubbed me with a thick towel. I slipped on my nightdress and belted my robe around my waist.

I sipped my milk. As I drank, Annie rubbed my feet back to life. I drifted into a dream of warmth and love and safety. Of Roderick. I was not aware of time. So much had happened that day to disturb and confuse me. But a memory had blossomed in my mind, of Roderick in his rose garden on that first and wonderful day of discovery. Speaking of his roses, he had said, "I protect them." And now he had protected me. I was buoyed up with love and hope.

Then I heard footsteps running along the passage. Laura came straight to me to hold me in her arms, quite silently, for a long moment. Then she burst into speech.

"Oh, Janet. We were so worried. First the storm, and neither you nor Albert to be found. You did not come, and you did not come, and the storm was so wild. And then the evening wore on … Mr. Landless was back from Millcote. All evening he paced back and forth like a man possessed. When the storm eased, he went to search the roads. The Colonel was pinched and silent with worry. We thought you were lost on the moors. But now he is so angry—a white and icy rage. When Mr. Landless came in and said you were safe, that you had taken shelter at Thornfield and Sir Hugo had tried to molest you … He blames you, Janet. He called you 'wanton' and unprincipled. I thought Mr. Landless would hit him … They faced each other, glaring like mad dogs. The Colonel will not listen to any explanation. He has closed his mind against you. He will not storm at you this time. I think he will ignore you, pretend you do not exist in his world."

Laura's calm was quite gone. She was flushed and agitated in a way I had never seen her.

"I will make him listen. I am the victim here. I have been attacked, Laura. And Albert is hurt. We went to Thornfield to escape the storm, and Sir Hugo tried to force me to stay, to compel me to consent to marry him. He threatened to coerce the Colonel with threats of exposure of his son's marriage. The Colonel's rigid convention is causing us all harm.

"And he is my guardian! He promised my father that he would protect me in his absence. If he is indeed a man of honour—that honour that is his god—he must defend me from Sir Hugo and his threats."

"He says you bring trouble on yourself. That no lady would have ridden out today. That you lay yourself open to the opprobrium of the polite world. That it is no wonder Sir Hugo thinks you easy prey."

I looked at her in wonder. She looked and sounded feverish. Did she then agree with the Colonel's strictures? My quiet friend Laura, intelligent and filled with inner strength, who had defeated her own uncle's stratagems? What had changed her?

"There is something more, Laura. There must be. What is it you are not telling me? Why do you sound as if you are taking the Colonel's part? Is there some word from the East? From Mr. Briggs?"

"Oh, no, Janet. Oh, my dear. I do not want to hurt you further. Oh, I am so confused!" She hid her face in my shoulder. She was nine years my elder, but in her agitation, she seemed the younger.

"Janet, listen. Late this afternoon, you were away and Annie had taken Parvati for her bath and supper. I had taken tea with the Colonel, and we were sitting together—as you know we often do—and the rain began to fall and slash against the windowpanes. Quite suddenly, the Colonel proposed to me. 'I need you, Laura,' he said. '*We* need you. You love the child, and she loves you, and you can rear her here in the privacy she needs. Be my wife and let me give you security against the world. Marry me and stay at Highcrest and mother my son's little daughter.' I stared at him, Janet. I could not speak. I have sometimes felt he was fond of me— in a fatherly way, quite a fatherly way. And orphaned as I am, that has pleased me. I saw nothing to alarm me in such an affection. For I like him, Janet. You know that. I have always liked him.

"I sat for some moments in silence, and then I thanked him but refused him. His faced closed up. What he would have said I know not, for just then the storm broke, and hail clattered on the roofs and the terrace. And we waited and waited. Dinner was served, but none of us could eat. When the storm had passed, Mr. Landless went to saddle his horse. Then the Colonel sat in his study and drank port wine and would not speak to me. He is not reachable. I do not know what to do."

"Laura, dear Laura, we will talk of this again. First, I must deal with the Colonel. Dear friend, do not think I slight you. Be patient with me." I called to Annie. "Annie, I must dress once more. Pray, fetch my green woollen."

I turned to Laura. "I cannot sleep without seeing him. This hiding of truth, this false climate he imposes, is destructive to us all. Tomorrow Sir Hugo may come here armed with *his* story, *his* demands. The Colonel must be informed of the truth."

"He will not listen. He will order you away."

"Let him. I'll not go." Annie brought my clothes, and I donned them quickly. She brushed my drying hair back from my face and twisted it into a simple knot at the nape of my neck. I splashed my face with water to which Annie added a *soupçon* of eau de cologne. Warm, refreshed, feeling in order in my person and my thoughts, I slipped my feet into my house shoes, threw a paisley shawl about my shoulders, and was ready.

If I had another battle to fight, if I must face another angry man, I should at least do so warm and comfortable, in decent array and in full possession of my wits.

CHAPTER SEVENTEEN

Concept of Honour

"And now," he resumed—"now I can think of marriage; now I can seek a wife."

⊰ SHIRLEY ⊱

I WENT QUIETLY DOWN the grand staircase.

Pilot was lying outside my door, and he rose to his feet with a grunt and followed me. I put one hand on his great head and felt as if I had at least one ally. The house was silent, although it was not that late; I had made my dramatic entry not much past nine o'clock. It was now almost ten. In fact, as I turned towards the Colonel's study, the grandfather clock began to strike with its rich, resonant beat.

His door was not quite closed. The mingled glow of firelight and lamplight made a halo around the door. I pushed it open.

"Colonel Dent," I said. "I wish to speak with you. It is important that you hear me."

He sat in his great oak chair behind his desk, his face turned away from the light. His chin rested on one thin-fingered hand. He did not move as I spoke. He did not turn towards me.

"But I have no wish to speak with you, Miss Rochester. There is nothing you can tell me that will assuage this present blow to your family's honour. Your continued misconduct, your wilful behaviour, your lack of even the appearance of propriety—all are abhorrent to me. In the future, you will not leave the house unaccompanied. Your hoydenish ways cannot and will not be tolerated in this house. Now leave me."

"Colonel Dent …"

"Leave me!" he shouted. "I will be obeyed!"

"No," I said. I was shaking, suddenly so tired I could scarcely stand before him. Pilot pushed against my fingers. I held a tuft of his fine hair in the palm of my hand, and suddenly, it was as if my father was there with me. I straightened.

"No," I repeated. "I will *not* go. *I* am wronged. I am injured. It is your duty to assist me, protect me. You gave your promise to my father. Are you not a man of your word? You shall not take refuge in stiff-backed pride and outmoded prejudice.

"Sir Hugo Calendar has threatened me. He claims he has the means to compel you to coerce me into marriage. He tried to keep me at Thornfield by force to compromise me, and he has abused Albert, my groom, who came to my defence. Mr. Landless has been my champion. Thanks to him, Albert and I have escaped Sir Hugo and have found refuge at Highcrest. But you are my guardian, *one* of my guardians, my protector in Yorkshire, and it is for you to reassure me and protect me from any further outrage.

"If you are indeed a man of honour, you will prove it now."

Before I had finished speaking, the Colonel had pushed back his chair and risen to his feet. Now his features were in full light, and I could see that he had flushed a dark crimson. His right hand was clenched into a fist, and he made as if to pound it on his desk. But my last sentence stopped him, as did another voice from the open doorway.

"Aye, and prove it in more ways than one."

Mr. Landless, his cravat loose at his throat, his unruly hair falling about his brow, leaned against the jamb.

"Now is the time for clear and open speaking, Sir. I have for years accepted your reticence. You have stood in the place of a father to me as I grew up, and I have respected you and have been grateful to you for providing me with a home and the shelter of your name. But that now falls short. It is my own name I need. You know the truth of my birth, you know the name of my true father. I am not a boy. I have long been a man. And it is time I was made aware of the full circumstances of my birth and the trust that was left for me. At one time, I believed you were the originator of that trust. Now I do not. I will know the truth, Sir!

"It is my wish to marry this lady who stands so proudly before you, and I believe it is her wish to be my wife. But until we have full knowledge of my birth, my ancestry, we cannot cleave together."

"How dare you, sir, how dare you approach her without my consent and not knowing your true relationship!"

"But you know it, don't you, and yet you keep silent! You could spare us this distress, the heartbreak of not knowing. *Tell me now. Who was my father?*"

"I am sworn, sir, sworn to silence. I cannot with honour speak."

"Honour?" I could no longer stay silent. I was aglow, alive once more; the blood in my veins had turned to wine. Roderick loved me, he wished to marry me! "What reason have we to believe in your honour? What is honourable in denying your son's marriage, in hiding a child away—his orphaned child, your own granddaughter—as if she were not fit to see the light? You know nothing of honour, Colonel Dent. You are enmeshed in pride, selfish pride and arrogance. Your son loved and married a woman of another race. They left a charming and delightful daughter. True pride would acknowledge her as a beautiful feather in the Dent family's cap.

"But thanks to your false pride and that concealment, you have laid yourself open to possible blackmail and me to coercion. For shame, Colonel Dent. There is no honour here but considerable dishonour."

The Colonel's colour had drained from his face, leaving him grey and old. He sat down again, slumping against the back of his chair. But still he did not give in.

"If I tell you, Roderick, if I assure you that Miss Rochester is *not* your sister, will not that suffice?"

"No, sir. Glad though I am to hear it, I must know the full truth of my birth. Justice must not just be done, it *must be seen* to be done. Malicious gossip must be quelled. The County also must know the truth."

"Then leave me now. Let me think. We shall meet again in the morning—but now, leave me to think."

The Colonel looked so old and ill that I doubted the wisdom of leaving him. Roderick moved swiftly forward and poured him a glass of brandy from the decanter on the shelf.

"I will send your man to you," he said. "Come, Janet. We will leave the Colonel to his thoughts."

Roderick took my arm and led me from the room into the dining room. "You too should take some wine," he said.

"Yes, indeed," I said somewhat tartly. "I, too, am suffering from shock!"

He placed a glass of sherry wine before me. He was smiling as he looked down at me.

"My warrior maid," he said softly. "My passionate love. Was I remiss in my declaration of my intentions? May I now propose to you—now that we are alone? Janet, my Janet, will you be my wife? Stand by my side and face the world? Whatever my condition, whatever fate holds in store for us, will you marry me?"

"Yes, Roderick," I said. "If our relationship is not a forbidden one, I will marry you. With all my heart."

His arms were becoming familiar, the curve of his shoulder the truest place for my head to rest. His embrace was home to me. When he kissed me this time, there was no shock of *surprise*, but of excitement, an enormous growing sensation of enjoyment, of awakening pleasure.

When we parted at my bedroom door, I felt as if I were bidding good-bye to that naïve young girl, Janet Rochester, and opening myself up to womanhood. Janet Landless? Whatever should be my name, I welcomed it.

Annie was dressing my hair the next morning when I heard the carriage. At least four horses were being driven at a hard pace up the drive. I peered out the window as the coach drew up. A servant leapt down and lowered the steps. A short, stout body, heavily overcoated, began to dismount. It was Mr. Briggs.

I plucked my tortoiseshell comb from Annie's fingers and thrust it into place. Holding my skirts in one hand, I ran from my room in time to see, from the landing, his entrance into Highcrest.

Mr. Briggs entered the Manor like a small, balding thundercloud, his brow furrowed, his whole person tense with anger. His face was thinner and pale, but his vigour was that of a far younger man. I heard him demand to speak to the Colonel in a tone I had never heard from him.

I called to him. "Mr. Briggs!" I cried. "Mr. Briggs!"

He looked up at me. "My dear," he said. "I shall speak with you shortly. First, I must confer with the Colonel."

"No, no, Mr. Briggs. There is news the Colonel does not know. Please, first hear me out."

He looked at me intently. No doubt my deep perturbation showed in my face. "Very well. Come to the library, my dear. I will hear what you have to say."

"But are you well, Mr. Briggs? We heard such ill reports of you."

"Well enough, my dear, for my age. Well enough to do my duty. Come down, come down. We cannot halloo to each other in this fashion."

He made me smile, and I ran down the stairs with lighter feet than had been mine for some time. I led him to the library, and he closed the door behind him.

There I poured out to him my story: how Roderick Landless and I had come to love each other; how a malicious story had set us apart; how I had learned Roderick's story and then uncovered his mother's true name; and, finally, how Sir Hugo Calendar had declared him legitimate, the child, repulsively, of my father and Bertha Mason Rochester. His face grew still grimmer.

"This is wrong, very wrong, Janet. It was never your father's wish that you should be abused in this way. And even your grandfather, that odd, sardonic man, did not intend his testaments to bear this consequence. Well, all shall be put right. Be a little patient; I must see the Colonel at once. So command your soul in silence, and we will sort out this merry tangle."

"May I not be present at your interview? I am no longer a child. And Mr. Landless—Roderick—surely has the right to attend you?"

He pondered, then nodded. "Yes, it will save time and explanation if we are all together, though I do not expect the Colonel to be pleased."

I rang for Ramsbotham and asked him if the Colonel were in his study. On his assent, I sent him to announce Mr. Briggs. We followed at his heels. I did not know how the Colonel would react, and I was determined to force his hand. When we entered the study, I sent Ramsbotham for Mr. Landless.

The Colonel faced us as he must have faced enemy guns in the Khyber Pass. He greeted Mr. Briggs with cold courtesy. But Mr. Briggs made short work of greetings. He came straight to the point.

"I have come, Colonel Dent, in great haste on finding, on my return to my offices after my illness, that my staff has been tampered with and one of my clerks bribed to betray my confidence. I now find that much damage has been done, but, fortunately, we can set all right. This confusion must not be allowed to continue, Colonel Dent. Whatever old Mr. Rochester's words when he first set up the trust, it was not his intention to deny Roderick all knowledge of his birth. Mischief has been done, sir. It must not continue!"

The door opened quietly, and Roderick Landless slipped inside in time to hear the last of Mr. Briggs's words. He stood behind me with his hands on the back of my chair.

The Colonel shot him a glance, then faced Mr. Briggs once more. "I am a man of honour, sir, I'll have you know. I was sworn to secrecy by old Mr. Rochester in the matter of Mr. Landless, and I have kept my word!"

"And would you have your notion of 'honour' destroy your ward and harm Miss Rochester? For I now find that she has been told—she has been living with the belief—that Roderick Landless is her illegitimate brother. More recently she has been blackmailed—yes, I repeat, blackmailed by the suggestion that he is her *legitimate* half brother, daughter of Edward Fairfax Rochester and Bertha Mason Rochester, and as such entitled to inherit Thornfield Hall and all Mr. Edward's estate! All this time, you have known the truth; you could have spoken out what you knew: that Roderick is the son of Verbena Hawksley, daughter of a former Rector of Hay (and commonly known as Mrs. Verbena Gray), and Rowland Rochester; that they considered themselves betrothed and that it was Rowland's avowed intent to marry Miss Hawksley at the time of his death in a riding accident; that the match was opposed by both the rector, Miss Gray's father, and Mr. Rochester Senior, who knew of his son's intentions and, on his son's death and the birth to Miss Hawksley of a son, established a trust for mother and child, which is still in operation.

"I suggest, Sir, that you temper your overheated concept of honour with an infusion of the cooling waters of common sense."

I heard Roderick's deep exhalation. My own breast rose and fell with emotion. My cousin! Not my brother, my cousin.

Then I rose and faced him. "Welcome to the family," I said, "dear cousin." He raised my hand to his lips and continued to hold it as he turned me to face the two older men.

"Colonel Dent," he said. "Mr. Briggs. Miss Rochester has consented to be my wife. I realize and accept that there is no question of marriage as yet, but I wish our betrothal to be announced with all due speed so that she may openly have my protection."

"And Mr. Briggs must be shown to a bedroom where he can refresh himself and then return to take hot tea with us; indeed, we are all in need of breakfast," I said.

There was much still to be explained and discussed. I went in search of Laura and was drawn into her warm embrace when she heard my news. We all sat down at the breakfast table, hungry for sustenance of mind and body.

Mr. Briggs led the way. Mr. Rochester Senior had called on a senior partner of the same firm to draw up a trust for his illegitimate grandson. Mr. Briggs himself had entered the matter through a side door, so to speak, when his legal connection with my mother's uncle had introduced him to the younger branch of the Rochester family. On the death of the senior partner, Mr. Briggs had quite naturally inherited the family affairs. "Mr. Edward Rochester was in Jamaica when Mr. Rowland was thrown from his horse and killed. He knew nothing of his brother's involvement with young Miss Verbena, daughter of that ice-cold Christian parson, Aubrey Gray Hawksley. Old Mr. Rochester and the Rector never got on. There was arrogance on both sides; the Rector came from an old but impoverished family, but he claimed dominance in God's name. Mr. Rochester found nothing to admire in a family without wealth. Neither man would bow down before the other.

"Mr. Rochester made sure his grandson was properly provided for, but it amused him to mark the boy with the name 'Landless.' And then he died himself. When Mr. Edward came into his inheritance, he was informed of the existence of this trust among other bequests, but he did not know the details of Roderick's birth; he thought it some whim of his father's. He barely glimpsed the boy, who went from school to college and then overseas, and thought of him as Colonel Dent's ward. Then, after Nigel Dent's death, when the Colonel called Mr. Landless home, your father had already left in his turn for foreign parts. Had your parents met Roderick, Janet, when he had reached this man's estate, they would, of course, have been struck by the family likeness, and I cannot imagine they would not have made themselves thoroughly familiar with the story and the relationship. Certainly your father did not realize that he was giving you into the care of a household of which your cousin would be so much a part."

It all seemed quite reasonable when it was explained. All those tears, I thought, all that anguish, gone, smoothed away by truth. I plied Mr. Briggs with hot food and drink and made sure he had everything he needed to be comfortable. He had long been my trusted friend; now it seemed he was my salvation. I had never met my Uncle Rowland; he had died long before I was born. It was not perhaps remarkable that I should never have considered him as part of this family conundrum. My feelings for my father and my growing involvement with Roderick had left my mind in a turmoil not conducive to rational thought.

Mr. Briggs returned to London, and Roderick and I began the engrossing process of learning to know each other. And I remembered what I owed to Laura. She was very quiet these days. The Colonel, after two days of silent withdrawal, became once more not unlike his old self. He dealt with Laura with careful politeness, as did she with him. But he watched her, I noticed, when she was occupied, his eyes filled with pain. Laura, on her part, turned her attention to Roderick and me. I made haste to get her to myself and, in the privacy of our sitting room, revived the subject of the Colonel's proposal.

"I can but apologize for my selfishness, dear Laura. My own affairs have driven your problems from my mind. Please tell me, if you can, what is making you so unhappy. It cannot be the Colonel alone."

She seated herself by the window. The scene beyond the windowpane was a picture of snowy beauty. A robin skipped along the stone balustrade of the terrace and piped a tentative song.

"I have never told you, Janet, of my early love. I knew Duncan Monroe in Scotland, and he followed me to England. We were engaged—newly engaged and oh, so happy—when he died. There was a boating accident, a trivial thing in shallow water—we laughed, we helped each other out of the lake, I called him my hero—he caught pneumonia and was dead within the week. He was a dear man, so kind, so gentle with me. I had my whole life planned in my mind, making a home for him, bearing his children (they would, I hoped, have hair as red as his), spending my life with him as my companion. He was an actuary, with some money inherited from his grandfather. There were no barriers to our marriage." Her hand had been at the locket at her neck. She slid the chain over her head, opened the locket and held it out to me. A lock of hair, red-gold, was nestled inside.

"This is all I have left of Duncan. I made up my mind that I should never marry. And I was happy here, in this new life, with you and the Colonel as friends, and then the child. I watched you and Mr. Landless as you grew towards each other. It made me wistful yet happy for you, and I thought—and hoped—you might have what I had missed."

"I thought perhaps you cared for *him*, Laura."

"Oh, no. Oh, no. But I like him very much. I think you will have a good life."

I went to her and hugged her. I kissed her cheek.

"Dear Laura. There must be happiness for you as well as me." And then I left her.

More and more Laura devoted herself to Parvati, whose health improved rapidly and whose understanding of the English language grew apace. The winter wore on. Gradually the storms slackened, the frosts and snows became less severe. It was March, and I had seen my first snowdrop in the garden and my first kestrel hovering overhead, when the letter came from Mr. Briggs.

My parents were rescued. They were safe. They were on their way home.

CHAPTER EIGHTEEN

Return of the Wanderers

. . . a joy of the past and present, of memory and of hope.

§ SHIRLEY §

*M*Y PARENTS RETURNED WITH the spring.

My nineteenth birthday had come and gone. We had celebrated quietly, and Parvati had blown out the candles decorating my cake. My twentieth year began.

On the day they returned, I picked my first daffodils of the season. Their nostalgic scent filled my nostrils as I entered the house, taking me back to that fateful day when my mother announced I was to go to London to school. I stood by the terrace door with my bouquet to my nose. At that moment, a carriage swept into the driveway.

Two people descended: a gaunt man, his hair iron grey and his beard shaggy, and a small, upright woman with a face browned by exposure in a way no English lady should accept. It was Pilot, of course, who recognized them first. No outward change could deceive his keen nose. He hurtled forward, long legs skidding on the wet stone slabs of the terrace, and flung himself at the man with grey hair.

It was a lead I could not fail to follow.

"Father!" I cried. And the next moment, I was in his arms.

"Janet. My dear Janet," said my mother's voice at my ear. And I turned to find her gazing at me with a look in her eyes and a smile on her lips that I had never known.

"Oh, my precious daughter," she said.

Tears cascaded from my eyes. It was some moments before I could see clearly. Then I pulled out of the multiple embraces and took a few steps back to look my fill at these dear strangers. I was startled at once by changes. My father no longer stood a head higher than I. Had he shrunk? No, it was I who had grown. His hair, full and long, was quite grey and his beard a pepper-and-salt mixture of black and white. His face was lined. I had always seen him as the same, unchanging, dismissing the passing of the years. Now, yes, at sixty-five he was growing old. Even as I came to this conclusion, I recognized the reason for my change of view. Now there was someone to contrast him with. Someone who looked as he had once looked: Roderick Landless.

But such thoughts must wait. It was my mother who held my attention. My mother, yes—the same but not the same. Her skin was sun-browned, her hair streaked with lighter strands. Nor was it so tightly dressed, so smoothly worn. There were curls escaping above her forehead from beneath her bonnet, wisps about her ears. Her face was, if anything, younger than my memory, despite the wrinkles at the corners of her eyes, softened, warmed, very alive. Her eyes, as she in her turn looked at me, were full of expression, no longer cool and analytical but overflowing with love and—yes, liking!—that word some think a cooler expression of feeling but meaning to me acceptance, pleasure in one's company, sharing one's interests. Her form was somewhat thinner than of old. Her whole port gave the impression of an open, friendly nature. Her arms were outstretched.

"Mother! Dearest mother. Oh, how wonderful to see you once again. I feared you lost to me for ever—though I never gave up hope!"

"Janet! My daughter! Oh, Janet, let me embrace you."

She held me close. As I wrapped my arms about her form again, I was conscious of change. Yes, indeed, it was I who had grown. I was now a head taller than my mother.

"Edward, see. How beautiful she is, our daughter! And so grown up. I carried a picture of you in my mind, my dear. But that picture was of a child, a quiet, earnest child. You are a young lady now."

I laughed and denied I had so changed. Colonel Dent had stood quietly by. He now came forward, and close behind him was my Roderick.

My parents turned towards them—and then stopped short.

"Mother," I said. "Father. May I introduce to you my cousin Roderick, who is also my betrothed."

"Roderick? My brother Rowland's son? We met Mr. Briggs in London two days ago, and he brought us up-to-date on the essentials of your story; he left it to you to fill in the details. But I believe I have to thank you, sir, for your protection of my daughter." My father stood face-to-face with this man so like himself and shook him warmly by the hand. I could not help but note Roderick was at least three inches the taller. I had thought him a true copy of Edward Fairfax Rochester in shape and size, but that was not the case. My father, a Colossus to his worshipful daughter, was not in truth a giant.

My mother was more impulsive and more direct. She had been gazing at Roderick with a wondering smile on her lips.

She went straight to him now with open arms and pulled him into her full embrace.

"But mother, where is Oliver? Has my brother stayed in London?"

"Farther off than that, my dear. Oliver chose to stay on Anjing, our tropical island. He is engaged to Mary Elizabeth, the daughter of our saviours, Mr. and Mrs. Hathaway, the missionaries. He chose to stay in the islands and to take their way of life as his. Mary Elizabeth is a sweet girl, warm and gentle, and will make him a loving wife."

This was something of a shock. My brother had stayed in Southeast Asia and was to marry, and perhaps I should never see him again. It was a blow, but even as I frowned with dismay, I caught a glimpse perhaps of some of his motivation. He had always needed to come out of the shade cast by my father, that oak tree of a man. There are seeds that only grow when the parent plant dies or is removed. Oliver might well be of this breed. Now he could be himself, grow to his full strength, and not be just a pale copy of his father.

I took my parents upstairs to the room prepared for them, Pilot snuffling at our heels and giving excited grunts and wriggles. When they joined us downstairs in the drawing room, my mother's eyes were wet. She seated herself next to me on the sofa and took my hand. My father stood by my lover's side at the window. Laura was there to be introduced, and Parvati came wriggling out from her favourite hiding place, under the grand piano. There were so many stories to tell!

Mrs. Brotherhood and Millie brought tea and macaroons, and when we were all served, the talk began. By popular demand, the wanderers led the day.

The day of the storm had been overcast and strange, the sun obscured, the sky a dull yellow. The air was full of electricity, so that things—locks, railings, anything of metal— carelessly touched gave off sparks and small electric shocks. The captain, apprehensive, had hauled in his canvas and battened down all hatches, making sure of the cargo. My father was not inexperienced with the climatic freaks of the area. He insisted my mother be warmly dressed and that she tuck some oddments of importance into the pockets she wore in her uppermost petticoat. She had felt it quite a game and had stowed away her sewing kit and scissors, as well as her toothbrush, soap, and some simple medications.

The typhoon struck hard and fast, with torrential rain and winds of galvanic force. The mast snapped and the boat, bucketing like an untamed horse, broke its back and capsized. The crew tossed my parents into one of the boats. As it was lowered, two seamen, with Oliver, scrambled after them. The boat plunged, and one sailor missed his aim and was swept away at once by the roiling waves. The second hit his head on the side of the boat as the ship rolled and partly submerged.

For some considerable time, my parents clung to each other and the boat, intent only to preserve life. When the seas fell and they came to themselves, they found the seaman unconscious. My father had struck his shoulder and could not raise his left arm. Oliver was lying in the water at the bottom of the boat, half drowned, but he recovered once he vomited out the sea water he had inadvertently swallowed. My mother was bruised and shaken, distressed because she had lost her cap and her clothing was torn and disarrayed (one shoe was missing), but my father had held her close and saved her from worse harm.

My family were adrift for several days. On the second day, the seaman, who had been tossing in delirium, leapt overboard and drowned. They discovered a supply of ship's biscuit, dry and hard but edible, under the prow and a small barrel of fresh water. They found lanterns and lamp oil and rope and some canvas, a bucket and an axe, and my father carried safety matches with his pipe. They rigged up an awning to protect them from the fierceness of the sun and managed to catch a fish or two, which they cut in strips and ate raw with biscuit. The seas were shark-infested, and sight of the ominous fins had filled them with alarm.

About the fourth day (for they lost track of time), they floated near a coral island. Fortunately the sea was calm at that time, and no shark fins could be seen. Oliver sprang overboard and, swimming behind the boat while father rowed one-handed, helped to navigate it inside the coral reef and so to shore and safety. And then their adventures began.

"Your mother was our salvation," said my father. "Her strength, her will, her practical energy kept us alive. We made a shelter out of saplings roofed with palm leaves. We had to husband our matches and after a while were able to make a fireplace with rocks and to keep a fire in day and night. We found coconuts and papayas and tiny bananas, like fingers, and crabs, which we roasted, and a great clutch of turtle eggs buried in the sand, which greatly restored our vigour. My arm gradually regained its strength. Oliver fished and explored. We all scavenged on the beach."

"Your father kept us alive," said my mother positively. "His great heart, his courage, his perseverance, his knowledge. It was he who deciphered the turtle tracks on the shore and found where the she-turtles had buried their eggs. He was indomitable."

It had been the end of the monsoon, and they had stored all the rainwater they could in the bucket and in coconut shells. But while they needed fresh water to drink, they also needed to keep as dry as possible. My mother was ill for some days with the ague, but luckily her small stock of medicine included quinine. Mosquitoes were a problem, and tiny biting sand mites and fleas. But after a while it seemed they became acclimatized, and the insects ceased to trouble them so much. By the time the rainy season ceased, their explorations had led them to a freshwater stream, and they moved their camp nearer its banks but still within easy reach of the sea.

"It was a desperate time," said my mother, "but strangely beautiful. Such sunsets! Such silver sand stretching as far as we could see, with the sea so deep a blue—yet green withal! Each day when the tide was out, we would walk along the shore and the reef, which extended some way out, hunting for driftwood, flotsam and jetsam, shellfish and small fish stranded in the pools. We found large, flat shells, which we used for dishes and cups. There were crabs of many kinds, both land and sea, some with one big blue claw, which they snapped at each other. Oh, and hermit crabs. At first they frightened me—I took what I thought was an empty shell and found claws waving at me—but later I found them amusing. They left distinctive tracks in the sand. In a way, it was a return to childhood, but a childhood I had never known, of physical freedom and loving company." She laughed a little and glanced at my father.

"After a while your father taught me to swim, inside the reef. It gave me great pleasure! You would have stared, my dear, to see me diving for shells in the pools or floating on the surface in the heat of the sun. You know, Janet, my life had not taught me to indulge in much pleasurable physical activity. Orphaned as I was and living with uncongenial relations, I never learned to play. As a child I did not ride and oh, my dear Janet, how I envied you when you became so proficient! I was afraid you would notice." I caught my breath; my mother, *jealous* of my riding ability! "Swimming was a great joy to me. Freedom to splash and kick, twist and turn, dive under the water, float on top as buoyant as a duck feather! In fact, the whole way of life, despite the constant struggle to feed ourselves and stay alive, was somehow beneficial. My daily walks on the beach with your father or Oliver (one of us always stayed with the fire) and my swimming lessons! I even took my turn at climbing trees! I fear it was most self-indulgent, if not unseemly at my age. But there was no one there to censure me.

"There was one day, one early morning, when I ran on the beach alone in the glow of the rising sun. My feet were bare, and my hair was loose and, as I ran, I thought I heard you calling me. 'Mother!' you cried. And I called back, 'Where are you? Wait for me!' Your father heard me cry out and came to me. But you, of course, were far away. It was a dream, a waking dream."

I stared at her. My mother, so neat, so controlled! Swimming, beach-combing, climbing trees. And suddenly I remembered my dreams of a smiling, freckled-nosed mother running on the sands, her hair blowing loose about her face, her feet bare. I held my peace but could only wonder at this meeting of our fantasies.

"After some weeks, we began to explore with more precision. Oliver drew a map with charcoal on canvas of what we knew, and daily we extended our territory. And so it was that finally we saw signs of human life and found a mission settlement on an adjoining island, connected to ours by a causeway when the tide was low. The missionaries, Mr. and Mrs. Hathaway, and their children kept in touch with their head mission in Singapore by a trading ship, which pulled in two or three times a year. They were good people, living a quiet and simple life among the indigenous villagers. They had a young son and a daughter, Mary Elizabeth, who was twenty. It was obvious, quite soon, that she had won Oliver's goodwill. The Hathaways made us welcome, and we helped with the work as we could. My nail scissors, which I had tucked into one of my petticoat pockets, were enough to make us welcome, since

Mrs. Hathaway had mislaid her own some weeks before. Strange, the importance of little things. After that, it was just a question of waiting for the next schooner.

"If it had not been for the anxiety we knew you must be feeling, we should have been content. I shall always think kindly of our tropical idyll."

It took more than one day for all the stories to unfold. Roderick's life, our meeting, our growing affection, were told in much detail. Parvati's history and Colonel Dent's struggle with himself, the intrusion of the tenants of Thornfield. Within two days, my father and I set out for Thornfield. There we found Sir Hugo and his sister had already decamped, left with all their baggage for London. It was a joy to me to see my mother's sitting room stripped once more of the oriental art and embroidery that had rendered it alien. The servants greeted my father with delight. They had been left unsettled by the events of the past months—with the quarrels of the tenants, my attempted abduction (which had lost nothing in the telling), Mrs. Deveraux's hysterics, a visit from Mr. Briggs (who had been closeted with Sir Hugo for some time), and then the departure of Thornfield's tenants, bag and baggage.

My parents moved back into their own home, and I joined them within a week.

Albert Higgins, my trusty servant, came with me to Thornfield, and Annie returned to her own childhood home at the Lodge. And, at the end of a year, they married, and I made Annie happy with a choice of my London dresses for her bridal gown.

The terms of my father's trust for me were concluded. Laura, to my regret, chose not to accompany me to Thornfield, but her reason was unarguable. She had, after considerable deliberation, agreed to marry Colonel Dent. She told me her news with sober eyes. Only after I had hugged and kissed her and promised that we should always be friends did she smile at me. "I think I shall be happy," she said in thoughtful tones. "I intend to be. I came to believe I should not live in the past, that Duncan would not have wished it. The Colonel has a strong regard for me and I for him. He will be a good husband, I am sure. We all dream of romance when we are young, but there are other good things to be found in this life. I love Parvati, and she needs me badly."

The locket was gone from her neck.

Laura would always be my dear friend, and I was glad to have her for my neighbour, mistress of Highcrest, to restore openness and trust to that stony stronghold. Whatever the reaction of local Society to my family's return and my forthcoming marriage, with one household our relations would always be good. It had been Colonel Dent's intention, so he said, to make Roderick his heir. Now it seemed he would bide his time. With a young and healthy wife, he might yet father another son. And Parvati would marry. The future was suddenly full of promise for the Colonel.

With Oliver's decision not to return to Thornfield and with his full agreement, my father proposed to bequeath Thornfield to Roderick and myself, in joint possession, after our marriage. Oliver would not lose by giving up this portion of his inheritance. My father was not about to repeat his own father's error; Oliver would receive his fair share of family wealth.

To the neighbourhood, the revelation of Roderick's true parentage and our betrothal and subsequent marriage were yet more delicious scandals to add to the Rochester repertoire. I am sure we enlivened dinner conversation for many a month.

What became of Sir Hugo Calendar and his sister—whether they stayed together or went their separate ways, in England or abroad—I never knew. Nor, indeed, did I wish for such knowledge. There are times when I still see in my mind's eye her tragic face and hear her voice as she revealed their incestuous connection and accused her brother of betrayal. I was intent only on clearing every trace of their tenancy out of my beloved Thornfield before Roderick and I became one.

For yes, Reader, I married him—Roderick Landless, the man who combined my father's likeness with his own very individual temperament. My girlhood longings came true; I found a man who was my father's equal and more.

Although Roderick was happy to move with me and live in the house of his true family, he could not but regret his gardens at Highcrest, into which he had poured years of labour and learning. Thornfield shared the same climate but had not the same quantity of old flint walls. With Colonel Dent's agreement, he continued to work at his established beds while, with my father's ready consent, he began to create rose gardens at Thornfield within walls built by local labour to his own dimensions.

Pilot came with us to Thornfield, but I carried out my plan, and we found him a suitable mate; soon Parvati, who had wept sorely at his departure, was made wildly happy with a puppy as closely resembling its father as could be.

Some two years after our marriage, however, we found a new adventure. Accompanied by a well-equipped expedition from the Royal Horticultural Society, Roderick and I travelled to China on a plant-hunting expedition. It was an occupation I loved to share with him; I had always a longing for action and adventure, and I was granted this in plenty. But that is another story. When, as inevitably happened, I bore him a child (a girl; we named her Jane Verbena and called her Jenny), we settled down at Thornfield to raise a family as well as roses. A boy, Rowland Edward, followed. And finally a second daughter, Laura. Roderick published papers on the propagation of roses in northern England for the Royal Horticultural Society and made a name for himself in the annals of horticulture and, with time, I won sufficient skill in my drawing to make a worthy record of each of his prize specimens.

And so we made our life together. When, as inevitably I did, I asked him how he came to love me, he told me it began that very first night, when he stood in the shadows of Colonel Dent's study and watched me, illumined by candlelight, stand up to Colonel Dent.

"You stood with your head high—looking so young, so very young and brave, my love—and spoke in defence of your mother. Your hair was tousled, your habit wet and muddy, your hat—the one I recovered from a hawthorn bush—flattened and its feather drooping. I watched a raindrop trickle from your forehead down your nose. Not for a moment did it upset your poise. You brushed it away with an unheeding hand and told Colonel Dent that never again should he speak disparagingly of your mother! I was wholly engaged with your flashing eyes, your flushed cheeks, your proud defiance. I, who had, in my own youth, known and rejected slighting comments on my birth and parentage, could only rejoice at your mettle.

"And it was then that I thought how proud I should be if it should turn out we were related in some way, if I *were* to prove to be a Rochester, never dreaming what fate had in store for us."

And when, dear Reader, did I first love him? Oh, the spark was ignited at our meeting in the lane, of course. Though it was not until the night Pilot and I met him in the passage that my body began to respond so strongly to his presence.

And I learned that I was right in my youthful assessment of love. To love someone devotedly meant to want him close by, ever near, to exchange a hundred small caresses every day, to allow eyes to meet, fingers to touch, arms to brush, words to be spoken in low, deep tones meant for one ear, for one listener alone among many. When Roderick and I retired at night to our bedroom, our arms entwined, I remembered my early fantasies. In the privacy of our bed, I told him my dreams, and he laughed and held me close and taught me with much love and some passion how far reality soared above those dreams. "With my body I thee worship."

I am no longer an isolate. I am surrounded by those I love best. My father is once again my dear friend and loving companion. And in my mother—my new mother, who even in middle age had found in her adventures in a far country the seeds for development of a freer, more open personality, who had grown and expanded in the warmth and liberty of a tropical climate and a South Sea island—I found someone who was able to love me (and like me) in a way I had hardly dared to dream.

My children, when they came, were reared with her help in a house full of laughter.

EPILOGUE

My Mother

"I wonder what she has been through?"
"Strange hardships, I imagine."

❧ JANE EYRE ☙

*I*T IS ONLY FITTING that my story should end, as it began, with my mother.

So I paint you a picture illustrating her castaway life, echoing and enhancing the vision that flashed across my inward eye when first I knew she was shipwrecked. Watch with me as she comes to the beach early one morning, with the sun, golden as a newly minted coin, filling the heavens with light as it rises out of the night blue sea.

Jane Eyre Rochester, middle-aged mother of two, devoted wife of a beloved husband, stands at the mouth of the path that leads from their camp through the tangle of coconut palms and vines and thorny bush to the edge of the beach. "Made by *our* feet," she thinks proudly, looking down at the narrow, sandy track. The sand is coral, ground fine from centuries of waves thrashing over the reef and onto the shore. It shines with a silvery light in the early morning sun.

She is wearing what remains of her dress, the skirt hacked off somewhat jaggedly (she had used her husband's pocketknife, easier to handle than her nail scissors) to just below her knees, the once high neckline cut low for comfort in that hot and humid place, the long elaborate sleeves with their shoulder puffs and dozens of tucks and small pearl buttons removed so that her arms are bare and free. All cloth is useful. Of her numerous petticoats only one remains in use, and this she would sacrifice in a moment. The others are now reduced to narrow strips braided to make cords and larger cloths used

for washing and straining; the whalebones from her sometimes imprisoning corsets have become utensils.

Her face, once sheltered from the elements by close
bonnets or by wide-brimmed hats of straw, and her neck, her
arms, and her legs and feet, are bronzed by the sun. Her waist
moves easily inside her dress. Her hair, once so primly and
closely confined in its neat bands and braids and surmounted
by a matron's lace cap, is uncovered and loosely braided over
one shoulder. Her slippers are plaited from palm fronds, just
a thickish sole for protection and a strap between the toes to
keep them on. She slides them off and lets the dry sand run
over her feet and through her toes. The soles of her feet are
callused, her ankles scratched and marked with insect bites.
She steps towards the sea, below the tidemark, to where the
sand is wet and resilient. She looks with pleasure at her foot-
prints: small imprints of toes and heels barely joined by a
narrow bridge illustrating her high instep. Her eyes, sea-green
and brilliant, scan the beach, noting driftwood and seaweed,
shells and stranded jellyfish. Her nose is freckled, peeling a
little. There are more scratches on her arms.

Crabs dimple the sand with bubbles. Some heave themselves into sight and scuttle away to scavenge. Inland, a bird
gives a long strident call; a monkey chatters. A gull sends its
shadow ahead of her up the beach. The sun clears the horizon.

"God rose each morning on that island, golden, beautiful," she tells me. "How easy it must be to worship the sun."

She is there to gather from the overnight bounty of the
ocean whatever might be of use in her family's survival, but

first of all she makes her way down to the sea and paddles in the clear, cool water. Beneath the ripples, her feet show pale, blue-veined, and her toenails shine like pearls. The sensuous pleasures of the moment—the silk of the seawater slipping over her ankles, the rough softness of the sand beneath her feet, the gentle early morning breeze kissing her neck and bare arms, the warmth of the rising sun like a blush on her upturned face—bring her close to tears.

She flings out her arms and runs along the beach.

The End

About the Author

Elizabeth Newark is a Londoner by birth but a Californian by choice. She was educated at The Tiffin Girls' School, Kingston-on-Thames. On leaving England in 1954, she lived and worked for two years in Kuching, Sarawak, and eight years in East Africa. Her children, Penelope and Hugh, were born in Nairobi, Kenya, and it was there that she began to write, inspired by the country and the animal life. She and her family immigrated to California in 1964. She now has seven American grandchildren.

Under the pen name Betty Dinneen, she wrote and published seven children's books: adventure stories of children and wild animals, all set in East Africa. Under the name Elizabeth Newark, she has written two sequels: *The Darcys Give a Ball* (previously titled *Consequence*), a sequel to *Pride and Prejudice*, and *Jane Eyre's Daughter*, a sequel to *Jane Eyre*. She has also written essays on the works of Jane Austen and Charles Dickens (for the fun of it) and, more recently, poems. She is the author of the world's only mouse version of *Pride and Prejudice*, titled *Eligibility, Or, An Account of the Romance between Miss Elizabeth Mouse and Mr. Fitzwilliam Souris*.